THE DANDELION CLOUD

To M.tch —

Thanks for

Your Support !

THE DANDELION CLOUD

———

Dale Boyer

ISBN: 0997013400
ISBN 13: 9780997013405

..."the root of all wisdom comes from having loved someone."

EVELYN WAUGH,
BRIDESHEAD REVISITED

to
John and Dan,
in Friendship

And to Scot, with Love

BOOK I

CHAPTER 1

———◆———

FALL, 1979

J USTIN STOOD IN THE HALF-LIGHT of his dorm room, looking at his body in the
mirror, thinking, *6'3", 6'3"*, the phrase a little litany of self-chastisement. He
didn't weigh as much as Kyle -- was taller than him by about four inches -- yet
he didn't have Kyle's good proportions. Looking now, he saw with awful clarity
each straining rib, the sunken chest, the limbs that flailed about like planking
breaking up and rising from a wreck. He hated his body: chest straight up and
down, the waist too high, his butt as rounded as a woman's. *Not like Kyle's physique
at all*, he thought: that warm brown beard and hairy torso, shoulders round and
firm as boulders underneath the cotton of his shirts. Even the "V" Kyle's back
made was as perfect as a clothes-store mannequin's. Justin slipped his T-shirt
on, then pulled the shoulders out to where he imagined Kyle's might be. He
dropped the shirt, then pulled the shoulders up again, as if to magnify the scare-
crow nature of his frame. He did this time and time again. Then, noticing the
spindly bulge his biceps made, he thought back to the day when he'd seen Kyle
lifting weights, the biceps nearly popping as the thick veins swelled along the
center of the muscle. Justin held the shoulders out again to mimic Kyle's proportions, swelled his chest out in a parody of male virility, then felt his penis stirring.
Was it just a general feeling of sexiness that was to blame, or was it something
else? He stopped, ashamed, and dropped the shirt again about him: sacky as
an old-time baseball uniform. And yet, Kyle would look good even in those
baggy clothes, he thought despairingly. Kyle was the perfect athlete: elegant,

1

coordinated. Justin remembered his own experience with baseball back in grade school: out in right field, wandering; the spring day cool; distracted from the game in progress by the musings of the bumblebees that ambled from one clover to the next; occasionally arcing out one cleated foot to swish the dandelion seeds onto the ground; and sometimes in that instant hearing some left-hander's dreaded crack as bat met ball and he looked up, sun-blind, to see the small black dot that centered its unswerving and implacable trajectory upon him; moving dreamlike underneath it; suddenly aware of all eyes focusing on him; and dreading how this thing was going to smack when finally it landed in his glove.

That's when he heard the knocking on the door.

Justin scrambled for his clothes, embarrassed, terrified. He hoped the door was locked -- that Kyle and Craig (his other good friend) would not just walk into the room and find him here undressed, erect, his penis yearning like a seedling toward the light. He hopped on underwear and pants, the zipper's "V" caught in his underwear as suddenly the door swung open and both Kyle and Craig stood looking at him from the hall.

"Are we a little early?" Craig said playfully. Craig's scruffy beard and gentle manner always made him seem like some lost sage -- some 19th century mystic tilting dazed, Quixote-like against the windmills of the hour.

Kyle didn't even wait to hear an answer, pushing past Craig in the room and saying in that charming, boyish way, "Looks like we caught *you* with your pants down." Kyle winked at Justin slyly, manfully, as if to say, *You dog, is there some woman in this room?*

As though there were a chance of this, thought Justin: *the slightest, faintest chance.*

Standing with his shirt unbuttoned, pants half on, Justin felt Kyle's arms around him, wrestling him into a playful headlock. As he yielded to it awkwardly, Justin was relieved to see that neither Kyle nor Craig had seen he was erect. He felt Kyle's hard warmth through his terry cloth shirt, the bristle of Kyle's chest against his face, then felt his pants begin to slip as Kyle paraded him submissively around the room. He reached down frantically to hold his pants in place, and with his other arm, reached out to grab hold of Kyle. Was it just for balance, he asked himself? As he felt Kyle looming huge and masculine beside him -- felt the firm protectiveness of Kyle's embrace, the muscular exuberance of this friend -- Justin wondered once again if he was wrong, if what he felt at times like this was just affection. Kyle was such a loving person. Was it possible that's all it was?

———◆———

Justin had initially become aware of Kyle the first week of his Freshman year when Kyle, apparently an upperclassman, had been standing just in front of him in line for a picnic on the quad. Justin's first impression, even then, was of the gentle beauty of the man, of how immense his shoulders seemed: how firm and square and strong. And yet, belying that athleticism was a warmth and friendliness that emanated from him like cologne. He later learned Kyle was a Peer Group Counselor, or "PGC," on campus -- someone who was assigned to mentor other kids. In fact, Kyle reminded Justin of the counselors he'd had at camp -- those warm, athletic, older brother types he'd idolized through all those gawky adolescent summers. Once, when Justin and the other eight-year-olds were out in their canoes one summer on the Mississippi, a counselor had even saved his life. That August day, they'd been paddling peacefully in their canoes until a game of war erupted. Justin remembered watching as the counselor's face slid instantly from laughter into horror as the boys in one canoe rammed into theirs, and everyone went spilling into the river. He could still recall the rush of water, hear the counselor saying, "Oh, my God," and taste the warm silt of the Mississippi flooding into his mouth; could still recall how swift the river currents were that grabbed him as he floated loose-limbed in his small, orange square of life-vest; could still recall the anxious helplessness he felt until the counselor hoisted him -- at last -- to safety in his strong, sure arms.

So Justin looked at Kyle that first time in the food line, as if thinking even then that Kyle might similarly rescue him. He had watched Kyle's face turn unselfconsciously an inch or two in front of his own, answering someone who'd called him from across the lawn: the eyebrows dark and masculine, the face both boyish and adult, a quiet wisdom and intelligence suffusing it. He had had the sense that -- for the first time ever -- he was understanding what a man could be. From that first day, Justin wanted more than anything to get to know Kyle and be near him.

A few days after that, he'd seen Kyle once again as Justin stood there cold and goose-bumped in the shallows of the pool at the school gym. The blue lines of the swim lanes wavered like nerve endings in the water all around him as he watched Kyle swim his laps before emerging like a Colossus. Cascading water ordered every chest hair perfectly on Kyle's magnificent pectorals and abdomen as Kyle stood towering beside him, shaking off the rush of blood. Kyle smiled -- this god-like, adult male -- said "Hi," then shyly moved away. He'd felt like such a child then, just the way he'd felt that day at camp when the counselor had pulled him back into the boat, or as he had once when he'd clung onto the shoulders of his older cousin in the pool when he was small, his cousin striding through the water powerfully, his grown-up shoulders seeming unimaginably broad.

Later, as he saw Kyle in the locker room, a similar childlike sense of awe and wonder filled him. Kyle had stripped and pissed, and then walked naked to the showers just as unselfconsciously as if he'd worn his clothes. Meanwhile, Justin stood in the thin, small curtain of the water opposite him, suddenly uncertain where to put his arms; trying not to look, and yet unable *not* to; watching as Kyle lathered up the black hair of his chest, held up his arms and soaped the full, deep pockets of his underarms, then swished the soap around his swinging man-hood and his legs. As Justin watched Kyle, privy to the nonchalant, unconscious sacrament that Kyle performed, he felt again the onrush of emotion that had gripped him on the day when he'd first seen him. Kyle rinsed off, then turned and padded wetly to the lockers for his towel. As Justin turned his own shower off and headed back, he placed his feet inside the same tracks Kyle had made: the thrill he felt was visceral.

The way he had eventually met Kyle was via Sam, the Peer Group Counselor for his freshmen dorm. Peer Group Counselors (PGCs) were students -- mostly seniors -- who'd been trained in counseling techniques. They lived in single rooms and were assigned to every floor at Thornton College. "You have to take a counseling class, then spend a week before school starts bonding with the other counselors, doing role playing and trust building exercises -- things like that," Kyle had described it offhandedly once, which made him seem to Justin like an initiate into a secret cult: one Justin felt immediately sad that he was not a member of.

4

Justin's PGC was Sam, a burly, friendly type who was more-or-less a friend of everybody on the campus, including Kyle. Sam was the first person Justin had met on campus, in fact. That first, crazed day when Justin's father had abandoned him with typical befuddlement after the four-hour drive through central Illinois to Thornton, Sam had helped Justin move his things into the room, his presence in the white-walled, cinder-block cell seeming oddly comforting. Sam had a blacker, fuller beard than any Justin could recall on anybody even close to his age, and as Justin's father (currently in the process of divorcing his mother) stood in the stark room watching in the helpless way people have when they aren't quite certain what to do, while hoping someone else will seize the reins and do it for them, Sam's authority had helped to ease the situation greatly. Sam had gripped his hand broadly, masculinely (it was the first time Justin really remembered shaking someone's hand, and the contact of it -- intimate and male -- registered with him fully). Sam said, "Don't worry, we're going to take care of this guy," and winked. As Sam held onto Justin's hand an instant longer, Justin had immediately felt as though here he might truly have a friend and ally -- an unfamiliar feeling for some time now, especially lately: with his mother and father going through their current phase, Justin often felt as though he had no one he could turn to. Everything at home at present was territorial -- mom's or dad's side: it had made him afraid to show an interest in anyone.

This sense of camaraderie remained when they had met Justin's roommate, Jacob, who turned out to be from Nigeria. Justin could feel his father tensing beside him, and recalled the few odd, derogatory comments he had heard his father make down through the years regarding African-Americans. The whole situation of race had been as distant to Justin growing up as, say, news reports about riots brewing in Chicago during that late 1960s. Since there had been just one black person in his entire graduating class in high school, Justin had little or no exposure to other races, even other religions. The entire populace of his hometown, Moline, seemed to have been blond-haired, blue-eyed, and Scandinavian Lutheran -- everyone, that is, except Justin who -- though part Swedish (the other half was English) -- had black hair and green eyes. This fact alone had made him feel different from nearly everybody else growing up. Justin, then, was cheered to see his roommate was someone who, like him, might not feel as though he belonged. As he shook Jacob's hand -- the second such instance of contact that day -- and took in the handsome, deep-set eyes, the dark espresso of his beautiful, unblemished skin, Justin's only disappointment was that Jacob was already there with several other friends, a fact that made him wonder how much he would really get to know him: if Jacob already had a ready-made group of friends he hung around with, how much would he be around? Still, Jacob seemed energetic and friendly, and was impeccably polite (his British education and accent served to heighten this impression), and Justin felt glad of the opportunity to be his roommate.

Later, Justin's father bid him farewell, and perhaps because of his nervousness at the roommate situation, or perhaps thinking to make up for some of his recent lapses in regards to divorcing Justin's mother, he had urged Justin in a lamentably bluff, over-compensating manner to "stay out of drugs and in a condom." Then, departing, he shook Justin's hand as obsequiously as if he were a member of the local Moose lodge. Not only was it the first time his father had ever shaken his hand, but the gesture -- even in comparison to the other handshakes that day with Sam and Jacob -- felt tepid and tentative, emblematic of his dealings with his father as a whole. At least with Sam and Jacob, he'd felt a spark of something -- a certain connection; with his father, there had never been anything more than a wish for something firmer, stronger, more definite. Certainly, the circumstances of his father divorcing his mother was playing a part in that; but there was this gap between him and his father where Justin had always craved more affection -- a spot where he'd always wanted an older brother to be. Instead, there had often merely been a void.

After Justin's father had left, Sam asked both Justin and Jacob up to have a beer; and even though he wasn't old enough to drink (Jacob might have been -- Justin couldn't tell), and even though Sam and he were well aware he wasn't old enough, Justin tried to act as though an offer of this kind were completely natural.

Sitting in Sam's room -- a room that looked to be in the process of being moved into or out of, but which Justin came to learn was its perennial state -- Justin learned that Jacob was, indeed, older than he (22, in fact), very into women and cars ("I like my women like I like my cars: fast"), and in the process of trying to get an American business degree ("Is the American dream, no? To make a lot of money? What better place to do that than in America?"). Hearing all this, Justin's heart sank as he found himself doubting that he and Jacob would wind up having much in common after all.

A week or so after that first invitation, still early in the school year, Sam had asked Justin up to his room again, and this was how he'd finally met Kyle and Craig, who, along with Sam, were seniors at the school. Thornton College was a small school of about 500 students in southern Illinois. Justin had chosen it primarily because it was one of the few schools his parents could afford, but also because it was liberal arts. Most of Justin's other friends had gone to the larger state schools, but here he was now, stranded in the middle of the Illinois cornfields, alone and confused.

As soon as Justin walked into Sam's room that night, he noticed Kyle. The room was still the way he'd noticed only loud rooms were, and semi-dark with incandescent lighting. The cinder block white walls were lined with an array of damaged sofas, their ticking spilling out of arms and seats like socks stuck in an over-filled sock drawer. A golf flag tucked into a huge wood electric cable drum stood in the center of the room, and served as a cocktail table. The carpeting was blue-green, frayed, and badly stained with beer. As Justin entered, he saw Kyle standing at a makeshift bar, deep in conversation with Sam. Justin would have liked to talk to Kyle, but still felt too shy. As Justin was on the verge of backing out entirely, a body from a nearby group of people bumped into him, and he felt a warm and startling liquid surge across his stomach.

"Oh, God, I'm sorry," said the man.

"Cut Daniels off! He's drunk!" a woman in the man's group yelled. She had a page boy haircut straight out of 1925, and smiled at the two of them impishly, as if delighted by the complication.

"Oh, don't you wish," the man said good-naturedly. "You're just looking to take advantage of me if I am."

"Me? Oh, not me. But I do think you should take that shirt off."

"Oh, right," said the man. "You're just trying to get us all to take our shirts off."

"Ooh, baby!" said the woman.

"All right. You go first."

"Don't tempt me," said the woman, smiling at him flirtatiously.

The man turned to look at Justin now. He had scruffy, long blond hair the color of pinewood sawdust, a patchy, not-quite grown-in beard, and was tanned a startling reddish-brown. Hearing the woman talk about all the men in the room taking their shirts off made Justin wonder what this smooth, tanned torso would have looked like if he'd done so, and Justin found himself staring at the man's throat and collarbone almost involuntarily. The man took hold of Justin's shoulder now and said, "I'm sorry. Did I soak you?"

At the man's touch, Justin felt a charge -- electric -- running straight into his loins. Embarrassed by this, but also by the fact he wasn't sure exactly what to say, he fumbled awkwardly. His shirt *was* wet, and yet he didn't want to seem unfriendly. He was also very conscious suddenly of everybody's eyes on him.

"No, that's okay."

"Shit, I did."

"No, no, it's okay," said Justin, trying hard to wave it off. Yet, suddenly, the man had raised the beer above his head and was pouring it on himself.

"You *are* a wild man!" said the 1920s woman, looking at him with renewed appreciation.

"It's my Indian blood," said the man, looking at Justin a little sheepishly, his hair dripping. "My grandmother was a full-blooded Cree."

"I'm sure she'd be very proud," said Justin.

"I'm sure she would," said the man, laughing, extending his hand. "My name's Craig. Craig Daniels."

"Hi, I'm Justin Lloyd."

They shook hands and, once again, Justin felt something moving through him, though this time it was more like a sense of grounding than anything else: the sense he'd longed to feel on meeting his roommate Jacob, but had not.

"Why did you pour that beer all over yourself?" said Justin as they moved away.

"I don't know," said Craig. "I'm way too willing to make a fool of myself sometimes, I guess."

The two of them began to chat, moving away from the group, and Justin felt increasingly amazed as time wore on that Craig was still devoting this much time to him, that he seemed so interested in getting to know him. Craig was not as attractive as Kyle was, Justin concluded instantly; still, Justin felt something unmistakable toward him -- some kind of a connection -- right off the bat, the way he had upon seeing Kyle that first day. From time to time as they talked, Justin cast a glance over towards Kyle and Sam, but they were still holding an animated discussion with each other, and it did not appear the much sought-after goal of meeting Kyle would be achieved tonight.

Craig and Justin were sitting now on one of the tattered black naugahyde sofas, the music (Tom Petty wailing, "You don't... have... to live like a refugee") having died down to a steady background murmur, and a number of people having left for other parties. The conversation had veered from origins (Craig was from Downer's Grove, near Chicago) to majors (Craig's was painting), to music. The mellow strains of *Netherlands* suddenly began to play, shifting the mood, and when Craig said enthusiastically, "God, I *love* this album!" Justin knew he liked him.

"I know. Dan Fogelberg is great."

"Actually, I think *Home Free* is his best album, though I love this one a lot, too," said Craig.

"Is that the one with the drawing on the cover where he looks like Jesus?"

"Yeah."

"Did he do that drawing himself?"

"Yeah, I think he does all the art for his albums."

"I think that's so great, when people can draw *and* sing. I can't draw at all -- can't even imagine what it would take to be able to create a self-portrait."

"You know," said Craig, suddenly expansive, "talking about him looking like Jesus, isn't it weird the way Jesus is always painted in that skinny, scrawny way? Because he was 30 when he started preaching, and before that, he'd been a carpenter his whole life, so all those skinny pictures of him always seem wrong to me. Wouldn't he more rightly have been a little beefy -- even burly -- if he'd been a carpenter?"

Justin was a little surprised at this: was Craig really religious? "But people back then weren't as well fed as they are now," said Justin cautiously. "I don't think he'd have looked as bulked up as you think."

"You've got a point. But still, I think he would probably have looked more athletic than ascetic, which is the way he's always shown." Craig scrutinized the people in the room now, looking -- as Justin subsequently grew accustomed to him doing -- as an artist does, with a kind of x-ray vision capable of looking deep down through the clothes and skin to actualities of joint and bone. "More in the line of Sam," said Craig. "Or maybe better, Rhodes. I think he'd be a lot more likely to have looked like Rhodes than like some starving monk."

At hearing mention of his name, Kyle turned around to look at Craig and Justin.

"Are you guys talking about art over there?" Sam called out jovially, the amiable, black-bearded Friar of the party. He took a swig of beer, then yelled warmly to Craig, "Hey, Daniels, this is supposed to be a party, for Christ's sake. Quit corrupting that Freshman, will you?"

On seeing Kyle advancing towards them, Justin seized up. At first, he hadn't recognized who Craig was speaking of when he'd said, "Rhodes," though he'd been conscious all night long that Kyle was there, so tantalizingly close. Now, as he gradually became aware that this was who Craig was referring to, his shyness quickly turned to panic as Kyle sat down next to him.

"Did I hear my name?" said Kyle, turning that awesome countenance suddenly on Justin.

Justin froze. It seemed that he and Craig had been caught in something very dangerous: a critical appraisal of another man's physique. And, while Justin sensed that Craig was doing it on pure artistic grounds, his own appraisal hadn't been so innocent.

Craig looked casually at Kyle and said, "Oh, we were just discussing your god-like body."

"You were what?"

"We were just talking about religious paintings," said Justin hurriedly. "Craig was saying it didn't seem right that Jesus was always portrayed as being so frail."

"I see," said Kyle, perplexed, his forest-floor brown eyes and ruddy beard making Justin almost too flustered to think. "And how exactly did my name come up?"

"Oh, we just thought you looked like God," said Craig.

"Oh, well, I can see that," laughed Kyle.

"You can? Jesus, you are *so* vain," said Craig, at which point all of them began to laugh.

"Have you two met each other?" Craig said.

Justin stammered a minute, uncertain what to say. He wasn't sure whether Kyle remembered seeing him that day at the pool.

Before he could respond, however, Kyle was saying, "No, I don't think so. I'm Kyle Rhodes."

"Hi, I'm Justin." As he shook Kyle's hand, the room and everybody else inside it vanished. Shaking it was like being lost in someone's arms, like a tearful face pressed deep in sympathetic shoulders: for a moment, all the world blocked out. Enveloped by Kyle's grip, he had to fight to let it go, to bring the world and all its clamorous cacophony back into focus. As he did so, he was fighting hard to hear Kyle's words.

"So, Justin, where are you from?"

"Moline," said Justin, gathering himself. Then, because he felt their eyes still on him, "You've probably never heard of it. It's nowhere."

"Oh, I know Moline," said Kyle. "West of Chicago, on the Mississippi, right?"

"Yeah," said Justin, surprised. "Not that many people down here seem to have the slightest idea where it is."

"I've never been there, but I've heard of it," said Kyle. "I'm from Stevens Point. It's about half way up Wisconsin, north of Madison."

"Oh," said Justin, conjuring up already in his mind an image of a small resort town: gorgeous people raising huge and healthy sons.

"You're from Chicago, right?" said Kyle to Craig.

"Well, I *used* to live outside Chicago, but my parents just moved to Tennessee."

"Really? Why Tennessee?" said Kyle.

"My mother's family is from there. My dad's retired; they decided to move back."

"Is that where you were this summer?" Kyle asked.

"Hell, yes, that's where I was," groaned Craig comically. "I spent the entire summer driving post holes on my uncle's farm."

"So *that* explains the tan," chanced Justin, still gun-shy of saying anything that indicated he'd noticed something physical about another man.

"Hell, yes," said Craig. "And let me tell you, tan's about the *only* thing I got this summer, down in bumfuck Tennessee."

"I see. Not a lot of action down there, huh?" said Kyle, interpreting for Justin a remark that otherwise would probably have gone right over his head.

"No, not unless you count my hand."

Justin cringed at this, and looked to Kyle to see if he had also thought it crude; but Kyle seemed nonplussed.

"So," Kyle said, after a moment's pause. "No women, and an entire summer driving post holes. That was pretty Freudian."

"Let's just say, after three months in Tennessee, my *sister* was starting to look pretty damn good to me."

"I see," said Justin. "When in Tennessee ...."

"Something like that, I guess," said Craig.

"So, mister god-like body," teased Craig. "Tell us all about your summer screwing *everything that moved.*"

"No, no," said Kyle, vaguely embarrassed again. "I have a girlfriend."

There was a pause, during which time Craig looked comically at Justin, then turned back to Kyle. "*And?*" said Craig, making them laugh. "You have a girl-friend and you *didn't* screw all summer? What's wrong with this picture?"

Justin watched Kyle struggle with the right way to respond, a small, self-conscious smile appearing at the corners of his mouth. Then, Kyle said finally: "I respectfully refuse to answer that, on the grounds my answer may incriminate me."

"Thank you, John Haldeman," said Craig.

"*John Haldeman,*" said Kyle. "Geez, get some more up-to-date references, will you, bud? It's almost the '80s."

"Well, pardon us, Mr. Ford," said Justin, at which they all laughed again.

"Oh, Jesus, forgive me, " said Craig, looking prayerfully toward Kyle.

"All right, since you already started this," said Kyle. He picked the plastic cup of beer up off the table near him and began to pour it over Craig's head.

"*In nomine patris, et filii, et spiritus sancti.*"

As the focus of the room began to center on them again, Kyle poured beer not only over Craig, but over himself and Justin, too. It was like a laying on of hands: a curiously visceral, strangely erotic sensation that traveled from his scalp straight to his belly button and his toes.

"Cut them off! Cut them all off!" yelled Sam from behind the bar.

Despite renewed attention from the whole room -- or maybe due to it -- Justin felt more pleased by this than any other thing that could have happened. It seemed to him they'd been anointed as friends now, marked for everyone to see -- that he'd become, through Kyle's own gesture, one of the elect.

The next day, walking on the campus after his Intro Psych class had ended, the late-September day still warm and beautiful, a high, clear, angular light streaking the quad as if through cathedral windows, Justin stumbled into Craig, and felt the little thrill of familiarity again, a connection like the one he'd felt as they had shaken hands last night.

"Hey, how you doing?" said Craig.

"Great," said Justin. "That was a fun party last night, huh?"

"Yeah. Sorry again about the beer."

"Oh, no problem," said Justin.

"Speak of the devil," said Craig, and before Justin knew it, there at his side was Kyle, making the picture complete and giving him again a sense of inclusion and bondedness such as he had never had before.

"Oh, sure," said Kyle. "One minute I'm God, the next minute I'm the devil."

Craig laughed. "What can I say? Sometimes it's hard to tell the difference, I guess."

"Hey, guy," said Kyle now to Justin. Never before had Justin been called "guy" with such import; never before had he felt such a tingle on hearing it from another man's lips.

"Hey," beamed Justin.

"What are you guys up to?" said Kyle.

"I was just thinking about heading out to the plaza," said Craig. "You guys want to come?"

"Sure," said Kyle.

"Sounds good to me," said Justin, thrilled to be included in their company once again.

They walked out past the outer dorms onto the road behind the campus, past tennis courts and late-summer hedges, and they could see the edge of campus bordered by the rows of cornfields browning in the sun. Despite the fact that it was fall, the air had something of the feel of spring about it, and indeed, Justin had noticed in the past that -- since the angle of the light was just about the same in either season -- there were days in spring that could have passed for days in autumn, and vice versa: you could have made yourself believe it was either one. If he had not been certain of the date upon the calendar, this mid-September day might have been one in April.

Behind the soccer fields and run-down houses on the cindered road behind the campus, the fields began to open up and lose their fall appearance. Some of them had been plowed under already, and as they walked along, the sense of being suspended somewhere in time increased. The rich, turned furrows of the earth -- as dark as brownie batter -- and the fresh-washed feeling in the air, did indeed give the appearance of spring. Looking at the plowed rows, Justin could almost make himself believe the crops were just about to appear, rather than being at an end.

Suddenly, cresting the rise of a small field beside the local shopping center, they came upon a huge expanse of fields entirely covered in white. For a moment, Justin thought wildly that it was snow, but the weather was far too warm for that.

"Oh my God," said Craig. "Will you look at that?"

"Jesus," said Kyle.

"What is it?" said Justin.

"It's dandelions," said Craig. "Millions and millions of dandelions. I've never seen anything like it."

As Justin's eyes narrowed, he saw Kyle was right: the field, indeed, was like a dotted Swiss lace curtain, rolling grey and undulant as far as they could see. Almost before this image coalesced in his mind, however, Kyle was racing out into the field, a trail of dandelion seeds raising up behind him, leaving in his wake a swath like a lawnmower makes on the first May grass.

"Come on," yelled Kyle, and, in a moment, they were racing out to meet him, dandelion fluff ascending in a cloud around them, rising up into the blue glass of the sky like bubbles to the sunny surface of the ocean. Justin ran out laughing, stirring up as many seeds as possible by running, waving arms, and swishing them into the air, the soft grey heads all smushing to the touch like slush. In a moment, through the veil of seeds ascending and descending all around him like a blizzard, Justin felt a body hurtling through the cloud mass, wrapping both arms firmly to his torso in a tackle. With a thud, he fell into the softness of the dandelions, and someone's body -- Kyle's, he now concluded -- molded into his. Then, in the stunned and unimaginably silent instant following, he grew aware of how it felt to have Kyle laying there on top of him. Kyle's face pressed into his, and he let his body slacken in the warmth and feel of it. Then, the welter of seeds above them dissipating and clearing finally, he grew aware of Craig standing again above them, looking at them comically. "Well, was it good for you?" said Craig, amused.

Kyle laid his head a brief, full moment of repose on Justin's chest, both arms still locked unshakably around Justin's torso, and said agreeably, "Hey, *I* just shot my wad."

Craig laughed and looked around. "My, my. You are prodigious."

Kyle stood up now and tackled Craig, another, smaller cloud ensuing as they landed.

Justin lay for a moment in the spiky grass remembering the feel of Kyle, not wanting anything to take away the feel of it. Another moment passed, the world still and the sun warm on his body. Lazily, he pulled the dandelions from his hair, his mouth, his clothes. Then, suddenly self-conscious, he stood up finally and tackled Craig, and after they had landed on the ground and all the particles had settled, set out more gingerly to tackle Kyle.

Standing in the shower's steam that evening in his dark dorm pondering the afternoon, the way they'd laid waste to the field -- as many dandelion heads dispersed as possible -- Justin still could not erase the feel of Kyle as he'd embraced him when they landed, nor the memory of Kyle on top of him: Kyle pouncing on him like a fumbled football, squarely, sexually, as if announcing to the world: *You're mine. I've got you.*

As he lay in bed that night, he pulled the pillow hard against him in a vain attempt to counterfeit the feel of it once more. Was he in love with Kyle? And did this mean, then, he was gay? For some time now, he'd been aware that he felt something sexual toward men -- exactly what, he was afraid to think; yet, there was something there. He'd felt a worrisome attraction and awareness all through high school for a few boys in particular, but had never dared express it, let alone act on it. The high school dates he'd made half-heartedly, the nervous dances he'd attended with the kind, plain, girls, had left him on the verge of understanding something in himself that he was not prepared to know; and yet, a statement of that truth seemed somehow unavoidable. Now, as he thought about that day when he'd stood in the shower room with Kyle, he tried again to sort out what he felt. If what he'd felt toward Kyle was attraction, and therefore physical, why hadn't he been fighting an erection then? And what had Kyle meant by his comment as he'd tackled him out on the field, that he'd just shot his wad? If Kyle was feeling something toward him, too, why hadn't there been any other signs of it? For his part, Justin was aware of something burgeoning deep down inside toward Kyle, and yet, he couldn't figure out how much was love, as in desire, and how much was an outgrowth of their ever-growing friendship. Thinking once again about the feel of Kyle on top of him, the casual nature of Kyle's comment, Justin asked himself anew: if this was love, which he was petrified it was, was love like this? This unexpected landing on your ass? This scared and breathless accident that left you dazed and not quite certain of its tone?

———◆———

Sitting at the bar one night some weeks later, still pondering these questions, Justin looked, distracted, at the beer inside his glass. It was the same gold color as the light that bathed the wood floors and the coat racks, mounted moose and elk heads lined up on the wall above them. It swirled up near the pressed tin ceiling and the huge, stuffed crow that perched in the corner looking down on them, as if forever on the verge of saying, *Nevermore*. It was the same hue falling on the beautiful, black walnut bar surrounded by the tacky chrome-and-lime-green vinyl bar stools, the same hue lighting up the face of Craig across from him and Kyle beside him in the vinyl booth, so that, as Justin pondered this light suffusing everything, he suddenly thought savagely, *Everything's the same hue in and out but me -- I am the only one with shadows*. Then he felt the fear again, the lie inside him. He tried to think if it was true, that he loved Kyle; felt conscious of his friends' eyes upon him as he grew aware of how much Kyle and Craig didn't know. He wished he could tell them -- wanted so to talk about his indecision; but the fear was always there: the fear that he'd risk losing them as friends if he confessed.

And so, he sat in the warm cave of Kyle's body, Kyle's thick arm extended unselfconsciously around him on the booth's back -- once more, Kyle's protected ward -- and marveled at the way the bar light underlit and softened Kyle's moustache. He looked across and saw the light glint in Craig's beard as well, and thought about the setting sun through wheat fields, turned back and watched as Kyle's words stirred the hairs about his mouth as gently as the kelp in oceans. He watched Kyle's lips caress the syllables, looked down and saw the soft black hair on Kyle's chest, and once again grew fearful of his thoughts.

"Are you all right?" said Kyle, and Justin realized that no one else was speaking; no one else had spoken for some time.

"Yeah, I'm just tired," he said, then cringed. How stupid could he be? Why not just wear a sign announcing it: *I am in love with Kyle. I'm* ... but the word too dangerous to think of, let alone to speak. He looked down at his beer, then saw that Craig was looking at him from across the table, eyes fixed upon him with a strange intensity. Justin looked away.

Kyle said, "Oh, God, there's Stacey Neal."

As Justin looked, the 1920s woman from the party walked into the door behind Craig. Craig turned back to look at her, then turned around again.

"How come, "Oh, God?""

"Didn't I tell you guys what she did to me at that party?" said Kyle.

"No, I don't think so." Craig said.

"Oh, man," said Kyle, embarrassed now and laughing at the same time. "I was standing leaning up against the wall drinking a beer, minding my own business. Anyway, she walks up to me and, without saying anything at all, slides her hand into my pocket. I'm talking *way* down into my pocket -- she was practically touching my 'nads. Then, she looked me straight in the eye and said, 'Maybe I could borrow this sometime?' Well, you know what *I'm* thinking. Anyway, I look down and she's holding my car keys. She just smiled, handed them back to me, and walked away."

"That was the party we were at?" said Justin, confused.

"Yeah, must've been earlier, before I talked with your guys."

"She's a wild one," said Craig, looking suddenly envious. "So, why the hell didn't you go for it?"

"With Stacey? Yeah, right, that's just the kind of girl I want: shy, demure. Besides, I'm a one woman man, and I'm very in love with Maureen. Even if she is, what, 300 miles away at another school and I won't be seeing her again until, when, Christmas?" At this, Kyle bit his fist and groaned.

Hearing mention again of Kyle's girlfriend, Justin asked, "How long have you two been going out?"

"About five years."

"Wow," said Justin, trying to assimilate this fact, and look as cheerful and unflustered as possible.

"I don't know," said Craig after a moment. "If Stacy threw herself at me, I'd go for it. Why not? Of course, it might help a little if I had a bod like yours."

"Who are *you* trying to kid, you old smoothie?" said Kyle. "You've got that artist thing going for you: suave, sensitive. A good-looking guy like you? I'd think the women would fall all over you."

"Yeah, right," sniffed Craig. "Not like you, Mr. Christ-like figure."

Hearing these mutual compliments of the other's attractiveness, Justin wondered again: if even Kyle could admit to noticing these things, why should he think he had a problem?

"Hey, cut that out, will you?" said Kyle. "I may not be that great of a Catholic, but I don't exactly want to tempt fate, either."

"Sorry," said Craig. "Speaking of being damned to hell forever .... "

"Thanks," said Kyle.

"Sorry," said Craig. "But seriously, did you guys hear what happened with Jennie Martinson and her roommate?"

"Who's Jenny Martinson?" said Kyle.

"She's that weird girl who's always trying to hold Bible discussion groups. I keep running into her all over campus."

"I know the one you mean," said Justin. "Always wearing black, with that huge wooden cross dangling on her chest."

"Oh, yeah," said Kyle.

"Anyway," said Craig, "turns out her roommate is a lesbian who thinks she's falling in love with her. So, she decides to confess it to her."

"Oh, God," said Kyle, his head falling into his hands.

"Yeah, and not only that," said Craig. "After her roommate confesses she's in love with her, Jenny Martinson decides she's going to try to do an exorcism to 'cast Satan out' of her roommate's body."

Justin was almost too afraid to move, let alone say anything. At last he managed to ask nervously, "What happened?"

"Well, get this," said Craig. "At the end of the ceremony, Jenny Martinson's roommate -- and nobody seems to know her as anything other than 'Jenny Martinson's roommate,' by the way -- at the end of the 'ceremony,' the roommate goes screaming down the hall and throws herself off a third floor balcony into the parking lot below."

"Jesus," said Kyle. "Is she alive?"

"I guess," said Craig. "She's in the hospital, obviously."

There was silence, during which time Justin tried anxiously to think whether he was really going to ask the question which was chafing at him. Finally, knowing he'd never rest unless he asked it, he said to Craig, "Which one of them do you think is damned to hell forever?"

"What?" said Craig, startled.

"At the start of the story, you said, 'Speaking of being damned to hell forever.'"

"Oh," said Craig. "I didn't really mean anything by that."

Justin wanted to say, "Which one of them do you *think* is damned," but couldn't find the courage to say it. As he was mulling over some kind of a response, heart pounding with fear, Kyle said,

"Sounds to me like they were *both* in hell, in one way or another."

Craig murmured his assent, and Justin merely let the matter drop.

Walking home that evening, down the dark side streets that led off from the square, past grand, old late-Victorian houses on a main street that looked to be straight out of 1910 -- huge Queen Anne's with multi-gabled roofs and striped awnings -- Justin thought about the conversation at the bar, pondering both Craig's and Kyle's responses. How could he talk to them about his fears tonight? Much as he'd wanted to, he'd felt blind-sided by the news about Kyle's girlfriend, and the story of Jenny Martinson and her roommate. Now, as they stumbled through the frosty, blue-black darkness, moonlight etching tree limbs, empty screened-in porches, curbs, and uneven sidewalks, he could hear the alcohol at work behind their boisterousness, could sense that -- even if he wanted to -- both Kyle and Craig were in no state to talk to him right now.

At last, they walked into the entrance of the campus, passing through the lane of trees and the low, brick wall proclaiming THORNTON COLLEGE on the right.

"I think I'll call it a night," Kyle said. "I'm bushed."

"Me too," said Craig.

"I guess me, too, then," Justin said. Even though he had decided not to talk to them, this sudden ending of the night seemed hard. He felt the need to linger, somehow -- wished they'd ask him whether anything was wrong.

Instead, Kyle said, "I'll see you guys tomorrow, then" and walked off handsome, unattainable, back toward his dorm.

Craig clapped Justin on the back and said, "You take it easy, guy. Goodnight." Then, Craig was gone as well.

Justin walked the cold, long silence to his dorm and wished he'd had more nerve. How long could he put off having this talk? How long could he expect to wallow in this indecisiveness before it drove him crazy?

As he opened up the door into his room, Justin sensed right away that something was amiss: the darkness was too dark, the quiet too intense. Now, as he flipped the room light on, he saw a woman holding up a sheet beneath her chin and, over her, his roommate, poised in mid-thrust, glaring back at him.

"Could you come back a short time later, please, Justin?" said his roommate. Even *in flagrante delicto*, Jacob was scrupulously polite.

"Oh, I'm sorry," said Justin. He flipped the light out in embarrassment, then opened up the door to leave. "I didn't realize."

"We presumed you'd be a little longer," Jacob said. "I do apologize. We should be finished here quite soon."

As Justin shut the door, he stood for a moment, looking at the harsh fluorescent glare upon the white tile of the hallway. It was 1 a.m., a Saturday, and he was not sure where to go.

CHAPTER 2

———◆———

S ITTING IN SAM'S ROOM A few days later, Justin had resolved to talk over the whole situation with him, and was trying to work his courage up to broach the subject. Sam was his Peer Group Counselor, after all; why not try telling him about his fears? About this strange, persistent doubt about his sexuality, this fear that hung down like a cord protruding from a closet door and wouldn't let it close -- a cord Kyle yanked whenever he was near?

Yet, as he sat in Sam's room on the dusty, worn-out sofa, empty beer cans littering the floor and people streaming in and out to say hello, he realized he couldn't do it. How could he talk about these things with Sam? What would Sam think? What if he was appalled and spread the word that he was gay? How could he stay at a school this small if everybody knew?

At last, Sam stood up, closed the door and said, "What can I do for you, bud?"

Behind Sam's head, a poster of a half-nude, buxom blond with very prominent nipples underneath her stretched white tube top proclaimed, "Study Hard."

He had thought he couldn't broach this subject. But with the door closed, in the sudden stillness of the room, he wondered whether he should risk it. Sam sat there in a nubby green chair that reminded Justin of a chair his grandmother had -- a similar, severe, uncomfortable material -- Sam's jovial, full-bearded countenance inviting him to speak his mind, to say for weeks what he'd been wanting to. Then, just as quickly, Justin knew he wasn't ready, that he couldn't bring this up today. He sat there panicked, trying to think of something else to talk about. But how else was he ever going to know?

"I'm feeling a little confused about sex, I guess," he said at last.

"Oh, sex," said Sam affably. "The big one. Is there something that's bothering you in particular?"

"Well," said Justin, already sorry he had started down this path. "I don't know."

Sam let him sit there for a minute, gathering himself, then said: "What are you feeling confused about?"

Justin squirmed a moment more, then said, "What if you're feeling something for somebody, but you're not sure they feel it, too?"

"I see," said Sam, a little half-smile playing suddenly about the corners of his mouth. "You feel attracted to someone, but you're not sure the feeling's mutual?"

"Yes," said Justin, startled and relieved to have the issue finally articulated.

"Well, Justin, let me tell you," Sam said. "Half the time -- most of the time -- I think you'll find out the girl you're interested in is interested in you, too. You just kind of have to go for it. Now, I'm not talking about sex. As far as sex goes, I would have to urge you not to let yourself rush into that. But if you're interested in seeing someone, let her know. More times than not, I'll bet she's interested, too."

Justin hardly heard a word past "girl." Of course, Sam would presume the person whom he was attracted to was female. What else would he think? Justin felt constricted. What else could he do now but endure the rest -- just wait and smile and try to act as though his fears had been assuaged?

"Does that help you any at all?"

"Yeah, a little bit," said Justin. "I guess I just have to take the bull by the horns," he added uncomfortably.

"That's right. These things all have a way of working out. By the way, is it anybody I know?"

Justin froze at this, panicking as he realized that Sam knew Kyle, too. And if Sam found out about it, how long would it take to get back to Kyle?

"No, I don't think so."

For a moment, Sam sat looking at him patiently. "All right," he said at last. "Is there anything else I can help you with?"

Walking back into his room, Justin heard his roommate playing Donna Summer again. *The Talking Heads* and *B-52s* were blaring alternately down the hall, but Jacob, being from Nigeria and lagging somewhat behind American trends, was playing her as though she were something new. He was also very into *The Supremes*.

As Justin walked into the room, he saw that Jacob was completely naked, standing at the mirror shaving carefully. Jacob was utterly without self-consciousness about his body, something Justin envied. Justin looked away, yet still, he saw how well-built Jacob was: his chest and limbs all broad and strong; his body that of an adult, which Justin never felt as though he was himself.

"You going out somewhere?" said Justin.

"Ah," said Jacob sagaciously. "One never knows what one will find, does one?" He pulled on a pair of light blue underwear, then said, "Why for do you not seek out the women, eh? They are all waiting to be opened like ripe fruit."

"Well," said Justin shyly and uncomfortably. "I just haven't found the right one, I guess."

"But I think you are too bashful. What difference does it make, right one, wrong one? Why not sample them all?" He grabbed Justin's crotch suddenly and said, "You have a nice, big organ dere, eh? Why be ashamed of it?"

Justin was shocked and confused at the contact, not sure what to make of it. No one had ever touched him there before, even in play. Was he perhaps just overly sensitive and prudish? Was it really not that big a deal at all?

After Jacob had left, Justin sat down on the bed, still reeling and embarrassed. Was Jacob right? Should he try going out with women more? Was he too prudish, and too bashful, and was he simply confusing this bashfulness with something else?

That evening, after supper, Craig and Justin sat in Kyle's room. They were about to head out to the library to study for a while, but Kyle had said he'd like to call Maureen first. The hall was strangely quiet for a weeknight, and as they sat, they heard Kyle speaking quietly on the pay phone at the end of the hallway, though mostly what they heard was an occasional assent, a murmur. Something in the tone of it had caught their ears, however, and Craig and Justin sat there listening, not talking to each other. Soon, they heard Kyle hang the phone up, and a second later, he was in the doorway.

"Fuck," said Kyle as he flopped upon the double mattress on the floor. Kyle had a single room by virtue of his role as PGC, and he'd pulled both his mattresses onto the floor to make a king-sized bed.

"What's wrong?" said Justin, looking at the mass Kyle's body made upon the cocoa-colored blanket. Everything in Kyle's room seemed to be in shades of brown or yellow: blankets, woodwork, desk. Shot glasses lined his bookshelves, along with textbooks, notebooks, dictionary, and a hardback copy of *The Executioner's Song*. Plaid brown and yellow curtains, which Kyle's mom had made, held back the light.

"This long-distance relationship is killing me," he said. "And now, I feel like Maureen's jerking me around, telling me she's suddenly not sure about the wedding date again."

"How come?" said Craig.

"Oh, it's just jitters, I think. We're supposed to get married right after graduation in May, but now she's wondering about changing the date, so she could do a summer internship in Washington. I don't see what the problem is. Why can't we be married even if she *is* going to be gone a few months? But she says she doesn't want the wedding to be a hurried-up affair." Kyle sighed, a long, exasperated sigh, then flopped completely supine on the bed. He lay there for a moment more, and then his hips began to pound the mattress rhythmically, faking masturbation. He stopped, then looked at them and laughed. "Sorry. I just had to get that out of my system."

Justin laughed as well. Still, he was shocked. The sight of Kyle's butt muscles clenching and unclenching as he fucked the mattress was an image he was certain he would not be able to forget.

"Well, there's always Stacey Neal," said Craig. "Seems like she'd be willing to lend you a hand."

"God," said Kyle. "I should have grabbed her while I had the opportunity."

"Oh, right," said Craig. "Like you're such a womanizer. I think if I ever saw you cheat on Maureen, I'd fall over."

"I guess I *am* pretty pussy-whipped at that," said Kyle. "I've known she was the one for me ever since my sophomore year in high school."

"How did you know?" said Justin, trying to make the question sound as innocuous a possible.

"I don't know," said Kyle. "Just did." Kyle paused, then looked at Craig. "How come you don't ask out Linda Cates? You know she likes you."

"Yeah, well, I don't know," said Craig. "I sort of thought I might ask Vicki Jones out. I suppose that lines me right up there with every other guy on campus."

Kyle frowned at this. "So what? You're a good-looking guy. You want to ask her out, then do it. The worst she can say is no."

"I know," said Craig, though without inspiring confidence he'd follow through.

"To tell you the truth," said Kyle, "Vicki really doesn't seem like your type to me. Isn't she a little, I don't know, stand-offish?"

"Maybe. I don't know," said Craig. "She certainly hasn't been that friendly to me." He said this with a pained smile, and Justin noticed Kyle backing off.

"I shouldn't say that," said Kyle. "I don't really know her. If you want to ask her out, you should. Don't sell yourself short."

"Maybe," said Craig haplessly.

"Oh, you knucklehead," said Kyle, springing up from the bed and wrestling Craig into a headlock. "I see I'm going to have to pound some sense into this head of yours."

Kyle and Craig were now a kind of push-me pull-you, tussling around the room. Kyle reached down and gave Craig's head a rub, but as he did so, Craig grabbed both Kyle's ankles, sending them both sprawling into Justin. As they fell en masse, Kyle said, "You're not safe from me either, bud." Reaching around, he locked both Craig and Justin in his arms. Once again, enveloped in Kyle's arms, Justin marveled at Kyle's strength, his warmth, his unselfconscious gesture of affection. As they sprawled into the half-made bed, exhausted, laughing, Kyle said suddenly: "I love you guys."

Talking to his mother on the pay phone in the dorm late that evening, Justin tried in vain to fill her in on what was happening. Since the divorce proceedings had begun, his mother had been almost irrationally protective of him, worrying incessantly about the dangers he might be exposed to, being "fatherless." The white-tiled hall was nearly blue with smoke from someone's bong, yellow beer stains splotched the floor from one end to the other, and the drone of music seemed to signify little in the way of learning was going on. Still, he felt exuberant and happy, and assured her everything was fine.

"Have you made some friends?" his mother asked in that desperate way only the newly bereft have. Justin's father's leaving had left her as naked and exposed as a cabinet without a door: all the neatly ordered things lying somehow pitiful and exposed.

"I've made some *great* friends, mom," he said, suddenly conscious of how woefully inadequate those words seemed. Justin felt as though Kyle and Craig were brothers he had never had; were closer to him than anybody he'd ever known, almost as close -- wasn't it really true? -- as lovers. At any rate, he felt a greater sense of affection from them than from any other people he'd ever met, including his family.

"That's good," his mother said. "I worry about you in that environment, though, sweetie. You're not getting into drugs, or anything like that, I hope."

"Oh, mom," said Justin, praying that the people with the bong kept quiet.

"Are you meeting any nice new girls?" his mother asked hopefully. "That would be nice to hear about." One of the other things his mom had been obsessive about lately was the subject of Justin's dating. She seemed to fear that unless Justin found somebody immediately -- anybody, it didn't really matter whether he was happy in the choice or not -- he was destined to wind up as alone as she now felt.

"Mother," said Justin, exasperated, defensive. "I'm not worried about that. I'm studying hard."

"Don't study *too* hard, dear. College is probably the best chance you'll ever have to meet someone."

I have, he almost said in annoyance, thinking of Kyle and Craig, but caught himself.

"I have to go now, mom," he said, uncomfortable with all the raw emotion in the air between them. His mother at the moment was rather like a wounded bird one picked up from pity, and then was not quite certain how to handle.

"All right. I love you."

"I love you, too, mom."

Love, thought Justin, hanging up. Kyle loved Maureen, but he had also said, "I love you guys" as they'd been horsing around. Justin's father had once loved his mother, presumably, but he was not *in* love with her anymore. His mother had just said, "I love you," but obviously she was not *in* love with him. Did he himself feel merely affection for Kyle, sexual love, or was this the kind of love that wasn't *love*? And what the hell did any of it mean?

CHAPTER 3

———•———

A FEW NIGHTS LATER, KYLE, CRAIG and Justin were sitting together at the bar. A peaceful, amber colored light suffused everything; the stuffed crow was perched as always on a rafter overhead, and the stereo was playing "Sixteen Tons." Because the bar was frequented by the local miners, it was a popular selection on the jukebox.

The bar they went to was, strangely, also a college hangout, though because most of the students were under age, there was a constant threat of being asked to leave. Kyle, Craig, and -- in their tow -- Justin, had never had a problem getting served, but they were always conscious of maintaining low profiles.

As they sat in the booth tonight, however, they grew conscious of a group behind them that was coming dangerously close to getting tossed out.

"Screw Addison," said one of the older students, referring to the college's drama teacher. "He can kiss my ass."

"Oh, God, theater majors," droned Craig.

As they listened, the group was rapidly becoming more and more risque.

"Shit, he'd probably like that, the little poofter."

"Yeah, fuck 'em all," said a student seemingly much younger than the others. The way he said it managed to convey not only that he wasn't used to drinking, but also that he was new to swearing.

Kyle glanced back at him in a kind of warning, looking up at the bartender at the same time to see what impression the group had made. The bartender gave a "Keep it down" motion of his hands, though Justin knew the other people hadn't seen it.

"Hey, guys," said Kyle, acting partly in his Peer Group Counselor role and partly, Justin thought, because Kyle would have done this anyway: "You might want to keep it down a bit. Frankie's giving you the evil eye."

"Fuck Frankie," said an older student. "Fuck you, too."

"Fine," said Kyle curtly. "I'm just trying to do you guys a favor."

Turning back to Craig and Justin, Kyle said stiffly: "They're going to be out of here in about 30 seconds."

Before the bartender could do anything, however, Justin heard one of the crowd behind them say, "Fuck it. Let's get out of here. This place is a tomb."

There was a great deal of commotion suddenly as the group abandoned its empty beer-steins and garbage on the table -- the unwritten rule at Frankie's being that everybody always took his glass up to the counter when he'd finished, in order to stay in Frankie's good graces. Justin thought this would be the last of it: the bar would settle down, and they would have their intimacy once again. But now, one of the students -- the younger, inexperienced one -- was beside their table, asking, "May I join you?"

Kyle looked up, surprised, and said, not quite whole-heartedly, "Sure." Looking up at Craig and Justin now, he said, "Guys, this is Steve Norberg. Steve's on my floor."

"Hi," said Justin; Craig nodded as well. As Steve sat, Justin felt vaguely threatened, though he wasn't sure exactly why. He could also feel the tone shift as Steve pulled up a chair to join them.

There was a pause when no one was certain what to say, and Justin took Steve in. He was an unsettling looking creature, tall and gaunt: he had reddish-yellow hair, a hooked nose, round, gold, wire-rimmed glasses, and a mouth of crooked teeth, which were stained yellow and uneven as a stand of cattails at the water line. The skin seemed exceptionally tight around his forehead, so one could see the blue veins underneath, and which gave his whole visage the appearance of being like a death's head. Steve had on a baseball cap, which seemed studied, and as Justin watched, his long, thin fingers dipped into a package of Virginia Slims: in Justin's mind a woman's brand of cigarettes.

Kyle said, "You need to tell your friends that when they come here, they should keep it down, or Frankie won't be serving them again."

"Why? Can't they have a little fun?" said Steve, giggling nervously. "God, what a fascist place."

"Look," said Kyle, impatient now. "You think you're old enough to drink? You need to pay attention to the fact that Frankie doesn't have to serve us. All he asks is that you keep it down, don't call too much attention to yourself. He could get into serious trouble for serving us, so if you want to drink here, try to act like an adult."

"Okay, point taken," said Steve, looking like a scolded dog.

"Are you a theater major?" asked Justin, straining to make some conversation. Steve seemed almost defiantly effeminate, and he couldn't believe that Kyle and Craig hadn't noticed this.

"Oh, God knows what I am," said Steve dramatically. "I seem always to be in a state of perpetual identity crisis, so I guess the theater's as good a place for me as any." He paused, then said, "So, what are you guys up to tonight?"

Kyle looked at Craig and Justin, mystified, as if thinking, *This is what we're up to,* though he said: "Not much. Just sitting around, talking."

"Aw, you guys need to liven it up a little," said Steve. "We should head back to the campus and party."

Justin looked at Kyle and Craig, afraid they'd acquiesce in Steve's suggestion.

"No, this is fine," said Kyle firmly.

Justin felt both grateful and embarrassed. He would have liked them to be rid of Steve, and yet, he wasn't sure how they were going to do it: Kyle and Craig were too polite to say a thing.

"You're smoking Virginia Slims," Justin observed. Even though he didn't want to play into Steve's obvious need for attention -- the way he was sure Steve wanted someone to ask him about the perpetual identity crisis comment -- somehow he couldn't quite let this detail go.

"Yeah, I like the menthol," said Steve matter-of-factly, looking at Justin intently. There was such a mixture of challenge and insecurity in his look that Justin, embarrassed and uncomfortable, said at last, "Well, you've come a long way, baby."

Steve merely smiled -- a little, pained smile of defeat -- when Kyle and Craig laughed. Justin felt a twinge of guilt for having said this -- for mocking him with the advertising campaign which had made the brand famous -- yet, he didn't like Steve's affectation, either. He assumed they'd have to endure Steve just a little longer, then he would get bored and leave them to themselves.

But Steve didn't leave. All through the rest of the awkward evening and the crimped conversation his presence there engendered, Steve hung on: a burr they couldn't shake.

The next day, Steve was there at lunch as well, all studied red baseball cap and eagerness. Unlike most baseball caps, which were sweat-stained and faded, Steve's was pristine, and looked to be a souvenir someone else had bought him: Steve didn't give the impression of someone who was a rabid baseball fan himself.

"Oh, God," said Craig as he saw him approaching. "Here's our friend again."

"Hey, guys," said Steve, sliding his tray onto the table next to theirs. "Thanks for humoring me last night. I had a really good time."

Justin cringed at the overly polite diction, the Beaver Cleaver cheerfulness. Despite Steve's surface mannerisms, there was something nervous and unstable about him, as if all his energy were covering up some inner sadness. Justin wasn't certain whether Kyle and Craig had noticed it. He was also almost positive that Steve was gay -- his speech and mannerisms made it seem so obvious -- although he didn't want to be the one to bring that up. After they suffered through lunch and Steve departed, Craig said, "So who *is* this guy?"

"He's a freshman on my floor," said Kyle. "He's a bit clingy. I've tried to kind of introduce him to different people, but he doesn't really seem to fit in anywhere."

"Man," said Craig. "I'm glad you're the PGC, not me."

"Why?"

"Because you have to be nice. I don't."

"Oh, he's not so bad." said Kyle. "He's just trying too hard."

"Well, I'll agree with you that 'trying' is the right word," said Craig. "But not the way *you* mean it."

"Now, now -- not very nice." said Kyle.

"No," said Craig. "But honest."

Justin felt the same way Kyle and Craig did -- that Steve didn't fit in with them. But the thought that also came to him was: How different was he, really, from Steve? Steve was just a needy kid who wanted friends, same as Justin.

"Maybe he got the clue today -- maybe that'll be the end of it," said Justin hopefully.

"Hmm, I don't know," said Craig. "He seems like a pretty insistent little lad."

"Then, there's also the fact that I *am* his Peer Group Counselor," said Kyle. "It's not like I can, or should, ignore him, even if I wanted to. Which I don't."

"Like I said," said Craig. "I'm glad it's you, and not me."

⸻

That evening, Justin, Kyle, and Craig were sitting in the library studying together. Kyle had a Counseling paper to do, Craig was working on some Art History, and Justin was wrapping up a study of William Carlos Williams' "Asphodel, That Greeny Flower" for his Lit class. He hadn't thought much of the poem when he'd first read it -- hadn't even realized it was a love poem. Then, upon seeing W. H. Auden's comment that it was "one of the great love poems of the twentieth century," and upon learning that asphodels were, mythically, the flowers that grew in the Elysian Fields, Justin had imagined a field very similar to the dandelion field they'd seen that day earlier in the year, and had begun to look at the poem with renewed interest. The three of them had lapsed into a comfortable, connected silence when, suddenly, the glass doors of the reading room swung open with a bang, and Steve walked in. Everybody looked up toward the noise, annoyed. Justin wasn't sure if Steve had meant this entrance as a way of getting noticed, or if the banging of the doors was just an accident, but as they watched Steve now, he looked at them expectantly and called out loudly from across the room, "Hey, guys." A shushing noise was heard from somewhere near, and Steve -- his eyes upon the three of them the whole time, looking for reaction -- called out toward the general area of the shusher: "Oh, hush yourself!" Steve smirked as though he thought his cockiness had pleased the three of them, then continued walking toward them. Justin turned his gaze from Steve to Kyle, who watched as Steve approached. Justin's stomach fell as he anticipated Steve would crash their group once more, irrevocably altering the dynamics. Steve reached their table, but then hesitated, as if waiting for Kyle to signal to him that it was all right to sit. Kyle looked at Steve a moment more, then seemed to come to a decision.

"Sit down and be quiet, Steve," Kyle said. "This is a study area."

Steve looked defeated momentarily, but pulled a chair out opposite Kyle. He gave a sickly little smile to Craig and Justin, then said with heavy irony, "Sorry."

Kyle said nothing in return, and for a while they sat uncomfortably, each trying to resume his studying. But Steve was fidgety, and in a short time he was up again, walking out to get a drink of water.

"Oh, man," said Craig. "This guy's a royal pain in the ass."

"I know," said Kyle. "I think I'm going to have to have a talk with him: he just doesn't seem to be getting it."

Justin wasn't certain what to say. There was a part of him that felt sympathetic toward Steve, and yet, he didn't really like Steve any more than Kyle and Craig did.

"Make it snappy, will ya?" said Craig. "I can't take this guy much longer."

Next morning at breakfast, Kyle was telling Craig and Justin about his chat with Steve:

"Do you believe it? This guy's mad at *me* for last night. He knocks on my door at 10:00 and says I had no right to talk to him that way -- as he put it, 'ordering him around like a little kid.'"

Craig laughed. "What did you say?"

"I told him if he was going to act like a child, I was going to treat him like one. End of story."

"And did he seem to accept that?" asked Justin.

"I guess. Who knows?" said Kyle. "We'll see."

At lunch that day, Steve conspicuously steered away from them inside the dining hall. Instead, he took his tray and plopped it in the midst of all the other theater majors; but even though he steeled his gaze away from them, Justin knew that his attention was acutely focused over Kyle's way, trying to see if he had made his point. As nonchalantly as they could, considering this scrutiny, Kyle, Craig, and Justin finished up and left. As they were exiting the dining hall, however, Justin glanced back and saw Steve looking after them forlornly. It was a look that nearly stopped him in his tracks: like an unwelcome puppy lurking at the edge of the crowd, waiting for scraps. It was a look he thought must not be too far from a look he'd worn himself at night, alone, whenever he was thinking about Kyle.

CHAPTER 4

———◆———

CRAIG AND JUSTIN WERE STANDING in Craig's studio. Craig was working on a nude -- a semi-cubist painting of a woman -- which he couldn't quite get right. They were surrounded by Craig's other canvases, one of which caught Justin's eye.

"What's this?" said Justin.

"Oh, *that* thing. It's a copy of a Gericault painting called 'Portrait of a Tubercular Man.' Everybody here thinks it's Kyle."

"What? But it doesn't look anything like him."

"I know," said Craig. "At least, *I* don't think so. But put a beard on someone, and people get confused."

"I like it. It's got a really haunted, introspective look about it."

"That's what I was hoping for," said Craig. "Actually, if anything, it's more a self-portrait than a portrait of Kyle. And it's not a copy, really -- more like a starting point. I call mine 'Portrait of a Lunatic,' which is pretty apropos, for me."

"Oh, stop it," said Justin. He knew Craig had been despondent since his date with Vicki Jones hadn't panned out. Somehow, despite his popularity with seemingly everyone on campus, he didn't seem to have much luck with women.

"I can't get a date for shit. Nobody loves me."

"Sure they do," said Justin tentatively, somewhat nervous about using this construction: "Kyle and I do."

"Sorry, bud, but that just doesn't cut it."

Justin felt a little stab of hurt at this. After a moment's pause, he said, "There are a lot of girls I know who'd like to go out with you."

"Like who?"

"Oh, you know who. Linda Cates, for one. But there are lots of others, and I know you know who they are."

"I guess you always want what you can't have," said Craig, dabbing at the woman's breast half-heartedly. "Anyway, what about you? Aren't you interested in anybody?"

Justin flashed on Kyle immediately, thought of echoing Craig's "always wanting what you can't have" comment, but said instead, "No, not really."

"No?" Craig stood back and looked harshly at the painting in front of him. "Oh, God, this sucks."

"It does not."

"It *does*," said Craig, then sets his paintbrush down. "Oh, don't mind me. I'm just feeling sorry for myself. Sorry and crotchety." He moved away from the easel and stood before the copy of the Gericault, appraising it again. "Maybe people aren't so wrong to say this looks like Kyle."

"What do you mean?" said Justin. For one brief second, he thought Craig meant this as an insult.

"I don't know. I have to say, I thought of Kyle when I was working on the color of the beard and hair -- these sort of chestnut-colored highlights here and here." Craig's fingers brushed the canvas lightly on the upper lip and chin, and Justin was startled. The years of being told one shouldn't ever touch a canvas made him unprepared to see Craig touch it like this: intimate, familiar, its creator. "Maybe Kyle crept into it more than I thought."

He wasn't sure what to say to this. To him, the picture bore only the slightest possible resemblance to the Kyle he knew, and yet, if someone were to parody Kyle's features, it might look something like this: Kyle's soft, brown eyes becoming hollow, inwardly reflective; square, firm jaw and bright, rouged cheeks becoming shallow, sallow; and finally, the rich, dark beard becoming sparse and scruffy, giving him the hangdog look this portrait had. At last, he said only the obvious: "But this man is diseased, tubercular. Surely, you can't mean this looks like Kyle."

Craig hesitated a moment, thinking, then said: "It might reflect some ambivalence on my part, I don't know. Don't get me wrong, I love Kyle. I love *both*

37

you guys. I'm awfully glad we've become friends. But I have to say, I guess I feel resentful sometimes. It's not like Kyle is God or anything, despite the way we kid him. But he *is* good looking, athletic, and the women just fall all over him. To a certain extent, I have to say, I do resent that."

Despite dismay at hearing this -- he liked to think the three of them were perfect friends, that there was absolutely no disharmony amongst them -- Justin said reluctantly, "Well, I guess I know what you mean."

"Do you know the women call him "Cute-butt Rhodes?""

"They do?" said Justin, though he was hardly surprised.

"Yeah," said Craig. "You and I should be so lucky. Anyway, I think the two of us are more alike than Kyle. We're both quiet, and reflective, and I think we share a kind of artistic 'outsiderness,' always feeling we're on the outside of things, looking in."

Despite having many of his own thoughts about this -- a kind of sadness at the confirmation that both he and Craig weren't nearly as attractive as Kyle was, yet also a sense of joy at the bond between the two of them Craig was articulating -- he felt duty-bound, but powerless, to defend against what Craig had said.

"I guess you're right," he said at last, unenthusiastically.

"I shouldn't say it, I suppose," said Craig. "I'm just jealous."

"I know what you mean," said Justin.

"Hell, I wouldn't be surprised if Steve Norberg was in love with him, too, the way he runs around after him."

Later, Justin sat with Kyle alone in Kyle's room. Kyle was changing to go jogging, and Justin watched him as he walked around the room unbuttoning his shirt, the green-and-orange plaid pattern setting off the black hair on his chest, his shirt tails trailing in the air behind him.

"Where's Craig tonight?" said Kyle.

"He's over at his studio." Justin was thinking about Craig's comment about Steve, and about to mention how ridiculous he thought it was that people thought Craig's copy of the Gericault looked like Kyle, when Kyle said:

"Is he still working on that nude?"

"Yeah," said Justin, startled. "Why?"

"God. That guy is never going to finish that. He's been working on that thing ever since I've known him. It's things like that that really make me think Craig's a bit of a masochist, you know? I mean -- God love him -- he's a great guy, but it's been almost three years now, and I really don't think it's that good of a picture. If you ask me, he should just hang it up and move on."

Justin felt a flash of anger and resentment similar to what he'd felt when Craig had made his critical remark about Kyle earlier. For a second, he could sympathize with Craig in his ambivalence about Kyle: everything with Kyle was easy, effortless. He could never understand the patience and the diligence required to work at something like a painting long-term.

"He's just trying to get it right, I guess," said Justin weakly.

"Yeah, but I think it's more than that. Look at the way he sweated over Vicki Jones, and she just wasn't interested in him, not to mention she wasn't really his type. Then, last year, he was after this girl named Martha something. Let me tell you, Martha was this emaciated vegetarian virgin who looked like she was afraid of her own shadow. I never understood the attraction then, and I still don't, but you should have seen the way he mourned the fact that it didn't work out. They went on exactly two dates, I think, which -- even at the time -- I could have told him wouldn't work out."

Justin wasn't certain what to say. He hardly felt prepared for this barrage, and yet he'd noticed something in Craig, too, that rang true to these words. For someone who was so popular, Craig always seemed to pine for girls who weren't the least bit interested in him. Perhaps it *was* some masochistic streak, some strange self-punishment that made him seek out girls he couldn't have.

"So, you think his working on that painting is a sort of symbol for the fact he can't quite get his feelings toward women right?" said Justin

"I think there's a lot of truth in that. I just wish the guy could get past that sticking point, you know? He's a great guy. I just wish it would happen for him somehow."

Kyle slipped off his pants and pulled on shorts despite the chill, then stood there trim and muscular: a vision of athleticism. As Justin looked, he tried to think again what he was feeling toward Kyle. Was it admiration, attraction, or -- dare he even think it -- love? Were he and Steve Norberg the same after all? Kyle rubbed his head affectionately, then said, "Sure you don't want to come with, bud? A good, brisk jog might be just the thing you need to clear your head."

Justin felt flustered and embarrassed and cursed himself as he felt the voltage again. "No, that's alright," he said awkwardly. "I have to get ready for a test."

Walking agitated back across the dead quad to his room, the light from dormitory windows falling on the late October grass, now stiff and yellow, the windows of each room lit up like postcards from some normal life that he would never quite feel part of, Justin thought about Kyle's comments. What was wrong with him? What was it that eluded him and Craig? Why did others, now and all through junior high and high school, have no trouble pairing off? With meeting people, feeling something spark, then following up that urge with dating? Remembering how Craig had touched the lips and beard about the mouth of the man in the painting -- how erotic that had seemed -- he wondered: was Craig, perhaps, as troubled as he was? Was he, perhaps, attracted to Kyle, too?

Justin walked into the student union, alive as usual with the smells of coffee, the sounds of video games, and the voices of students taking a break from studying. After grabbing a cup of coffee, he took a chair off in the corner of the room to start reviewing for his Psych test. Looking up after a while, feeling peaceful and cozy in the warm, bright, cathedral-ceilinged and wood-paneled room, he clutched as he saw Steve Norberg walk out of the bookstore suddenly, package in hand. Steve saw him immediately, and began to make his way directly toward him. He walked slowly and lazily, his heels brushing the floor at every step like a woman wearing slippers (the effect was somehow feminine and revolting), and Justin felt his stomach start to tighten. Steve sat down next to him and placed his plastic bag on the floor with a flourish. Justin wanted to run; yet in the next breath, he realized that Steve was enjoying this -- was enjoying his little moment of entrapment -- and Justin tried to calm himself, unwilling to concede Steve any victory.

"Hi," said Justin after a moment, striving for a normal tone of voice.

Steve merely sat, eyeing him, and Justin almost rose, thinking to himself, *Well, screw you, then.*

But suddenly Steve said, "Wanna see what I bought?"

"Okay," said Justin, trying to at least be civil, though he felt undeniably flustered and uncomfortable.

Steve opened the plastic bag beside him and pulled out a long, rolled-up poster encased in plastic, which he proceeded to shuck off. The poster was a large, horizontal cartoon drawing of a rainbow, which extended about three-quarters of the way across the page, then ended in mid-air like a half-completed bridge. Various black and white stick figures clambered over it like ants, and upon closer inspection, Justin realized that everything was encased in heavy scaffolding. "Building a Rainbow," it said in heavy lettering across the bottom.

"Oh," said Justin, thinking it was cute, but just a little precious. "That's nice."

"Thanks," said Steve, rolling the poster back up and putting it in his bag. "So, what's up?" He reached his long, El Greco fingers into the pocket of his carefully pressed, studiedly unbuttoned shirt, searching for a cigarette.

"Not much," said Justin, trying again to stave off his repugnance. Steve's every action was so effeminate, his lisp so pronounced, it was as if he could hear a lady's fur-covered mule dropping at the end of every word. Justin was about to say Kyle was off playing basketball, and Craig was painting, then saw no reason to volunteer this information: his relationship with Kyle and Craig was not a thing he needed to share with Steve, nor did he need to rub it in Steve's face.

Steve lit up a cigarette and sat silently again.

Justin grew increasingly annoyed by this wordless scrutiny, despite the seeming overture toward friendship the viewing of his poster had been.

"You going out with anyone?" said Steve.

"No. Why?" said Justin. For moment, Justin thought wildly that Steve might be working up to ask him out on a date.

"Just wondered. Guess you're waiting around for him too, huh?"

"What?" said Justin, suddenly outraged, and yet not certain that he'd heard Steve right.

Immediately, Steve looked afraid of what he'd said, and his demeanor changed to one of scared contrition. "Is Kyle going out with anyone?"

"Yeah, he's engaged," said Justin, surprised by his own abruptness.

"What's she like?"

The desperation of this was almost too much for Justin to bear. "I have no idea. I've never met her."

"I bet she's hot," said Steve. "She'd have to be, I think, to be Kyle's girlfriend."

Justin wasn't certain what to say: he simply wanted to escape.

"Don't you think she'd have to be pretty hot, to be with Kyle?"

"I guess so," said Justin, exasperated. "Look, what's your point?"

"I don't know, just trying to figure out a way to be Kyle's friend, I guess."

"I understand you want that, but I feel like -- and I think Kyle feels like -- you're trying to force it too much. These things either happen or they don't ...."

"You guys and your precious friendship," snapped Steve, suddenly bitter. "Why won't you let me be a part of that, too?"

A thousand things crossed Justin's mind to say. He felt sympathetic and defensive, guilty and indignant, and at last, said simply: "I guess you'll have to ask Kyle that."

———◆———

"Steve's really getting to be a problem," said Kyle. "He stops by my room four or five times a day now. And it's not like he has anything he needs to talk about: he just wants to be around."

They were sitting in Kyle's room, their papers done; Thanksgiving break was fast approaching.

"Don't you tell him you're busy?" said Craig.

"Sure, I do, but it doesn't do any good. The guy is like a fly -- I can't get rid of him. He's knocking on my door all day, he's there beside me at the sink in the bathroom at night..."

"Can't you speak to the head counselor about it?" said Craig. "Maybe you should refuse to see him again."

"Yeah, maybe," said Kyle. "Maybe I should."

"It's so unnatural," said Craig. "It's almost like he's trying to *make* us be his friends. But friendships can't be forced like that. There has to be a spark. I feel a little bad sometimes, but what can you do?

"I think Steve's attracted to you," Justin ventured, and immediately his heart began to pound. He wasn't sure he should have said this -- knew he was treading into dangerous waters -- yet felt he had to say it.

"Well, I guess I sort of realize that," said Kyle. "Actually, I asked him -- not exactly that, but I asked him whether he thought he might be gay."

"And what did he say?" said Craig.

"He told me he'd tried sex with a man once, but he didn't like it."

Justin's brain began to freeze. He had to struggle hard to comprehend the rest of what was being said.

"Love is one thing," said Craig, after a pause. "But obsession is another. Did you ever take this up with Mr. Tisch? I mean, he *does* seem to be obsessed with you, and you just keep on seeing him."

"Steve said to me last night, 'You *have* to talk to me, because you're my counselor.'"

"Well isn't that just what I said?" said Craig. "I mean, maybe you should just stop seeing him."

"I'm trying not to, but he makes it so damn hard. Mr. Tisch suggested I limit time with him, or send him to the other counselors. So, I told Steve I could only see him once a day."

"Maybe that's what you'll have to do," said Craig, glancing toward Justin for confirmation.

"Yes, maybe you will," echoed Justin, the roar of blood in his ears as he did so making it nearly impossible for him to think. He wondered whether he should have said what he'd said. He wondered, too: if Kyle and Craig knew about his own confusion, would they say the same thing about him? How would he feel if he, too, was told he couldn't see Kyle?

All that week, as Justin sat in classes, went to lunch or dinner with Kyle and Craig, he couldn't get that conversation out of his mind. He kept repeating parts of it to himself, analyzing, scrutinizing: how exactly had Kyle reacted to the speculation about Steve's sexuality? What exactly was Kyle's tone of voice when he had said he'd realized Steve was attracted to him? And what had Craig's look meant as he'd told Kyle that maybe he should not see Steve anymore? Had either

Kyle or Craig suspected that he, Justin, might be gay himself, and attracted to Kyle? What did they really think of Steve? In another vein, Justin wondered just how much of their dislike for Steve (perhaps as well as his own?) stemmed from his sexuality. Was that the reason they hadn't wanted to be friends with him? And why exactly *were* the three of them friends? It wasn't like he, Justin, had that much in common with Kyle or Craig. So what, then, was the draw? What was the quality that made them friends but so eluded Steve?

As Justin walked out into the weakening November light, the campus cold and windy, all the trees half bare -- a few stray, red and yellow tatters clinging to the limbs -- he wondered what attachment was: what led one thing to cling onto another? Why did Steve, for instance, cling to Kyle? Why couldn't he let go? And if Justin, too, was afraid he was in love with Kyle, why couldn't he just face that? And yet, he found it hard to compare himself to Steve. One day, he'd seen Steve horsing around with some of his theater friends just outside a classroom. They'd all been affecting British accents, throwing around faux Shakespeare due to the performance of *Measure for Measure* in which they were about to appear, saying things like:

"Fuck thee, good sir. Thou art a lout."

"Fuck thee in thy royal bunhole, sir. 'Tis what thee likes."

At this point, Steve had struck a pose and said grandiosely, "Ah, the bloody assholes of love."

Justin had never quite been able to forget the mental picture he'd gotten from Steve's *double-entendre*, nor shake the sexual disgust he'd felt upon hearing it. Somehow, the image and the disgust were both affixed forever to Steve in Justin's mind; and, as sorry as he sometimes felt for Steve, he could never quite get past it, much the way he couldn't quite forget Steve's innuendoes and his strange aspect that evening in the Student Union: was Justin waiting around for Kyle himself? Didn't he think Kyle's girlfriend would have to be hot? This week, Steve had seemed particularly pitiful. Kyle had forbidden him to visit more than once a week, and Justin had seen him lingering at the edge of the quad when they were around, waiting outside Kyle's door -- avoiding them, but staring at them in the cafeteria at meals. It was as if everything they and Kyle did was under scrutiny now; and after thinking of the general drift of the conversation about Steve that night, Justin wondered for the first time whether he was under scrutiny now, too.

That Friday evening, Justin and Kyle were walking down Kyle's hallway after supper. Craig had gone back to his room to take a nap; then, later on, they were going to hook up for the school basketball game in the gym. Justin was happy for this unexpected time alone with Kyle, yet as they neared Kyle's room, they saw Steve standing in his doorway, watching them. They both fell silent for a moment, and Justin could smell the stale odor of pot (so common to the dorm) mixed up with the sickeningly sweet odor of the clove cigarettes Steve had taken up smoking -- a cloying and affected odor that always seemed to hover about him, and which made Steve seem even odder and sadder to Justin. Kyle, at last, mustered enough enthusiasm to say "Hi, Steve," and Justin nodded reluctantly.

"Hi," said Steve weakly.

Kyle unlocked his door and Justin started to head in, but then Kyle stopped and said, "What are you up to this evening?"

"Nothing."

Justin wanted to kick Steve in the pants, the way he stood there eyeing them so pathetically, obviously fishing for an invitation to join them.

"What are you guys doing?" said Steve hopefully.

Kyle paused, looking at Justin, then said, "Probably heading to the basketball game."

"Might I join you?" said Steve in that irritatingly desperate, overly polite manner.

"I don't think so, Steve," said Kyle as gently as possible. "We already have plans with Craig."

"I see," said Steve.

Kyle hesitated, hand on the doorknob, then said, "Have fun, whatever you decide to do."

"Probably not," they heard Steve say emphatically as Kyle shut the door behind him, erasing the sight of Steve bouncing back and forth against the doorjamb like a little child being reasoned with by parents.

"God," said Kyle, his hand still on the doorknob. "That guy can make me feel like such an asshole. But I'm not getting sucked back into his shit tonight -- I'm just not."

They sat there for a moment, silent, Justin feeling suddenly constricted. With Steve there lurking in the hall, he wasn't sure how they were going to sit and act like everything was fine, when everything seemed suddenly so strained.

"Fuck," said Kyle, heaving out a sigh and shaking his head. He looked at Justin now and shrugged as if to say, 'What can I do?'

They sat a moment more, both listening to the overlay of stereos and voices in the hall, as if dreading to hear Steve somewhere in the mixture.

"Well," said Justin, "You want to head out somewhere? Maybe to the Union?"

"Yeah," said Kyle. Just then they heard a knock upon the door, and looked at one another.

"Shit," mouthed Justin.

"Maybe just don't answer it?" offered Justin weakly, then felt bad for saying it.

Kyle rolled his eyes and stood up, moving toward the door. On opening it, however, they discovered not Steve, but instead his roommate, Mike.

"Kyle," said Mike. "Steve asked if you'd stop down." Mike had his books beneath his arm, and said this in the manner of someone discharging an unpleasant duty. Justin thought that, living with Steve, he must have realized how ridiculous the situation between Kyle and Steve was, and beyond that, he was trying to stay as far removed from it as possible.

"Do you know what he wants?" said Kyle, exasperated.

"No," said Mike. "He just asked me to have you drop by."

"Okay," said Kyle, and looked at Justin helplessly as Mike moved on.

"Kyle," said Justin, "Do you really think you should?"

Kyle paused, then said pointedly, "I'll just be gone *one minute*."

Justin sat and wondered how long it would be this time. Pessimistically, he was certain Steve would wind up there beside them at the game -- that again, their plans would be irreparably altered by Steve's presence.

But a moment later, Justin heard a clamor in the hall and saw Kyle bursting through the doorway.

"Justin, call an ambulance! He slit his wrists!" Kyle fumbled with his towels, and Justin stood there frozen for a second.

"Oh, my God," said Justin, watching as Kyle lifted up a towel, then dropped it, lifted it, then dropped it once again before he started back without it.

"Go!" barked Kyle.

Justin snapped out of his shock and now was running breathless down the hallway, moving as if in slow motion down the stairs, through the lobby, then banging on the blank door of the Head Resident's apartment. The door swung open in a moment to reveal an unassuming group of people gathered quietly around a TV set, and lounging on the floor around some chips and dip.

"Steve Norberg just slit his wrists," Justin blurted out, not sure he should have said this to them all, but too upset to think about the protocol.

The dorm's Head Resident, whose name was Neal, took this as calmly as if somebody had told him he'd been locked out of his room. He was a 30ish, plain looking man who might have passed for an accountant in a bank. Neal turned to a woman in the group and said, "Oh, dear. Jan, will you call an ambulance?" Then turning back to Justin, he said, "Has he lost a lot of blood?"

"I don't know," said Justin.

"Is he conscious?"

"I don't know," said Justin, feeling stupid and inept. "I wasn't with him -- I just got told."

"I see. Is someone *else* with him now?"

"Kyle."

"Why don't you take me to him," Neal said.

As they raced upstairs, the thing that most impressed Justin was how totally indifferent everything around him was: the television set was on out in the lobby, playing to an empty room, the hallways echoed with the sound of voices, music, shouts. If Neal had not been there behind him, racing up the stairs, nobody would have known that anything was wrong, that Steve had felt this hopeless, that he had crossed the line at last and done this desperate thing.

In Steve's room, cluttered with dirty clothes, books and papers, and reeking of the same sad, cloying clove smell, Kyle was bending over Steve, and for a moment, Justin thought they were holding hands -- that he had caught the two of them in unexpected intimacy, the same way he had had a jealously irrational flash once upon seeing Kyle return a basketball to Sam. Sam had simply opened up Kyle's door without knocking, and, in that moment of supposed intimacy, Justin had immediately wondered -- irrationally -- whether Kyle and Sam were lovers. Now, Steve was sitting on his bed, arms in the air, and Kyle was trying to wrap a towel around his wrists. Blood was smeared all over Kyle's shirt, his pants, and Kyle looked as though he might pass out. Meanwhile, Steve's face was turned up, looking into Kyle's, and what struck Justin was the rapt, adoring look upon his face. Steve was smiling, almost laughing, as he said, "You're touching me! I made you touch me!"

Steve's face changed instantly as Neal walked into the room. Steve tried to draw his arms away, as if made suddenly aware of what he'd done. Kyle kept his grip, and Justin saw a thin streak of running down his forearm, and dripping down onto the bed.

Neal walked up and took the towel from Kyle.

"Here, let me see," Neal said. "Hold still."

Neal started to touch the wrist, but Steve broke free and shoved his arm behind his back, ashamed.

"It's all right -- I won't hurt you," said Neal, kneeling down in front of Steve. Then, as Steve still held his arm behind him stubbornly, "Let me see it. I can't help you if you won't let anybody see it."

Steve was almost crying now, the tears beginning in his eyes.

Looking at the scene -- at the painfully naive "Building a Rainbow" poster hanging on the wall behind Steve's head, Justin suddenly felt like an intruder. The pain and nakedness of Steve's actions were upsetting him, and he began to back up. There was a crowd behind him in the doorway now, however, and Justin found himself trapped.

"What happened?" someone in the hallway said, and someone else said,

"Norberg hacked his wrists."

Justin turned back to the scene inside the room, and acutely felt Steve's humiliation. Steve was trying not to hear the voices in the hall, yet how could he not?

Neal had his hand extended, trying to coax Steve's wrists out from behind his back, but Steve was fighting now, embarrassed, looking at the crowd.

"Everybody out!" said Neal, to Justin's great relief. He turned and followed everyone into the hall, but as he closed the door, two men in white were there beside him, pushing it back open.

"What's happening here?" said the lead paramedic, a big, burly man who had the look of someone who had never personally contemplated suicide in his life.

"He's cut his wrists, but he won't bring them out for me to see," said Neal.

"The patient's not cooperating?" said the burly man, again with the authority of someone who always called the plays in football.

"No," said Neal.

"You want to show me your wrists?" said the medic in a voice too loud, and simply, as if speaking to a child.

"You can either show us your wrists, or we use the restraints," said the other man, who had a somewhat gentler look about him, but who also seemed somewhat stressed, and not nearly as in control as the first man. "Trust me, it's much simpler if we don't resort to the restraints."

Justin hesitated, then pulled the door closed and walked, shaken, back to Kyle's room. He sat and waited, but it was half an hour more before Kyle came back.

When he walked back into his room at last, Kyle was a sight: blood on his shirt and pants, his pallor ashen.

"Well?" said Justin. "What happened?"

"They just took him away," said Kyle, sitting, looking dazed.

"How long do you think he'll be in the hospital?"

Kyle looked thoughtful for a moment. "A couple months, I guess. I don't really know."

"A couple *months*?" said Justin, incredulous. "Why that long?"

"Well, whenever anybody attempts suicide, they keep them for a while."

"Oh," said Justin. "You mean they're taking him to a psychiatric hospital?"

After a moment, Kyle said, "Yeah, I guess they *will* take him to the regular hospital first, then to the psychiatric one. You know, it really wasn't that bad."

"I know," said Justin tentatively. "I can't believe anyone would actually do that."

"I mean the cuts," said Kyle. "The cuts weren't really that bad. In fact, he used a little Bic disposable to do it, so they didn't really go that deep."

Justin wasn't certain what to say. He felt scared and naked suddenly, and Kyle was confusing him. He wished Kyle would hold him -- really hold him -- in his arms, but was afraid to ask.

"You said he's gone?" said Justin, weighted to his chair.

"Yeah, they just took him." Kyle hesitated, as if attempting to decide whether he should say this. "I didn't use my towels."

"What?"

"When I first walked down there, Steve was standing up against the doorway with his arms behind his back, flashing me that pathetic little grin of his. Then, when I got closer, he lifted his arms up, and I could see the blood trickling down his forearms, and I just freaked. I ran back here to get my towels. That's when I was yelling at you to call an ambulance. But then, when I started to pick up my towels, I thought to myself suddenly: 'No, I'm not going to use my towels. I'm not going to ruin *my* towels by getting Steve's blood all over them. He can ruin his own, but he's not going to ruin mine.' That's why I ran back there without one, not because I was so distraught. "

Justin was appalled. "Yeah, I saw you fumbling with the towels, but I just thought .... " He stopped, because he wasn't certain how to finish.

"I'm not proud of it," said Kyle. "Or maybe I *am* proud of it. I don't know, but that's what I was thinking." He paused, then said, "Steve asked me to hug him goodbye when he left."

"He did?" said Justin uncertainly.

"He asked me if I'd hold him for a second, but I didn't think I should. I almost did, but then, at the last minute, I just shook his hand instead." Kyle looked at Justin now, his face both questioning and defiant. "That was really hard, you know? Part of me felt like I should, but then another part of me was realizing I probably shouldn't."

Justin felt shocked, and unaccountably bereft and sad. There was a timid knock upon the door, and he and Kyle both started.

Kyle opened up the door, and Justin heard again the casual, indifferent overlay of stereos, a few hushed voices in the hall. Neal stood in the white-tiled hallway on the other side of Kyle. Kyle's body made an "x" in front of him -- that body so often seemed to block out every other thing -- but Justin knew it was Neal because he heard Neal's voice.

"Kyle, I wonder if you'd come down to the apartment for a while," said Neal. "I'd like to discuss all this with you."

"Sure," said Kyle a little nervously. He glanced at Justin. "Do you want Justin to come, too?"

Neal peered in the room and saw Justin sitting on the couch.

"Hi, Justin. Are you all right? Not shaken up too badly?"

"I'm fine," said Justin, though, in truth, he didn't have the slightest notion how he felt.

"Good," said Neal. "No, I don't need everybody who was there. I'd just like to discuss the situation with you -- maybe get a better feel for what happened."

"Okay," said Kyle, as unsure as before. He turned to Justin now and said, "I guess you'll have to let Craig know what's up. Are you all right heading back by yourself?"

"Sure, sure," said Justin.

"I'm sorry. Maybe I can hook up with you guys a little later."

"Fine, don't worry," said Justin. He started to follow them out of the room, but Neal took a step into the doorway.

To Justin, now, he said: "Listen, I realize this isn't exactly a secret, but let's keep the details of this to ourselves, shall we? It isn't anybody else's business."

Justin nodded.

Kyle was about to follow Neal into the hall. But then, Kyle turned and blocked the door again.

"Come here a second," Kyle said.

Justin felt Kyle's arms around him, holding tightly, pressing all of Justin into him. He felt Kyle's flesh against his flesh, Kyle's beard against his face. Kyle whispered hoarsely now, "Take care, okay?" and Justin's eyes began to fog. His tears were not for Steve.

CHAPTER 5

———•———

S TRICKEN, JUSTIN WALKED ACROSS THE night-dark campus, loud with music, voices, and the ridicule of laughter. He could feel the cold dew from the dark November grass soak through his suede shoes, saw his breath before him like a cloud, and felt his body slogging slowly, leadenly to Craig's room. It was all he felt -- all he would let himself feel right now: the motion of his feet, the cold night air, his breath around him coming regular and loud. He crossed near to the Student Union, lit and warm, but skirted it, and ducked into the nearby outside stairwell of Craig's dorm.

This stairwell was a new addition, clean cement and cinder block, and it felt curiously cold and hollow as he climbed the stairs: as hollow as he felt right now. His footsteps sounded muffled, sodden, as he mounted. There was nothing else to hear except the dull thump of his heart: confused, almost inaudible. Coming to Craig's floor, the music blared as Justin opened up the outer fire door. He walked into the hall, and here and there along the bright red carpeting, an open door revealed an unmade bed, disheveled desks, but no one seemed to be inside the rooms. The world seemed empty, noisy, as he walked the whole length of the floor -- both he and Steve, it suddenly seemed to him, condemned to wander through a world of vast indifference -- then crossed to Craig's wing, which was mercifully quiet. He knocked and, in a moment, Craig stood there, as groggy as a springtime bear.

"Oh, God," said Craig. "What time is it?" Craig stretched and turned his unscarred wrists toward Justin as he yawned. His sallow skin was beautiful, unblemished, covered with a fine blond mat of hair. Craig looked so warm and dry that Justin had to fight the urge to throw himself around him. But that's what Steve had done, he caught himself. Upset, he managed meekly, "It's about 8:30."

"Oh. I must have conked out."

Justin came into the room and sat down. He was so confused and shocked and scared, he wasn't certain where to start.

"What's wrong?" said Craig.

A noise escaped from Justin now -- a high-pitched whine, and then a strangled cry. It startled even Justin as it emanated from him.

"What's wrong? Why didn't you come get me for the game?"

"We -- I don't know, we canceled it. Steve Norberg slashed his wrists." When Justin finally said this, he could feel his lower lip begin to tremble uncontrollably, and so he stopped.

"What? I *knew* it!" said Craig.

"Huh?"

"I *knew* Kyle was in above his head! I knew something bad was going to come of this. He let this all go on *way* too long."

"What do you mean?" said Justin, shocked. "He did what Mr. Tisch suggested. He told Steve he couldn't talk to him."

"And *kept* on talking to him," said Craig harshly. "Don't get me wrong. I mean, the guy's heart's in the right place. But you can't talk someone *out* of being in love with you; you break off contact -- just stop seeing them. By talking to him, Kyle just kept encouraging him."

Justin felt like he'd been slapped, and sat there, stunned. Was this what he should do, then, too? Break off contact with Kyle?

"It's just a hard thing," said Justin at last, unable even to imagine this.

"Oh, listen to me," said Craig, softening. "I'm one to talk. I'm Mr. Masochism. Spurn me and I'll worship you forever. Anyway, so what happened. Is Steve okay?"

"I guess. Kyle said he only used a Bic disposable to do it, so it didn't cut that deep."

"Oh, 'only.' Like he 'only' cut himself so deep."

"I know," said Justin, finally relieved that Craig had put his finger on a thing that troubled him: the sense that Kyle, with his comments about the nature of the razor and the shallowness of the cuts, had minimized the desperate nature of Steve's act. He flashed on Kyle's remarks about the towels -- another thing that bothered him. "Kyle didn't use his towels."

"What?"

"When it happened, I was sitting in Kyle's room, and Kyle came running in and screamed at me to get an ambulance. He fumbled with his towels, but didn't take them. I just thought that Kyle was panicking, but later on, he told me he'd decided not to ruin his towels by getting Steve's blood on them."

"Well, good for him," said Craig.

"What do you mean?" said Justin, shocked again.

"He drew the line at last. Don't you see? That's been the trouble all along: Kyle wouldn't set his limits. That's why Steve kept sucking him back in, appealing to that older brother personality of Kyle's, the one that wants to make things right for everyone. Steve played him like a song, and Kyle could never seem to grasp that."

"Oh," said Justin.

"Are you all right?"

"Yeah, I'm just still upset, is all."

"Did Steve go to the hospital?"

"I guess so. We're not sure which one: the general or the psychiatric."

"Where is Kyle?"

"He's talking to the dorm head resident about what happened."

"Should we go find Kyle?" said Craig. "Is he all right, you think?"

"I think so." Justin wasn't sure at all he wanted to go back. Yet, he was overjoyed that Craig was reasserting the bond the three of them had by indicating they should seek Kyle out to help him through this.

"What do you say we go and find him then?" said Craig.

When they got to Kyle's room, the blue-green strip of carpet underneath the oak door was completely dark; a few frayed strands, pulled out of the brass strip, were waving lonely and forlornly on the filthy white tile of the hallway floor. They knocked, then stood there for a moment, waiting.

"You think he might've taken off and gone somewhere by himself?" said Craig.

"He could still be with Neal, I guess."

Just then, Kyle's door cracked open and he waved them in. "Come on in." He flicked the light on as they came into the room. Closing the door behind them, he turned and reached out to pat them both awkwardly on the back. "I'm glad you guys are here."

Justin glowed in the touch -- didn't want him to let him go, and turned to transform Kyle's touch into a full embrace. On one hand, he was feeling scared that he was just like Steve; yet on the other, here was Kyle exhibiting affection toward him in that natural way he always had, as if asserting that he wasn't -- reaching out for *him*, when he had not done so for Steve. With Kyle now in his arms, he had the sense that Kyle had needed this hug as much as him. That's when the tears began, as if he were a tree stump felled in winter which the sap still rises in in spring: the liquid gushing from a wound that Justin hadn't even known was there until he felt Kyle touching him.

"It's all right," said Kyle, clasping him. "It's all right."

They parted finally, and Craig said, "You're sitting here with all the lights off?"

"I didn't want anybody to know I was here."

"Are you all right?" said Justin. Kyle looked so exposed, so vulnerable, that Justin felt his heart was going to burst. He wanted to enfold Kyle in his arms again, to try to soothe the pain.

"I'm fine. I've just been thinking."

"Is everything all right? They're not blaming you for anything, are they?" said Craig.

"No, everything's okay. It's just been real intense, is all."

"So how'd it go with Neal?" said Craig

"All right. Did Justin fill you in?"

"Uh huh," said Craig. "So what did Neal say?"

"He asked me what the background was, and also if I'd talked to Mr. Tisch. I told him I had, and that was pretty much it." Kyle hesitated, as if deciding whether he should tell them this next part or not. "He also said he wasn't that surprised it happened."

"What do you mean?" said Justin, feeling suddenly defensive.

"Neal said every year he's done this, he could look out at the Freshman class and almost tell which students might be a problem. He said the first time he met Steve, he thought he seemed unstable."

Justin wasn't certain what to think. In part, he felt the truth of this, and yet, he was appalled by this pronouncement, this ability to prejudge everyone. He wondered whether Neal had prejudged him, too -- had looked into his eyes and seen the doubt, the fear, the horrible uncertainty.

Craig said, "I guess you do a job for long enough, you get to know the types."

"I guess," said Kyle.

"So, what do you say about getting out of this place?" said Craig. "You shouldn't be sitting here all alone in the dark."

"I know," said Kyle. "Truthfully, I was kind of waiting for you guys, and kind of trying to decide whether I should call Maureen. It's Friday, though, and I'm not sure whether she'd be at home."

At hearing Maureen's name tossed suddenly into the mix, Justin felt betrayed. It made sense, certainly, that Kyle would want to talk to her -- would want to share this news with her. Yet, while he understood it intellectually, emotionally, he did not: the only people Justin felt he needed right now were the people in this room.

"Suit yourself," said Craig. "But maybe it'd be better to get out now and call her later on, when things calm down."

"Yeah, that's kind of what I was leaning toward," said Kyle. "Besides, I've got you guys. It isn't like I don't have some support."

"That's right," said Justin, cheered by this. "We're here for you."

"All right, then," said Kyle, at last his tone beginning to brighten. "What are we waiting for?"

———◆———

The bar was curiously quiet for a Friday; there weren't that many customers, and none of them were college students, so Justin felt secure and cozy as they sat there in the booth. The light was soft upon their faces, on the gold beer in their glasses, on the grey-flecked Formica tabletop and the white wainscoted walls. Justin thought how wonderful their friendship was: they were like Musketeers: the three of them united against the world.

"Thanks for getting me out of there," said Kyle. "This feels good, being here with you guys."

"Well, we're glad we could be here for you," said Justin.

"I just want you guys to know, you're really important to me, and I care about you both a lot."

"Thanks," said Craig, looking a bit uncomfortable.

"You guys really think I handled it okay?" said Kyle. "I keep on thinking maybe it's my fault: I kept on talking to Steve, leading him on, and then I shut him out, you know? I felt really bad earlier, telling him he couldn't join us tonight, but I didn't know what else to do."

"But that's just how you are," said Justin, rushing to Kyle's defense. "You can't be rude to someone. You just can't."

"Maybe it would have been better if I had."

Craig was looking at the table now.

"What do *you* think?" said Kyle.

Craig looked up at him and said, "Well, to be honest with you, I think it *did* go on too long before you tried to get some help. Steve being in love with you -- which it seems obvious he was, or at least he thought he was -- is one thing; but Steve becoming fixated on you is another. Maybe there's nothing you could have done about it anyway. But it seems clear to me it should have been nipped in the bud when it crossed over the line from love into obsession."

"How do you recognize that point?" said Justin.

For a moment, Craig and Kyle looked blankly at him, and Justin clutched.

"You're probably right," said Craig after a moment. "There probably isn't a way to see that when you're caught up in the midst of it."

"I guess that was my problem," said Kyle. "Hindsight is 20/20."

"So," said Craig. "You're going to call Maureen tomorrow?"

"Yeah, I guess so. It's just hard, you know? I can tell her what went on, but it's not like she's really going to understand. It isn't like she shared in it. I want to tell her everything, of course, but I have to say, I feel very distant from her right now. She just won't understand the way you guys do. She wasn't here to go through it with me like you guys."

Nothing Kyle could have said, short of a declaration of love, would have pleased Justin as much. Still, Steve was on his mind. "I *do* feel like we have a very strong, a very special friendship," said Justin. "I've never had friends like you guys before. But why did you guys become friends with me and not with him?" said Justin warily. "I mean, without too much of a stretch, it could just as easily have been *me* wanting to be your friend, not succeeding, and slitting *my* wrists, as well as him. So what's the difference?"

Craig looked at Justin strangely, and Justin felt his heart begin to pound. Had he said too much? Was there truly no difference between him and Steve after all, and had Justin just tipped them off to this?

"The difference," said Kyle interjecting, "is that we *are* friends. Something clicked with the three of us, from the moment of that first party. I'm not sure why, but it did. And it never did, and never *would* have, with Steve."

Hearing this, Justin felt somewhat assuaged. "You have no idea how important it is to me to hear you say that. You guys mean so much. I feel like we're going to be friends forever, you know?"

"Well, that'll be hard," said Craig, "but if we want to, we can. I do feel closer to you guys than to probably any other friends I've ever had."

Justin felt relieved to hear Craig say this. Suddenly, all was right again: here they were once more, bonded emotionally, experientially, seemingly inseparable.

"Hey," said Craig brightly, "did I tell you guys that I was thinking of asking somebody out?"

———◆———

As they stumbled home that evening, Craig turned off wearily toward his dorm, and Justin was just about to turn regretfully toward his, when Kyle said suddenly:

"Justin, would you mind sitting up with me a little while longer? I just don't want to be alone."

The campus was dead still, frigid in the cold November night: there seemed to be no motion anywhere.

"Sure," said Justin, surprised, but touched by this request.

"Craig wasn't there, that's why I think maybe this isn't hitting him so hard. But you were there -- you know how upsetting it was. Would you mind? For just a little while?"

Kyle's voice was hoarse, inebriate, but also cracking with emotion. There was something in it he had never heard before: unsteadiness, uncertainty, and neediness, and as they walked along, he had the sense that Kyle was asking him for something he had never asked him for before.

"Sure, Kyle." Suddenly, Justin wondered whether he was being dishonest. Here Kyle was, feeling vulnerable and hurt, and asking him for comfort; Justin felt in need of it himself. Yet, he was also conscious of his struggle all semester long regarding what he felt toward Kyle. Should he be doing this?

Now, as they stumbled up the frosty hillside to Kyle's dormitory, walked into the hallway with its eerie calm, flicked on the harsh fluorescent light inside Kyle's room and stood for a moment shucking coats, then sitting awkwardly upon the sofa, Justin almost said, "If you're okay, I should go." But then, Kyle clasped him in an exhausted hug, and Justin wrapped his arms around the warm, sweatshirted bulk of him and held on tight. Kyle smelled of hair oil, stale beer, sweat, and Justin stared a moment -- absent-minded -- at some long, black hairs upon Kyle's back. Then Kyle began to cry. *So this is Kyle*, he thought. *This is the absolute reality of him, locked in my arms.* With Kyle's weight half upon him, he was conscious of a fundamental need being met -- a sense of comfort and release -- and knew that he was not like Steve: here was absolute proof Kyle loved and trusted him. Yet, he was also conscious of a physical sensation rising up in him: a need.

"Thank you," said Kyle, his voice now wet with tears.

"Hey, no problem," said Justin, feeling timid; ardent and confused.

"I think Craig thinks I fucked up."

"No," said Justin. "I don't think he thinks that. You did fine."

Then Kyle was crying suddenly in earnest, waves of tears escaping from him; Justin holding tightly, trying to keep his balance on the sofa; falling backward, tearing up himself. As Kyle continued crying, Justin pressed his lips against Kyle's hair, so tenderly he wasn't sure if Kyle had even felt it.

"It's all right," said Justin. "Let it out."

Kyle cried until his tears abated, their bodies pressed into each other desperately. Then, Kyle raised up awkwardly and kissed him on the cheek, Kyle's warm beard prickling Justin's skin.

"Thank you," said Kyle hoarsely, emotionally, his face now buried back in Justin's torso. Kyle's weight was on him on the couch, and Justin held him, breathless, penis burgeoning inside his blue jeans suddenly, the blood drained from his brain. He lay there for a moment, stunned, too scared to move, then felt Kyle's body slacken, fade, and heard Kyle's breathing coming slow and regular. He felt again Kyle's weight upon him, thought again about the kiss, his penis growing rigid as a stone. He felt upset, confused, and scared. As Justin wrestled with his penis, cursing it for violating what he guessed on Kyle's part was a gesture of mere friendship, he felt the room began to spin. He looked at Kyle now nearly prone on top of him, took in the heavy shoulders and the graceful neck, and felt desire consuming him. His mind now spinning wildly, he thought again that he should leave, but he was trapped. He touched Kyle's shoulder gingerly, reassuringly, and wondered awkwardly how long he should remain. Just then, Kyle shifted suddenly, and with a deft half slide, he eased himself from underneath Kyle, stood a moment -- dizzy -- in the center of the room, his penis throbbing on implacably behind his zipper. He knelt, ashamed, and swung Kyle's legs up on the sofa, then leaned down and grabbed a blanket from Kyle's bed to spread it over Kyle as soundlessly as possible. That done, he hesitated, wondering whether he should kiss Kyle finally on the cheek; decided not, then grabbed his coat and exited.

The incident left Justin terribly upset, so much so he could scarcely think of anything else that whole week long. True, emotions had been running high that night, and they'd been semi-drunk, but he had gotten stimulated when Kyle kissed him! And he had very nearly kissed Kyle back! What level of depravity was that, to feel a physical arousal in the midst of someone else's need? He told himself he had to broach the subject somehow -- had to find a way to tell both Kyle and Craig about the things he'd wrestled with all year. Yet he was scared: despite the friendship he had built with Kyle and Craig, he wasn't sure what they were going to say, how they'd react, especially given what they'd just been through with Steve. Perhaps, thought Justin, if he tried Craig first, he'd get some indication of the way his news would go. But then, if things went horribly with Craig, could it be long before Kyle knew as well? Looking at the picture window in the dining hall, now black at mealtimes due to daylight saving time, he pondered, suddenly, a future just as blank as this: where once the scene had been a sunlit dandelion field, the setting for the wonderful relationship he'd forged with Kyle and Craig, might it be similarly dark and blank if things went wrong when he told Craig? How could he stand to loose them both as friends, if it should come to that? Yet, how much longer could he stand not telling them?

It was the night before Thanksgiving break, and they were sitting once more at the bar. Justin still had not found any opportunity to talk to Craig, and felt that, with the holiday upon them, he had better do it now, or he never would. How deceitful he had been! What made him any different, in the end, from Steve, if not, perhaps, worse? He had thought Steve ill: a sick man. Yet here he was, apparently in love with Kyle himself, and he had not been honest with his friends. What kind of person did that make him, guilty of what treachery? Sitting there beside them, Justin decided finally that -- whatever came of it -- he had to talk to Craig, at least, and had to do it now, before he lost his nerve again. But it was awkward; he had waited way too long. How could he find a way to talk to Craig without Kyle there?

"So, how'd your date with that girl go?" said Kyle to Craig.

"Oh, it went fine. We went to see *The Lady Vanishes* in Keil Hall. It was pretty good."

"And will we be seeing her again?" said Kyle impishly.

"I think so," said Craig, his face a mixture of shyness and bravado.

"Good man!" said Kyle. " What's her name?"

"Estelle."

"I still don't know who she is," said Kyle. "What does she look like?"

"She's got reddish hair, parted in the center; kind of medium-tall, lives in Franklin Hall. I don't now, how do you describe someone?"

Justin listened and wondered: how would he describe himself? What model was there out there for him? Steve? His Dad? Kyle? Craig? He wasn't much like any of them, or was he? Would someone looking at him think he was gay, the way he'd guessed Steve was the first time he had met him? And how was he ever going to figure any of this out unless he talked to someone? Justin felt the evening slipping slowly and irrevocably away -- felt he wouldn't have an opportunity unless he grabbed it soon. At last, a full beer sitting there in front of Kyle, he saw his chance.

"Listen, I'm feeling really beat," said Justin, looking specifically at Kyle. "I think I might head back."

"If you wait a minute, I'll head back with you" said Kyle. He squeezed Justin's shoulders with a warmth hard to resist.

"No, no, you stay," Justin practically decreed. Meanwhile, his eyes implored Craig: *Please, walk home with me. I need to talk to you.*

"You're walking back?" said Craig.

"Yeah, I could use the walk."

"Why not just wait a minute?" Kyle said. "We can all ride back."

Justin started to slide out even as he spoke: "No, that's all right, Kyle, really. I'll walk back."

"Is everything all right?" said Craig.

"Actually, I'd like to talk to you about something. Would you mind walking back with me?"

"All right," said Craig, surprised.

"I'm sorry, Kyle. I'll come see you before I take off tomorrow, all right?"

"All right." Kyle looked perplexed. "I'll see you two guys later."

For a second, Justin almost weakened. For a second, with the bar light on Kyle's face and Kyle beside him looking hurt, he thought how easy it would be to stay -- how easy not to ever say a thing; but that had not been easy. He felt Craig's hand upon his shoulder, urging him up to the door, and made himself press on.

Outside, the stillness of the dead square hit him and he hesitated for a moment, Justin waiting as Craig shut the screen door of the bar behind them. He could feel Craig's expectation as they walked past all the houses off the square, the huge, Victorian structures speaking of the comforts of another age. A red brick road ran up to meet the courthouse: one-time jewel of southern Illinois. It was a graceful limestone structure rising like some fairy palace sprung up inexplicably upon the prairie. He walked in silence, resolute, not even knowing that he'd passed Craig up until he felt Craig's hand go out to slow him, heard Craig saying, "Are we in a hurry?"

Justin didn't answer then because he could not: something made the words stick in his throat. In his mind now he imagined when he told Craig this that Craig, inebriated, unsuspecting, walking here beside him, would revile him; would think of times when they'd been intimate or even naked in each other's company without self-consciousness; that now all that would change; that this impending statement tolled the end, somehow, of everything; that he was on the verge of claiming something that he wasn't even sure about. He looked at Craig, into his blank face: beer-soft, simple in the moonlight, thinking: *God, I don't deserve this love, this trust*; remembered how alone he'd felt before he met both Kyle and Craig; how they had taken him into their fold as older brothers would have: warmly, lovingly, acceptingly -- the way no other male friends ever had; and how their love had made him feel so normal, growing naturally, it seemed, into a bond as warm as Kyle's embrace. Was he really going to throw all that away?

He grew aware of Craig beside him once again, and felt like somebody had stepped behind him at a urinal: self-conscious, trapped, and scared. He wished that he could sit and have Craig hold him -- really hold him, there and then, the way Kyle held him on that recent night. He knew, though, things would never change until, at last, he told someone.

"Craig, I'm sorry. I'm so sorry," Justin said.

"For what?"

But Justin couldn't speak.

Craig said once more, "What? What are you sorry for?" He touched Justin's shoulder, hanging on a moment.

Justin felt the touch beneath his winter jacket, walked along a moment feeling it. But then he stepped away.

"Look, Craig, this isn't easy for me, but I think I want to tell you." He went slowly now, to soften it -- for whom it wasn't sure: "I've thought about this for a long time, but I couldn't bring myself to say it." Justin took a deep breath, then said: "Craig, I think I'm a homosexual."

Almost instantaneously, he wished he hadn't phrased it that way -- that he'd said, "I'm gay," or no, perhaps not. He wondered which term would have shocked the least, and felt again the sordidness of using it about himself. He wondered, too, how Craig had felt to hear him say those words -- tried to anticipate the possible rejection. Instead, they merely walked a while in silence, Justin growing more unnerved.

"Wow," said Craig after a moment as they walked along, his face inscrutable. "I guess that's why this whole Steve Norberg thing upset you so much, huh?"

"Yes," said Justin.

"I'm not quite sure what to say, Justin. How can I help you?"

Craig's question took him by surprise. Justin had imagined saying this for so long now, yet he had never gotten past these initial words. He stammered, conscious of the fact that *he* was the one faced with making a response, expected now to stir the air in some way with his vocal chords, and yet unable to, his stomach feeling small and animal at this unwelcome shift.

But Craig, perceiving his confusion, asked him quietly, "What makes you think you might be gay?"

It was a shock to hear Craig say the word; he felt accused somehow, repeating to himself the question and again made mute by all the images that popped into his mind: Steve's crooked smile as Kyle bent over him; the bloody wrists. He struggled hard to think why he had come to this conclusion, then remembered Kyle: that curious dependent need he felt for him; the way he felt whenever Kyle embraced him; how he'd felt that day Kyle landed on him in the dandelion field; the way he'd felt that night when Kyle had kissed him. He was on the verge, at last, of trying to articulate some part of this, but now Craig asked him even more gently, "Have you felt this way for quite a while?"

"I feel it sometimes when I'm with you guys," said Justin, trying again to soften it. "I'm not exactly sure it's sexual. It's just a feeling -- I don't know. I'm not real sure I know what gay means, anyway. I find it hard to think I'm like that, like Steve..."

Craig leaned toward him slightly, thoughtfully, then said, "Justin, this has been a really stressful time for everyone. Freud says we're all bisexual, you know? Maybe you shouldn't be too quick to try to slap a label on yourself. Maybe we're all just running scared. Anyway, why should you say you're this or that when you're not sure? Take time, sort out your feelings. Maybe then you can decide."

Everything in Justin seemed to shift, yet not to move at all. He wasn't certain whether he was happy, sad, relieved, and said now oddly, distantly, "Have you ever thought I might be gay?"

"Not really, no."

But Justin didn't feel relieved by this; he wasn't certain what he'd wanted as an answer. He was merely trying hard to fill the void, the void where, suddenly and irrevocably, he was a gay man standing next to Craig.

"I wasn't sure how you'd react," said Justin. "I always thought I had enlightened friends, but then, I wasn't sure you wouldn't take a swing at me."

"Oh, Justin."

"Well, you never know." He stiffened as they passed beneath a streetlight and the light illuminated both of them an instant, then diffused into the darkness all around them once again. He grew distrustful of Craig's silence, wished that everything would stop -- that they could stop right here and talk this out. Instead, they kept on walking: everything just kept on moving all the time. After a moment, he said simply, "I just wanted you to know."

Craig said, "It's fine, Just. I don't see why anything should change. Will you tell Kyle?"

He felt a swift attack of panic, then mastered it, saying simply, "I'm not sure I could handle telling both of you at once."

"I see," said Craig. "It's something that'll probably get a little easier as time goes on."

But Justin blanched at this, this threatening scenario of having all these people know this thing about him. "Well, I think perhaps you're right," he added quickly. "Perhaps I shouldn't use a label on myself. Maybe I just need some time."

They passed into the gates of campus now, and Justin knew they'd have to part.

"Are you all right with this?" he said. The chapel tolled its late hour quietly behind them in the night, and Justin found it hard to concentrate. The bell kept saying the same thing: over and over, it kept repeating what it was. He looked down at the pavement as he waited for Craig's answer, saw the shadows of the bare limbs moving. He could see the motion, but he felt no wind, no movement anywhere -- even inside himself.

Craig said, "I think so, Justin. Look, I guess I've never really had somebody tell me this before. I'm not sure how I feel, you know? It doesn't seem like it should change things, and I hope it won't. I guess I'm just not certain what to say."

"I understand," said Justin. "I just had to tell someone: I've been so scared."

"I'm glad you told me." Craig touched Justin on the shoulder, smiling wanly. "Don't be too upset with me. All this is new to me."

Justin's mind was whirling, going through the range, repeating to himself the crazy syntax of that sentence: "Don't be too upset with *me*," approval shifted once again to him. He merely said, "Me, too," then, Craig removed his hand.

"It's fine, Just, really," Craig said finally, then gave his arm a pat.

"Thanks."

"I'll see you before you go tomorrow, huh?" said Craig.

"Okay."

Craig turned and made his way back to his dorm, while Justin stood a moment more in the uncertain light. He watched the shifting patterns on the sidewalk, thinking of tomorrow, listening. Then he, too, turned.

Yet, even on returning to his empty room -- dead-seeming now that Jacob had left earlier that afternoon -- he didn't turn the harsh light on: there, in the shadows and the chill, he stripped off all his clothing silently, and pulled the blankets weightily up on his naked frame.

CHAPTER 6

G REY, INDISTINCT LIGHT. JUSTIN LAY in the softness of the morning's ambiguity, its solitude and indecision, thinking of the conversation last night.
He felt something close to desperation on the one hand, something close to
absolution on the other. At least, the topic had been broached, he told himself;
at least, that much had happened and no skies had fallen. On the other hand,
he worried maybe he and Craig had not gone far enough for him to know what
consequences this would have: if Craig would, in the end, not quite be able to
condone what Justin wasn't even certain whether Craig would actually remember. Now as he thought of this: the quite real possibility of Craig's not being
able to recall what Justin had confessed (because they'd both been drunk), he felt
a swift, involuntary stab of joy. Perhaps that would be best of all, he thought:
to have Craig know, and yet not know; to have the benefit of knowing that, on
hearing this, Craig had condoned it quietly, yet in the clarity and shadowlessness
of the dawn, the memory of it all had fled. If that was how it happened, Justin
now concluded, maybe it would end up being better off for everyone.

He rose and, after he had packed and showered, set out timidly toward Craig's
room. He was thinking how he'd act if Craig did not, in fact, remember what
they'd talked about. As Justin neared Craig's room, he finally resolved that, if the
subject of the night before did not present itself, he wasn't going to bring it up.

Yet, that resolution wavered as he neared Craig's door. The stillness of the
hallway, vacant and deserted as a schoolyard in the summer, hit him with its implications as he stood there in the dimness and the silence. Was it truly wise of
him to bury this confession, dodge this thing that had preoccupied him for so

long? Wasn't Craig the perfect person he could talk about this with, this friend who'd been his confidant the whole semester long; who knew both him and Kyle, and seemed to understand?

He knocked and Craig's door opened, and before him in the hall stood Kyle. As if in shock, he wondered whether he had walked, somnambulistic, to the wrong room: if fear of what he felt toward Kyle had made him walk, ironically, straight to the wrong room. But then, a second later, in the bright light just past Kyle, he saw Craig lean out in the hall and peer at him.

"Hey, guy," said Kyle good-naturedly.

"Hi. How come you're here?" said Justin awkwardly, suddenly panicking. Had the two of them met just now, to talk about what he had said to Craig last night?

"I just came by to say goodbye," said Kyle. "I was hoping you wouldn't run off without saying goodbye, too."

"No, no," said Justin, "You just surprised me. I didn't expect to find you here."

"Is everything okay? You don't mind my being here?" said Kyle. He smiled, a little half smile of uncertainty.

"Yes, no, I mean: yes, everything's fine, and no, of course I don't mind your being here." Justin felt incredibly embarrassed and confused: not only was he sounding stupid, he was also sounding rude. Again, he wondered whether Kyle and Craig had had some sort of chat, yet Craig's was not the nature of a man who'd said a thing. "Listen, Kyle," said Justin, "I'm sorry about last night."

"I was kind of wondering. Do you want to talk about it?"

He could feel Craig grow alert beside him, listening with renewed but guarded interest. Still, his manner wasn't one of someone who was sharing a secret with Kyle; rather, with him.

"No, it's nothing to worry about," he said, stealing a glance at Craig.

"You're sure?"

"Yes. I'm sorry if I was rude."

"That's all right. As long as it's not something I did."

At this, there was nowhere he could look but down. "No," Justin said. "It isn't you."

"All right," said Kyle. "So, your dad is picking you up soon?"

"He should be here within the hour."

"Great. Well, I'm going to drop this guy at the train station," said Kyle, motioning to Craig, "and then, I'll be off myself."

Craig gave Justin a helpless, my-hands-are-tied look which Kyle didn't see, and Justin felt relieved. Yet, he was disappointed that now the holiday would intervene and he was going to have to worry over everything, exactly as he'd feared.

"Come here," said Kyle. Kyle embraced Justin with a force that nearly knocked him over. Justin felt the warmth of it, but was also aware of Craig beside him, watching.

"Have a great holiday," said Kyle.

"You, too," said Justin self-consciously. They broke, and Justin felt guilty and helpless as he hugged Craig.

"Listen, write me, okay?" said Craig pointedly.

"Okay," said Justin, thinking that writing might be the best answer after all, but wondering still what Craig might say to Kyle before they met the train.

As his father picked him up a short time later, Justin still could feel Craig's eyes upon him, questioning and helpless. It was a look that seemed to follow him the long way home, hovering beside him like his own reflection in the tinted window glass. At least, as far as he could tell, Craig seemed to be all right with the news; there was some consolation in that. But even Craig didn't yet know the whole of it: that, not only did he think he might be gay, but that he was also growing more and more convinced he was in love with Kyle.

His father drove on through the somber November fields of Central Illinois, the cornfields plowed into their light brown, corduroy corn rows, the grey skies still and barren. A few black crows stood listless and immobile, trapped beneath oppressive skies.

"How is everything going?" said his father as they rode with Justin's week-long luggage, packed like an astronaut's space-walk gear in what was once the family car -- a tired-looking, forest-green Chevelle; his mother had gotten a new car in the settlement.

"Just fine," said Justin. In truth, he was feeling alien and strange, exactly as if he *were* embarking on a space walk in a hostile atmosphere outside the school.

"I think it's good for you to get away from home, grow up a bit," said his father in that same, expansive, unconvincing, worldly-wise manner he invariably employed to make himself seem like a man's man, and which never failed to confirm ones impression that he was very much the opposite. "Your mother worries about you incessantly, of course, but I don't. I had the army, you see, so I know what it's like to get away from home and sow a few wild oats."

His father winked at him, and Justin winced at this -- this all-too-frequent mention by his father of his military service during World War II, as if his father needed to convince himself, by constant repetition, that he'd once done something manly and assertive in his life. Actually, for all his supposed bravado, his father had had a desk job in Ally-occupied Sicily; he'd also not volunteered, but was drafted. As Justin thought about it now, it amazed him that his father had the nerve to carry on a love affair behind his mother's back: he seemed so little suited to decisive action. His new love, Peg, must have done all the planning and plotting for them both.

"Speaking of wild oats, how's Peg," said Justin antagonistically, feeling bad about his remark even as he made it. Once, when Justin had been little -- maybe six or seven -- Justin remembered his father curling up against him on the living room floor, rubbing his beard against Justin's chin playfully, and hugging him as they lay down for a nap. It was the single incontrovertible instance of all-encompassing love he could remember from his childhood -- the solitary time he could ever remember his parents hugging or even touching him: it simply wasn't done in his family. Now, his father had run away with that -- run off with Peg: this overly perky, clothes store clerk, betraying and abandoning his mother and him.

"Peg's just fine," said his father, looking at him warily.

As he watched the dying countryside move past, the broken, weather-beaten cornstalks and the cinderblock gas stations, Justin felt bitter -- bitter and bereft: like someone who'd escaped his tribe and now -- kidnapped again -- was being forcibly returned.

"So, when exactly did the two of you start fucking?"

Justin's father stared at him so long and hard he thought they might have an accident.

"Listen, Justin, I probably deserve that," said his father, "but that's the end of it, you hear? I'm sorry if my relationship with Peg upsets you, but I finally feel like I've found happiness at last, okay? I'm sorry if you can't be happy for me, but I guess I don't really have any control over that."

"Oh, great," said Justin. "That's really convenient for you: you can ruin all our lives and then tell us you're sorry we can't be happy for you."

"Look, Justin, what do you want me to say? I love you and your mother. I *do*," he insisted as Justin rolled his eyes. "But the truth is, the passion was never there. You have to have felt that, growing up: it just wasn't a loving household. We were great friends in school, your mother and I -- always had been. But sexually, it isn't there for us and never was. We got married, I think, because that's what people who were such great friends were expected to do. But it wasn't -- isn't -- love. Something was always missing: some all-important spark. And now I've found that. Don't begrudge me that happiness, Justin. I really think in life the wisest thing for anybody to do is to follow their passion. If you hate me and don't remember anything else I ever tell you, promise me you'll at least remember that."

An hour later, they were on the outskirts of Peoria, then Galesburg. Another hour after that, the Mississippi valley farmland fell gracefully away to the bridge across the Rock River, and Moline lay across the river on the other side. As they crossed the bridge and Justin saw the old familiar strip malls, seemingly un-changed, he felt increasingly the daunting thought that -- contrary to what he'd thought before -- maybe *college* was the space-walk after all, and *this* was the sad reality: as if none of the friends he'd made recently were real, none of the things he'd learned, or any of the progress he had felt he'd made; that he was coming back in order to resume, once more, the role of gawky, unloved boy: the one who had no friends, whose family never touched; and any love he'd glimpsed -- however hazily, confusingly -- was just the aberration he had feared.

As they sat down for the Thanksgiving meal that evening in the same, squat, ranch-style house his parents had once shared, Justin's mom and dad were trying to be on their best behavior, but Justin knew how brittle the peace was: try as they might to come together for his first Thanksgiving dinner back from college (and this was no request or even desire of his own), he knew it was only a matter of time before his mother made some casual remark about his father's relationship with Peg, and acrimony would prevail. To Peg's credit, she was generously conceding this special night-before-Thanksgiving meal to them for old time's sake, but even so, emotions were running high. Justin's mother, a large-boned, red-haired woman who often gave off the air of a nervous poetess, seemed strangely in control tonight, like a Medea whose rage and indignation have given her a new purpose. If Justin had sometimes thought of her in the past as a wounded bird -- especially during the past year leading up to the divorce proceeding -- she now seemed more like one of those crafty mother birds who will sometimes act wounded in order to lead people away from her imperiled nest, thus saving her chicks.

"How are things going at school?" said Justin's mother, interrupting the general silence around the table.

"Just fine," said Justin.

"Are you seeing anyone? Is there a girlfriend down there yet?" his mother asked hopefully.

"No."

"Well, why not, for heaven's sake? There must be lots of pretty girls down there."

"I don't know, mom," said Justin, annoyed. "I guess maybe I'm just busy with all the wrong things: schoolwork, classes, studying."

"Now, now," said his mother. "You don't want to let this opportunity slip past you. You don't want to wind up in life all alone, do you?" She cast a glance at Justin's father.

"Leave the boy alone, Marge. Honestly, I don't know why you're so anxious to match him up with someone. It's not like marriage is the key to happiness."

"Well, don't I know that," said his mother pointedly.

"I just meant, I don't know why you keep trying to shove him into something that'll lock him in for the rest of his life."

"Obviously it didn't lock you into anything," said his mother. "You felt perfectly free to run away with Peg."

"O*kay*," said Justin emphatically, not used to the bickering after being so long away from it.

"What's your roommate doing for the holiday?" said his mother, attempting to rescue the conversation. "What's his name again? Jacob?"

"Yes, Jacob. He has some relatives in Chicago he was going to stay with."

"Did you invite him to come here? It would have been nice to meet some of your friends for a change. But then, you never did bring any friends home for us to meet -- not ever. He would have been welcome to stay with us."

Justin's first impulse was to say, "I never had any friends," but he squashed it, muttering instead, "Wouldn't *that* have been something to be thankful for?"

"That's enough," said his father admonishingly, his tone angering Justin. In Justin's eyes, his father had long ago abdicated any claim to moral authority in this household.

"Perhaps he would have liked to celebrate an American-style Thanksgiving," said his mother, ignoring the remark.

"I'm sure he's just fine," said Justin, envying someone who was actually free to do whatever he wanted with his life; who might have been free to tag along with Kyle or Craig to their family holiday, something that had occurred to him -- that he had, in fact, hoped *might* happen -- but which had not panned out. They continued in silence, and Justin felt utterly depressed. How could he ever expect to find love coming from a family like this? If this was the end result of love, why bother? But he was certain it wasn't; he was certain Kyle's and Craig's houses were nothing like this. Sitting there with his feuding, unhappy parents, he would have given anything to be at Kyle's.

Later, as Justin sat in his old room, still decorated with his high school things, he felt listless and defeated. At college, he felt as though he'd broadened, changed so much. Now, sitting on his old bed with the posters from his high school plays still hanging on the faded walnut paneling, the religious choral masses he had listened to so fervently in high school still there beneath the stereo, reminding him that even in his high school years he'd had this doubt, this struggle within himself regarding what he felt -- seeing all this, he felt as though his so-called progress was a lie. Not only that: his parents had no notion who he was, or who he'd been for quite some time.

And who exactly was that? Justin didn't know himself. What was Craig thinking of him now, since he'd made his half-assed, incomplete confession? Would things change once he was back at school? Would Craig steer clear of him now, as he had with Steve, now that he knew the truth? Would Craig tell Kyle about him as well? As Justin thought about it, he realized he had no idea what was going to happen once he got back: the wonderful friendship he felt as though he'd built with Kyle and Craig might all come crumbling down. He was reasonably certain their friendship was strong enough to withstand this, but what if it wasn't? What would he do then?

———◆———

One day, still at home for the holiday, Justin stood inside the local Waldenbooks down at the mall. Christmas carols were blaring already, and tinsel was draped gaudily from every rafter. With Thanksgiving now over, the Christmas season was upon them, though Justin hadn't given it much thought yet. He stood looking at the titles of the books aimlessly, half-heartedly, when suddenly, he saw a paperback whose cover showed two handsome, blow-dried men each gazing lovingly at one another, holding hands. The book was called *The Lord Won't Mind*, and Justin couldn't quite believe his eyes. It sat there bluntly, with its brightly colored cover facing outward from the copper colored racks, and he was too terrified to even touch it. He kept on hovering, scared to move, and yet afraid to call attention to the fact that he had stood there already for so long.

Then, finally, he reached out for the book as though it were an oddity, a curiosity which might bear closer looking at. He lifted it and flipped the pages nervously, fear robbing all the words of meaning. Suddenly, a woman came up near him, and he put the book back on the shelf, his only thought to get the thing out of his hands. But, in his haste, he missed the shelf, and several copies tumbled to the floor and landed face up. Justin snatched them up and then, incredibly self-conscious, took a copy with him elsewhere in the store to look at it in peace. He would have bought it and been gone, and yet, he was afraid of what the clerk was going to think. The cover illustration was so bold, so unmistakably a picture of two gay men, anybody would have known just by glancing at it what it was about. And yet, he thought, as he stood leafing through the pages near the yellow wall of Cliff's Notes, if Waldenbooks was stocking it, perhaps he needn't be afraid. This was supposedly the age of gay liberation, after all: recently, *Time* magazine had featured Army Sergeant Matlovich upon its cover publicly declaring, "I am a homosexual;" Anita Bryant's subsequent campaign against gays seemed to be achieving a reverse effect, and just last year, the gays in San Francisco had staged a moving, candlelight parade protesting gay rights leader Harvey Milk's death, and calling for an end to discrimination. Maybe in the world today, thought Justin, homosexuality was not so big a deal.

And yet, as Justin took the book up to the register, saw the bun-haired, middle-aged cashier take note of it, then look at him suspiciously, he knew that it was still the same world, still as big a deal as ever, here in Moline, at least. The cashier rang the book up without touching it. Indeed, to read the price, she merely cocked her head and glanced at him. Then, as Justin handed her his money, she took it from him, being very careful not to touch his hand. She tore the register receipt off briskly, slipped it in the book -- again, not touching it -- then turned as if dismissing him.

"I'd like a bag, please," said Justin, his anger and embarrassment acute.

The clerk looked at him silently, then peeled a brown bag off the stack and handed it to him.

He took the bag and picked the book up simultaneously. "Thank you very much," he uttered with some edge. Taking the book and walking from the store, he felt like he'd been slapped, as though he were some reprimanded house pet, skulking to a corner of the house in shame.

When Justin finally read the book (well-hidden in his room, the cover taken off and shredded carefully into a trash bag, which he then personally then carried out), he found it disappointing and depressing. The two protagonists were gorgeous, prep school types, so beautiful and confident that Justin found it hard to like them. It was not well-written, and the sex scenes -- which at first he'd combed the pages for -- seemed strange and lurid. They were so remote from anything he'd read before, so frightening and alien, that the book's main message -- that the lord would not mind any form of love, as long as it was love -- seemed unconvincing, and more wishful than profound. He wondered once again: was this the kind of life he was destined for? Was this the kind of person he'd just told Craig he thought he was?

CHAPTER 7

———◆———

COMING BACK TO THORNTON AFTER break was over, Justin sat in silence in his father's black-interiored Chevelle, watching as the blank fields passed. The sound was muffled in the car, his dad was curiously quiet, too, and Justin felt more helpless than he ever had. As they came into the town, he saw again the brick-lined square, surrounded by the Greek Revival Farmer's and Merchants Bank, the 1930s grey stone building holding Franklin's Restaurant and a gift shop; on the other sides were Woolworth's and a hardware store, an Inn, and Frankie's bar (where all the college students went); off to the right, down Main, was the limestone courthouse with its own square, flanked by huge, old elms and large, old houses. Not a thing had changed, it seemed, since 1935, and it was this -- the sense that everything was still the same (all things except that now Craig had been told) -- that bothered Justin as they pulled up finally outside his dorm. His father helped him with his things, then shook his hand in farewell. In its shy, embarrassed lack of warmth, the handshake seemed to signify to Justin everything he felt like he was missing in his relationship with his father: they might have been two people concluding a business lunch, so perfunctory was his father's parting; as if the whole drive down were nothing more than a duty to be dispensed with, a business proposal tentatively offered, then withdrawn. Actually, Justin sensed that his father *did* want to talk over their situation a little more -- break through the ice in some way -- but was too afraid of Justin's anger to attempt to do so, and Justin thought he was probably right: in truth, he couldn't wait to see his father go.

Actually, his thoughts were racing far ahead to other things as Justin crossed the campus toward Craig's room. He'd been thinking over the situation the whole way down, and thought he knew exactly what he had to say to Craig: he wasn't sure that he was right before when he had claimed he was a homosexual -- that he may have made a hasty judgement. He was going to follow Craig's advice, and see how things turned out -- just take it slow, and maybe later on he could decide.

As Craig opened up the door, however, the expression on Craig's face changed to one of such joy, such exuberance and energy, that for Justin, it was like pulling the shades in the morning expecting to find grey clouds, and instead discovering a dazzling blue sky.

"Justin!" yelled Craig, so unequivocally glad to see him, it was as though he'd never said a thing to him at all. "How are you, bud?"

"Okay," said Justin, overwhelmed, and feeling suddenly absolved and loved. He wondered whether they would embrace, but they did not.

"Come on in. I'm just sitting here listening to some Dan Fogelberg."

"Oh yeah? Which album?" said Justin, sitting on the window end of the bed. He could see the frozen yellow quad; Craig sat at the other end, surrounded by some of his artwork in process, pinned up hastily on the burlap-colored walls.

"*Home Free.*"

"Yeah? I remember we talked about that album at the party the first night I met you," said Justin, shucking his coat.

"We did?"

"Yeah," said Justin, a little taken aback that Craig did not remember. "That's what got us started talking, remember? That drawing on the cover, and how it looked like Kyle."

"Like Kyle?" said Craig, startled. "Dan Fogelberg looks like Kyle?"

"Well, not like Kyle. I guess we were talking about how that drawing looked like Jesus, and then we got onto a discussion of how Jesus was a carpenter, and wouldn't have been scrawny." He didn't want to add the part about how they'd said he would have had a build like Kyle's, but almost did before Craig finally said,

"Oh, yeah, yeah, yeah. Now I remember. You just threw me for a minute."

Thinking about Kyle made Justin clutch, and they sat for a moment, the music washing over them. Then, Craig said,

"God, I love this song! Don't you?"

Justin listened for a second, but he'd been too distracted to notice what was playing. "Which one is this?"

"*Hickory Grove*. Here, let me back it up -- it's my favorite song on the whole album."

Craig lifted the needle, moved it back, and immediately a bright sound of strings filled the room, falling almost immediately to the interval a fourth below. "God, don't you just love that opening? It's like liquid sunshine -- like the sun on an August day, streaming through the trees."

In that instant, Justin could have believed it was Craig he'd been agonizing over whether he had feelings for, not Kyle. Watching Craig's boyish enthusiasm, his infectious joy, there was nowhere else in the world he would have rather been than here with Craig, who loved him and, apparently, accepted him.

"So, how was your break?" said Craig.

"Just fine. My parents were a little weird, what with the divorce and all." Justin hesitated for a moment, then said, "I missed you guys."

"I missed you, too. Listen," said Craig after a moment. "I'm sorry we didn't get to talk before break. I thought maybe you'd call."

"Oh, it's not your fault," said Justin, sobering quickly. Then, because of the warmth and safety he felt being here with Craig, he said, "Craig, about what I said back then .... "

"Yes?"

"I'm not exactly sure I was right. I mean, I think maybe I should take your advice: just give it some time."

"Sure, whatever you think," said Craig.

Justin nodded, uncomfortable, and Craig said,

"Just remember, it's okay whatever you decide."

"Really?"

"Yeah, of course."

"Thanks," said Justin, feeling naked and exposed, until Craig said at last, "Come here. It's good to see you."

As they hugged -- some fundamental need within him being met -- he tried to think what this was called. Would this be love, this hug without desire? For as he hugged him, Justin felt no physical sensation, but instead a kind of centering, as if he'd found his place at last. Again, he wondered: could it be he'd been mistaken all this time, misguided? Was it possible he'd merely found some warmth and love at last -- true friendship and affection – and, on finding it, had not been certain what it was?

When they finally hooked up with Kyle that evening after dinner, Justin felt happier and more contented than he had since he'd left, as if here -- and not in Moline -- he'd finally connected with his true family. Kyle embraced them both hugely, like a bear corralling cubs, and soon they were heading back to Kyle's room as if not a second had intervened.

"How was your break?" said Justin as they walked across the spiky quad, their voices blowing steam.

"Fine. Quiet."

"How's Maureen," asked Craig.

"I think that's just a *little* too personal, bud," said Kyle.

"Oh," said Craig, laughing. "That wasn't what I was asking, but since you volunteered it …. "

"We had a great time."

"I see," said Craig suggestively. "And since we've started down this road, are you and Maureen, you know, doing the dirty deed?"

Justin watched Kyle struggle with the answer to this question, and sensed his own smile fading. He wasn't sure Kyle liked this question -- he wasn't sure he did himself; yet, he was curious himself, and knew that Craig had only asked it because he felt like he was close enough.

"Let's just say my parents were pretty cool about my not coming home a few nights last week."

"Ohhh," said Craig, arching his eyebrows. "And is this a new thing for the two of you?"

"It is," said Kyle shyly.

"Our little boy has become a man!" said Craig, hugging him playfully.

"Get out of here," said Kyle, pushing him off.

"I take it everything's still on for the wedding, then?" said Craig.

"Yeah," said Kyle, looking curiously unforthcoming about something. "We're getting married at the end of May."

"I see. So you figured, what the hell, why not just sleep together then?" persisted Craig.

"Something like that," said Kyle, laughing uneasily.

"So, what's up tonight?" said Justin. "You want to head on up to the bar?"

Kyle looked conflicted a moment, then said, "Actually, there's one thing I need to do. I need to go find Karen Taylor and talk to her for a few minutes."

Karen Taylor was, like Kyle, a Peer Group Counselor: a sweet, dark-haired, New England type with something very patrician, yet unmistakably warm, about her at the same time. She was one of those women who could hold her own with the boys, talking about sports or whatever, and yet still retain her femininity. At hearing mention of her name, Justin saw a look of vague jealousy flit over Craig's face.

"What's up, some PGC thing?" said Craig.

"Yeah," said Kyle. "Would you guys mind if I hooked up with you a little bit later? Maybe I could meet up with you at the bar?"

"Sure, whatever," said Justin.

Later, at the bar, however, Justin couldn't help feeling momentarily threatened and off balance when Kyle showed up with Karen in tow and joined them at their booth.

"Hey, boys," said Karen, sliding in next to Craig and immediately altering the dynamics of the evening as she did so. "What's new?"

"Well, well," said Craig, rising to the occasion like some nineteenth century suitor. "To what do we owe this honor?"

"Kyle told me that they served beer here, and I just had to come see for myself whether it was true. Not that I've ever had any, myself."

"Oh, neither have we," said Craig.

Karen leaned away from him at an odd angle, and as they looked at her questioningly, she said, "I'm just waiting for the lightning bolt."

"Oh, who needs lightning," said Kyle. "These guys are lit already."

Justin laughed with the others, even though, in truth, he'd never liked beer that much. He just knew both Kyle and Craig did, and somehow, the bar was always where they went. He was also feeling a little hurt that the intimacy of their first night back was being compromised by the addition of this relative stranger.

"So, what's new on the PGC front?" said Craig. "Hopefully no more crises to deal with?"

"No, I hope not," said Karen, looking a bit uncomfortable. "I think Kyle has had enough to deal with already this year."

"Any word on how Steve Norberg's doing?" said Justin tentatively.

"No, not really. He's not coming back, last I heard. I'd be very surprised if he did. How could you walk around with everybody knowing all that stuff about you?"

Justin stiffened.

"Poor guy," said Craig, surprising Justin. This was the first he'd heard in the way of sympathy for Steve, and Justin wondered whether Craig was saying it because of the talk they'd had before the break. Indeed, the remark created an odd kind of tension amongst them all, an interrupted rhythm which -- added to Karen's presence -- made Justin feel a little off all evening long.

Walking home later, Justin couldn't help feeling just a bit cheated and frustrated: here he'd been looking forward to getting back together again with Kyle and Craig -- brief as the time at home had been -- and though he was pleased that things between him and Craig seemed to be fine, he was miffed at Kyle for letting someone else into their little circle, someone who was not one of the three of them. And yet, why shouldn't Kyle have someone with him? What in the world was he upset about? That that someone was a woman? Or was it simply that, by bringing Karen with him, it seemed to Justin somehow that their friendship must not mean as much to Kyle as it obviously did to him?

Walking back, frustrated, to his late-night dormitory, Justin found his room alive with noise and people partying. The stereo was blasting Devo's "I Can't Get No Satisfaction," the door was open with every light turned on, and Jacob was sitting tipped back in his desk chair, three women sitting just across the aisle from him on Justin's bed. Despite disparaging remarks that Jacob had often made regarding drug use, one of the women was smoking a joint placidly, while the room itself was littered with dark green Heineken beer bottles, empty ashtrays, and deflated yellow bags of *Lay's* potato chips.

"Ah, Justin, my good man," Jacob called out cheerily, beckoning to him as if he wished to impart some confidential knowledge. "Come, please, and join in our merriment. We are all having a very good time." At this, he turned to the women gathered immediately around him like a personal harem: "Everybody, this is my roommate, Justin. He is very good man. But oh, he need someone to show him a good time. Is that not right?"

Justin grew uncomfortable, unsure exactly how he should respond. "Hey, Jacob. How was your break?"

"I was very lonely. But I am lonely no more," said Jacob merrily, looking at the women around him. "Will you not join us and have a drink?"

"All right," said Justin, realizing he had nowhere else to be.

"Wonderful. Most wonderful."

As Justin sat and took a beer, Jacob started introducing people in the room. "This is Sheila, Danielle, and her friend .... "

"Laura," said the woman.

"Hi," said Justin, barely registering all their names, but thinking that Laura, a slender, dark-haired, older-looking woman, looked familiar, and seemed very out of place.

"We have World Lit together," said Laura.

"Oh, yeah," said Justin, realizing now where he knew her from. "Job and all that Biblical stuff." He pronounced "Job" to rhyme with "knob," and Laura laughed.

"'Job,' huh?"

"I couldn't stand that piece." He began throwing his arms around like an Italian tenor: "'Why me, God. Why?'"

"I know what you mean. I didn't care for it either. You always ask interesting questions, though."

"Oh, thanks," said Justin, blushing. "I like all the other stuff: *The Iliad* and *The Odyssey* -- just not the earliest things. Are you a freshman?"

"No, actually, I'm a senior. I'm taking World Lit to satisfy my English requirement, but I'm a marketing major."

"Ah," said Justin. "I don't have any head for business."

"And I don't have any head for literature."

"Well," said Justin. "Maybe we could get together sometime and give each other head."

As soon as he had said this, Justin colored furiously. He rarely said anything this risque, but he was feeling devilish and out of sorts, and almost didn't care what other people thought right at the moment.

Laura laughed riotously, however, and seemed totally unfazed by it. "Maybe we could just compare notes sometime instead," she said.

"Sure," said Justin sheepishly.

After a little while, Laura looked at her friend Danielle, who nodded.

"I'm sorry," said Laura, "but we have to go. It's been a really long day."

"Well, nice to meet you, or, to be introduced at last."

"Nice to meet you, too," said Laura.

As Laura and Danielle left, Jacob turned to Justin and smiled. "Ahh," he teased. " I am thinking that she likes you."

"No," said Justin, starting to feel flushed from the alcohol or the compliment, or perhaps both.

"Oh, but I think so," said Jacob, taking a puff of a joint that Sheila was now handing him. "We must strike while the iron is hot, no?"

Justin watched the black hairs of Jacob's mustache wrap around the joint, the black-edged poppy of the cigarette's tip glowing as he inhaled, held his breath, then passed the joint to Justin. Justin took a timid puff, conscious of placing his mouth where Jacob's mouth had been.

"He's right," said Sheila, cuddling up to Jacob.

"Well, maybe," said Justin, taking his cue from Jacob and exhaling after a moment.

"Perhaps we have found the one at last, eh?" said Jacob, wrapping an arm around his shoulders and hugging him affectionately. "But I didn't understand what you said about heads. Why she laugh so, eh?"

"Oh, it was nothing. I shouldn't have said it," said Justin, blushing.

"But it worked! It worked! Ask her out! Do eet," Jacob said good naturedly, his mouth an inch or so away from Justin's.

Justin felt something vague stirring in his loins, but wasn't certain whether it was Jacob, Laura, the drugs or alcohol that had caused it. Jacob squeezed him tightly again, and at last, Jacob's arm still wrapped around him affectionately and his erection beginning to stiffen even more, Justin said at last, "Okay, okay, I'll call her."

As Justin thought about it the next morning, it occurred to him that maybe Laura *was* the answer to his prayers. She was attractive and intelligent, and Justin *had* felt something stirring as he thought of her last night, hadn't he? Why not test out the waters just a little bit and ask her out? What did he have to lose? He looked up at the poster on his white brick wall, a picture of a stalk of wheat at sunset which read simply, "Bend." Is that what he should do? He flashed back on the poster Steve had bought -- the picture of the rainbow -- saw again the blood trails running down his wrists, and felt a momentary stab of fear. Shouldn't he do anything in his power to avoid such a fate? And yet, he flashed on his few instances of dating girls in high school, the awkward kisses shared with someone who was obviously feeling something worlds apart from what he felt. But then again, he'd never really been involved with anyone intimately. Maybe if he actually got into a physical relationship with someone, things would come out right. Anyway, how would he know unless he tried? Then, if he still felt the same...but Justin wouldn't let himself think that far right now. He'd take this one step at a time, and just see how it went. Hadn't Craig himself said he should give himself some time, not slap a label on himself?

Still, as they sat at dinner the next day, the incandescent light bouncing off the white Formica table tops, the cafeteria now startlingly dark in daylight saving time -- like some surreal, other world -- it was with mixed feelings that Justin turned to Kyle and said, "I think I might ask Laura Dickinson out."

"Oh, yeah?" said Craig, looking at him with surprise.

"Yeah," said Justin, trying to seem as nonchalant as possible.

"Who's Laura Dickinson?" said Kyle.

"She's in my World Lit. class. I met her at a party last night. She was kind of flirting with me."

"Go for it," said Kyle.

"Sure," said Craig after a moment. "He who hesitates .... "

Listening to their reaction, Justin felt strange, and a bit dishonest. Despite the fact that Jacob was convinced of Laura's interest in him, Justin still had doubts. More importantly, though, he noticed that there wasn't really any part of him that was excited by this prospect. Was he just young and inexperienced, or was it something else? Once again, he wrestled with the thought of whether he should follow through with this. Still, as long as the opportunity seemed to be there, why not pursue it?

"Isn't she in *my* class?" said Kyle.

"Yeah, she's a senior."

"You hound dog, you," said Kyle. "An older woman." Turning to Craig, he said, "Look at this guy. He's only a freshman and already he's hitting on the women in our class. It's always the quiet ones you've got to look out for." He tousled Justin's hair, and with this gesture, Justin knew there was no turning back: that settled it.

"You were very chummy with Karen last night," said Craig to Kyle. "What's going on there?"

"Nothing," said Kyle, looking suddenly defensive. "She's just a great girl, is all."

"Great girl, shit! She's a ten in my book. You're not getting yourself into trouble with her, are you? I mean, should Maureen be worrying?"

"Oh, grow up," said Kyle. "Maybe Justin can give you some pointers, if you're so desperate."

Flattered as Justin was by Kyle's seeming confidence in him, as Justin sat in class that afternoon, he was still uncertain how this asking out was going to happen. Justin watched the oak chairs in the brown-tiled classroom fill with students, thinking for a while with some relief that Laura might not be in class today after all, so perhaps it was a moot point. Then, as class was just beginning, Laura snuck in, saw him in the back, and smiled as she sat down near the door. All through the lecture, which today was on Greek drama, Justin glanced up at her nervously, but she seemed quite engrossed, and did not look his way.

As class was ending, Justin made himself stand up to greet her.

"Laura, Hi. How are you?"

"Hi. Just fine. You've recovered from your roommate's party?"

"Yes," said Justin, blushing. He still felt shy about the sexual innuendo he had made: it was so unlike him. Jacob's party was also the first time he had ever tried marijuana, and he was a bit ashamed about it. As he thought about it now, however, he remembered that he hadn't smoked the joint until after Laura had left. Was that when he'd been erect, or had it been before? He couldn't quite remember. Still, as he looked at Laura now, she seemed very appealing. She was tall, willowy, and had a very pretty face, with long, brown hair parted in the center.

"Jacob's kind of a wild man, isn't he?" said Laura. "Still, he's pretty attractive."

Justin wasn't certain how to respond, and stammered uncomfortably.

Laura laughed. "Sorry. Why am I asking you?"

"He certainly seems to be a ladies' man," said Justin after a moment. "But he's a good guy. How do you know him?"

"He's in my Accounting class. Danielle knows him better than I do. She's on my floor."

"Oh," said Justin. They had moved into the lobby of the classroom building, and were standing in the entryway. Mauve and violet light from Thornton College's insignia in stained glass overhead fell trapezoidally upon the grey terrazzo floor, the oak door beams.

"What did you think of today's lecture?" said Laura.

"*Oedipus Rex*? It was all right, I guess." He thought a moment, then decided to risk a joke: "I can't believe Oedipus would go out with her, you know? I mean, she's like old enough to be his mother."

Laura roared, a throatier and earthier laugh than Justin would have expected. She was a sort of fragile looking person on the outside, thin, with an angular nose. Now as she laughed, however, Justin saw a different side of her, a side that wasn't quite as quiet or as fragile as he'd thought.

"That's pretty good," said Laura. "You're a quick wit."

"Well, thank you," said Justin, suddenly embarrassed.

"I must say, your joke at the party last night took me by surprise. You seem so straight, I wouldn't have expected it of you."

"Oh, I don't know that I'm that straight at all," said Justin, suddenly self-conscious about the *double entendre* -- about the fact that he was acting like some jaunty, cavalier, world-weary guy whom he was not. And yet, this *was* him, wasn't it? He was making Laura laugh -- could feel her interest in him as they talked.

"Maybe we could get together sometime," said Laura.

"Sure," said Justin. "I'd like that."

"Are you free Friday?"

"Yeah, I think I am," said Justin, surprised that he was the one being asked out, and not the other way around.

"All right, then," said Laura. "You want to stop by my room about 7:00? I'm in Norton 205."

"Great," said Justin.

Laura was about to leave, but Justin, feeling suddenly mischievous, reached for the door. "Here, let me get that for you." Justin pulled the heavy oak door with exaggerated emphasis, bracing first one leg, and then the other on it, so that, in a moment, he was hanging upside down, opossum-like, upon the long brass bar of the handle.

Laura laughed delightedly, and went to help him.

"No, no, I insist," said Justin. After struggling with it for a moment more, he stood up as if baffled. Laura pushed upon the handle simply, and the door flew outward toward the quad.

"How extraordinary."

"Doors are a problem?" said Laura.

"Well, you must admit, it was rather complicated."

"Apparently. I'll see you Friday night, then. That is, if you think you can manage the door .... "

"I shall learn from your example," said Justin, bowing as he watched her walk off, feeling both exhilarated and afraid. He had his date; indeed, it really seemed as though Laura might be interested in him. Maybe things were finally falling into place!

———◆———

As Justin walked to Laura's dorm that Friday night, he wondered suddenly whether he should have brought some flowers. Was this *that* kind of a date? He wished he felt a little surer of himself. The intervening days had given Justin lots of time to doubt himself; still, he was nervous and excited at the thought that now, at last, he'd have the chance to figure out if there was any hope for him with women. Jacob had been overjoyed to hear he had a date, and razzed him all week long about his "woman," speculating as to how long it would be before they slept together. Justin tried to let all this wash over him. Now, however, as he stood outside her door and knocked, there was a part of him that almost wished Laura wasn't there.

As Laura opened up the door, his first thought was: "My God, she's taken this so seriously." Laura's hair was piled high atop her head, and she was wearing makeup: lipstick, blush, mascara. As he looked at her, all dressed up in a silk dress, he realized with daunting clarity the risks and implications of what he was doing.

"Hi," said Laura.

"Hi. You look really beautiful." As soon as he said this, Justin wished he hadn't. Even just by saying that, he felt he'd started down a path: a path he wasn't certain he could follow to the end.

"Well, aren't you sweet. Come on in."

"Thanks," said Justin, entering. "You have a single?" He looked around the room, taking in the peach-colored walls, the scattered vases full of dried flowers, doilies placed with care beneath all objects, as if nothing should make contact anywhere. On the wall, a framed picture of a ballerina's toe was poised atop an egg. Laura also had actual furniture in her room: couch, bentwood rocker, and steamer trunk that functioned as a coffee table -- not the standard-issue dormitory stuff that everybody else had.

"Yeah, " said Laura. "One of the virtues of being a senior. Then, too, because I had an apartment for a while before I came back to school, I brought some of my things here."

"It's nice."

"Thank you. Would you like a drink? I have some wine."

"Sure," said Justin, startled at being offered such an adult choice. He watched as Laura opened up a small refrigerator, pulled a bottle out and grabbed two glasses from the dresser. She poured the right amount of wine distractedly into the glasses, picked them up and walked with one extended toward him, all in one unconscious movement. Justin took the glass and watched her settle next to him atop a white duck sofa. There was something very fine about her, though it was a fineness that also seemed a little broken somehow. She had the air of someone starting out again after certain failures -- what, he couldn't say.

"Would you like to head out to a movie?" he said after a moment.

Laura hesitated for a moment, brushing back a lock with one curt hand, then said, "Why don't we wait a while and then decide?" She set her glass down on the coffee table steamer trunk, then said, "It's so cold out. I'm not so sure I want to brave the weather."

"Sure," said Justin, suddenly perplexed. "Whatever you feel like." He felt a bit uncomfortable now, wondering what exactly Laura had in mind.

She rose and crossed the room to turn some music on, and Justin watched her hips sway gently as an ocean in her smooth silk dress -- an ocean he was sure most men would have wanted to dive into. Did he, he asked himself? Or was he more afraid he would drown in it?

Some gentle strings began to play, and in a moment, Justin recognized *The Moldau* from his musical appreciation class.

"I love that piece," he said.

"Yes, I do, too."

He watched her sit beside him once again, and focused on the wine glass clasped between his two hands like a dowsing rod, arms pointed floorward, as if here -- right here -- he'd stumbled on the spot all forces indicated was the source. He grew aware that she was looking at him, and began to feel uncomfortable.

"Nice music," said Justin.

"Um hmm."

"You said you took a few years off before you came to school. What were you doing?"

"Oh," Laura laughed. "Not much. I ran away from home when I was 17 -- before I'd even graduated high school -- to join my boyfriend in a rock-and-roll band that never went anywhere. Crazy. That lasted about two months. Then, I lived in San Francisco for a while, just hanging out, because I'd always wanted to go there. After a year or two of doing that, I realized what a complete dead-end that was, and that I had to get my act together. So, I finished high school with a GED, and decided I'd come back here and get a marketing degree."

"Wow," said Justin, dazzled by this history. It seemed so unlike anything he could have imagined for her, or for himself. "That's pretty impressive."

"Impressive? Oh, I don't know about that."

"No, really. You took some really big risks. I admire that."

"Thank you," said Laura, looking at Justin in a way that made him realize Jacob had been right: Laura was definitely interested in him.

"Do you still sing?"

"No," said Laura. "For a little while, I tried doing a few clubs around Memphis, but it was too much work for far too little." Laura looked at something in the air midway between them, then said, "Justin, can I tell you something?"

He raised his eyes to just beneath her gaze and said, "Sure."

"I find you quite attractive."

For a second, he was only conscious of the silence in the room, and Laura looking at him in that pointed way. Then, he became aware again of music rushing, pulling him along.

She laughed. "I didn't think I'd shock you *that* much."

"No, no. I'm sorry. Thank you. I think you're attractive, too." Instantly, he wished that he had not been so reflexive -- that he'd said she was pretty rather than attractive. Once again, he felt his words were pulling him along a fearful path.

"Oh, you don't have to be polite."

"No, really, you are very pretty," he insisted now, despite himself.

"Thank you. You're too sweet."

Justin heard the music rushing still, and knew that he should speak. He felt his body growing heavy, weightier, each wordless moment, like a stone, heart-flutteringly sinking to the bottom of a rushing stream.

"Would you like more wine?" she said, but Justin shook his head. He felt paralyzed, uncertain what to do. Then, Laura leaned to kiss him on the lips.

"My goodness, you're so nervous!" Laura said.

"I'm sorry."

"Oh, there's nothing to be sorry for!" She looked at him, amused and charmed, then leaned in to kiss him once again.

He reached his arm around her, kissing back against her pressure, feeling strange and awkward. It was as if he were an actor in a play: he knew what they were doing, what he was supposed to do, but none of it felt natural or spontaneous. And yet, as Laura wrapped her arm around him, and the two of them fell backward on the couch, he felt her pelvis pushing in against his crotch and something down there started stirring. Laura kissed him harder still, then pressed her face against his chest. Her hips moved hard against his, legs encircling him, and he was suddenly uncertain where to put his arms. He touched her hair, caressed her back, but felt mechanical and helpless.

Laura raised up suddenly and stared hard at his belt. She fumbled at it awkwardly, then stood up, switched the room light off, and moved out to the center of the room. There, in the icy silver light, she dropped both shoulder straps to let her dress fall free. He watched her standing like Diana bathing at some private lake, skin glowing like a hand held underwater, and felt both awed and terrified. Laura held her arm out, beckoning for him to come, and as he stood, his knees felt weak. He crossed to her, and as he reached her, Laura dropped her slip as well and stood there silently, the dark moons of her breasts both pointed floorward. He could see the blank swatch in between her legs, which looked asexual and alien to Justin, as if something that should be there wasn't. Laura wrapped herself around him, reaching down to grope his crotch, and he was hoping he was still hard from before. She squeezed his penis hard, then took him by the hand and led him to the bed, where she lay backwards, naked on the comforter. He realized that he should lie on top of her -- that he should take off all his clothes and join her on the bed. Instead, he dropped his pants and knelt beside her on the floor, the way a child swings out above a breathless chasm on a rope swing, makes his noiseless arc, then lands, undeviating, on his knees back in the same place he had started; dragging heels to try to stop, his face pressed in her humid lap, and pants now bunched around his ankles.

Justin stood up, feeling all the energy drain slowly from his penis as he pulled off socks and underwear, climbed into bed, and started kissing Laura once again. But somehow now, he felt like they were starting off from scratch, as if the ember had gone out, and in its place was fear, indifference, as cold and hard as stone. His penis wasn't stiffening, and Justin felt himself begin to panic. What if Laura should look down and see that he was not aroused? He touched her body, kissed her ardently, and still felt nothing in his loins. He looked down at her breasts, and suddenly grew bold enough to take one in his mouth, the nipple like a single ochre curd of cottage cheese. He sucked on it, and Laura undulated underneath him like a lake raft when a motorboat has passed nearby.

As Laura's urgency began to grow, he felt her reaching down to touch his penis, which was small and flaccid. He rubbed himself against her in embarrassment, then felt her moving down to take his penis in her mouth. The shock and the embarrassment of feeling Laura's teeth around his penis made him shrink up even more.

When she had labored at him for a while and Justin, mortified, endured as best he could, she came up wiping at her mouth.

"Is something wrong?" She tried to ask it delicately, not to sound judgmental.

"I'm so nervous," said Justin. He *did* feel nervous. It was more than that, however. He was feeling nothing -- absolutely nothing -- from her efforts.

"It's all right." She moved up next to him and lay there, still.

He felt like he was going to cry. He'd let down Laura, let himself down. Laura turned uncertainly and stroked him gently in the silver light.

"I'm sorry," Justin said. Time and time again he said it in the moonlight, lying next to Laura: tired, defeated, untransformed.

CHAPTER 8

———◆———

WHEN HE WALKED BACK IN his room next morning, Jacob woke up groggily, looked at him askance, and winked.

"You whoredog."

As he'd crunched his way across the early morning stillness of the campus -- frigid, crystalline in this December sunrise; body feeling weak and small inside his red down jacket (even his gonads small and hard as acorns in the cold) -- Justin had been dreading this: this walk back to his room, and the inevitable dealing with the fallout.

"Hi," he said as noncommittally as possible, and started taking off his clothes.

Jacob stretched and looked at him, smiling uncontrollably. "I'm thinking now you are a man, eh?"

"Yes," lied Justin, taking off his shirt -- this shirt that had so recently lain rumpled next to Laura's bed. He tossed it with some vague disgust into his laundry basket. He tried avoiding Jacob's gaze, but looking up now, saw that he was beaming.

"Ah! Come here. Come here!"

Justin crossed now shyly in the chill, dust-moted light, and Jacob rose up naked from the bed. He kissed him on both cheeks and hugged him heartily, and Justin felt his groin begin to stiffen.

"It is wonderful, no? Today, my roommate is a man!"

Later, after he had showered, all traces of last night -- of Laura, of his hopes with women -- washing down into the drain, he headed out to Craig's room.

He was hoping he could talk to Craig before he saw Kyle, though he wasn't sure what he was going to say to him. He only knew he had to talk to someone, get away from Jacob and his innocent assumptions -- from himself. The yellow grass was frosted white, the trees were bare, and crows cawed noisily from wet, black limbs. He walked past vacant tennis courts, now netless in the cold, past sleeping dorms, and down a gentle hill. Atop the next hill stood the main hall with its chapel on one end, its Gothic windows soaring dark and graceful. Justin stood there in the little hollow, red-brick buildings ringed around him, storm grate at his feet, and suddenly he wished he could sink right through the grate into the sewer and be gone. He felt the tears beginning, looked for someplace he could sit, but found none. He debated sitting on the ground -- somehow, it didn't seem that he could move another step -- but suddenly, two students walked across the grass obliquely toward him, and Justin forced himself to move.

Each leaden step he took, however, was an effort. Maybe he should leave, he thought, just leave and not come back. How was he ever going to face his friends, face Laura? Maybe he should take a cue from Steve and go. Yet, as he reached Craig's dorm, and saw his own reflection silvered in the shadowed pane, he knew there wasn't any place for him to go -- no place where he would not be at the other end to greet himself, just like this pale reflection in the glass.

He climbed the stairs to Craig's room, knocking timidly, uncertain whether Craig would be awake.

Craig opened with a toothbrush in his mouth, however, hair still wet from showering, his shirttails still untucked.

"Hi, Justin. Come on in. I have to rinse my mouth out. I'll be right back."

Justin came into Craig's room and sat as Craig headed down the hallway to the bathroom. Craig's room was filled with sunlight, almost over-warm. A slight musk rose from the crumpled sheets, and Justin looked at all the artwork on the walls: Craig's sketches of the still-unfinished nude, a reproduction of Corot's "The Gleaners," and Van Gough's "Room at Arles." Craig's room was a half-room single, long and narrow, with light oak trim along the soft white walls. Despite its smallness, Justin always felt more comfortable inside it than in any other dorm room -- even Kyle's. It was like a warm cave, filled with Craig.

Craig came back into the room and tucked his shirt in hurriedly. Justin watched Craig's hand dip underneath the waistband of his jeans and thought almost abstractly of his manhood wrapped up in the underwear. Craig had an organ down there, an organ which he wanted to insert inside a woman. Why did Justin have, apparently, a different urge?

"You had your date with Laura last night, right? So how'd it go?" said Craig.

"It didn't," said Justin, still staring idly at Craig's midsection.

"What do you mean?"

"I don't know," said Justin at last. He felt the tears again behind his eyes. His lower lip began to quiver, and the words came tumbling out. "I tried. I thought at first I could, but then, I got so nervous, and Laura was so aggressive, and finally I just couldn't do it."

"Wait a minute, wait a minute," said Craig, suddenly serious. "You mean you two got really hot and heavy last night?"

Justin nodded.

"Wow, you two really jumped right to it. So then, what happened? You had sex, or tried to?"

"Yes."

"But what, you couldn't do it, or didn't want to?"

"I wanted to," managed Justin, "but, I don't know. I couldn't."

Craig paused a moment, then said, "Well, do you think maybe you just took it too fast? That you were too scared and nervous? Or do you think it's more than that?"

"I'm afraid it's more," said Justin at last. He swallowed hard, then said, "You remember our talk on the walk home from the bar before Thanksgiving?"

"Of course."

"Can we talk about that?"

"Sure," said Craig.

Justin felt empty, hollow: like his heart, lungs, stomach -- all -- had been torn from his chest. He felt as though the door were swinging open on his soul, and now the sun was streaming in upon his trembling, shrinking fear, balled like a conch meat in the hand. "Does it bother you?"

"Have you decided, then?" said Craig after a moment.

He sat there squirming for a moment, thinking Craig meant: *Have you decided you're in love with Kyle?* Then, he realized he had not yet told Craig about that fear -- that Craig was merely speaking about his sexuality. He sat there wondering what the consequences were if he should answer yes to either question.

"It's all right, Just. Like I said, it doesn't matter to me either way."

"I guess it seems pretty obvious, doesn't it?" said Justin at last.

"Well, I don't know. What did Laura say?"

"Nothing, really," said Justin, thinking of the awkwardness and the embarrassment, the way he'd lain there afterwards, apologizing. She'd gathered him into her arms and held him silently a while. "She said it happens; that I shouldn't worry."

"Then, maybe you shouldn't," said Craig, giving him a tight-lipped little smile. "Maybe you're still rushing into making a decision too fast. Are you going to see each other again?"

"I can't believe she'd ever want to see *me*," Justin said. "Jesus. How am I going to face her from now on?"

"Oh, don't worry about it," said Craig, looking as though he didn't have a clue as to how that was going to work out, either.

"Craig," he said, then stopped. He'd almost said: "I've never felt the same way toward a woman as I do toward you and Kyle," but then thought better of it. "I'm just so scared. And I'm afraid I'm just like Steve."

"Oh, Just, you're not."

"How do you know? How do you know I'm not?" He thought of Kyle: the anguished cry he bore inside him that he thought was love, and which he still felt he could not confess to Craig.

"Because you're *not*," said Craig. "Steve was unstable. Not because he was a homosexual, but just because he *was*. He was totally obsessed with Kyle. And you're not like that. We wouldn't be such good friends if you were. It wouldn't be possible."

Justin still felt unrelieved, yet for the moment let it lie. He still felt reasonably certain what his failure with a woman meant, and yet was still not ready to accept it. He was also unconvinced by what Craig said of Steve. He loved Kyle, too, or thought he did: Kyle certainly consumed a great deal of his thoughts.

"Maybe you're right," he said at last, but it was just the way Craig had responded once when Kyle tried to convince him he could ask out any girl he wanted to: deep down inside, he didn't really think it was true.

———◆———

Later on, the two of them struck off across the quad for Kyle's, their Saturday wide open, even though the year was coming to a close. There were still two weeks until semester's end, but they were in a lull until their finals started.

"There he is," said Kyle on seeing Justin. "You old smoothie. How'd it go with Laura last night?"

Justin winced, despite expecting this. He looked at Kyle and saw the innocent exuberance, the handsome, robust expectation in his face.

"Okay," he said. He looked at Craig, expecting some accusatory glance, but Craig was silent, nonjudgmental.

"What did you guys do?" Kyle said.

"Oh, we got together and had a drink, and talked a while," said Justin, suddenly uncomfortable with lying. He was on the verge of telling Kyle what really happened when Kyle said,

"Good man! It's good to hear you're not rushing into things."

"What do you mean?" said Justin.

"People have sex way too fast these days. Too many times, the only thing they think about is scoring. It's natural, of course, but I still think it's a mistake."

"Wow, that sounds very, I don't know -- responsible and adult of you," said Craig after a moment.

"Well, I think it's true. Look at Maureen and me -- not that I want to hold myself up as an example or anything. But we've been going out for almost five years, and the first time we had sex was just before Thanksgiving. People need to take more time before they make that kind of commitment, not give in to momentary impulses and pressures. It sounds like Justin's doing the right thing, and I'm proud of him for that."

Justin was far too overwhelmed to speak. He looked at Craig again, uncomfortable with Kyle's innocent assumption, but Craig was still looking at Kyle appraisingly.

"Maybe you're right," said Justin, still feeling ashamed, but wondering, too, about what Kyle had said. Perhaps they *had* rushed things too fast. Perhaps that was his problem. Maybe if he'd just taken things a little slower, not jumped straight into sex, things might have turned out differently.

All weekend long, as he sat looking at the night-dark windowpanes, or moved about his room, he thought about Kyle's words. Could Kyle be right? Was it perhaps just fear and nervousness that had compressed and dropped inside him, like a cork shoved down into the wine, which ever afterwards inhibited the flow? Perhaps his impotence was simply a result of that: the pressure and the fear. But, even if that were the case, what then? How could he ever steel himself to test this theory out again?

———

As Justin walked to class that Monday, he absolutely dreaded seeing Laura. What in the world could they say to one another? Would she even talk to him? Luckily, he didn't see her as he entered and took a seat. As he sat, he felt the radiator's dry heat start to make him sleepy. Then, just as class was starting, Laura breezed in late again and -- smiling at him shyly, which surprised him -- took a seat across the room. All class long, Justin thought about that smile. What could that mean? She'd seemed almost bashful as she'd done it; but she hadn't seemed unfriendly. Midway through, he made his mind up he would try to talk to her after class; but then, he kept on trying to decide if that was wise. Their teacher wrapped up his discussion on Greek drama, then gave details about the final exam. As Laura stood and picked up all her things, he whipped his coat on, grabbed his book, and made his way across the room.

"Hi," said Justin tentatively.

"Hi," said Laura, moving out the door into the hall. He followed her a little awkwardly, not certain whether he should pursue talking to her after all; yet again, Laura didn't seem unwelcoming.

"Can I talk to you a minute?" he said at last.

"Sure. Why don't we go outside."

They walked out through the main hall's double doors (this time no monkeying: he boldly pushed them open), then stepped out onto the quad. The sidewalks intersected at a point, then radiated out from them to reach a red-bricked, 60s-era dining hall and several other dorms. The lawns were frozen yellow now, and hard. A massive, black-limbed chestnut tree stood nakedly off to their left, a gray squirrel foraging for something underneath. There, in the center of the quad, they stopped, both blowing steam.

"Listen, I know you probably don't even want to talk to me, but I just wanted you to know I'm sorry about the other night."

"Oh, don't be silly." Laura smiled weakly. "I'm the one who should be sorry."

"What?" said Justin, taken aback. "Why?"

"Because I always come on too strong. It's a problem for me. Anyway, don't worry. Looking back, I feel sort of ashamed, like I pounced on you. I think I scared you."

"Everything scares me," said Justin defeatedly.

"It does?" said Laura. "Funny, I can't get a bead on you. You certainly don't *seem* scared, or you didn't, anyway, until, well .... " Laura laughed, and Justin had to smile.

"Maybe if I hadn't come on like a freight train."

"No, no," insisted Justin. "It's not your fault."

"We probably just took things a bit too fast."

"Really?" said Justin, surprised but encouraged by this turn. "Because I was sort of thinking the same thing myself, and I'm sorry if that killed it."

"Well, does it have to?" said Laura after a moment. "I don't suppose you'd want to try to start all over again, but slower this time? Maybe we could go to a movie some night?"

"Wow, sure," said Justin in disbelief, only half sure he meant it. "When are you free?"

"I have to admit, I'm pretty booked this week, with papers and projects, but I'm free Sunday night. That's just before the start of finals, though. Is that all right?"

"That's fine," said Justin, not sure what his schedule was, but figuring he'd change whatever he needed to change: even it if was painful, he knew he had to seize this opportunity -- to put an end to this doubt once and for all. "How about I pick you up around seven?"

"All right," said Laura. She smiled weakly again, and Justin suddenly was not sure what to do. Should he kiss her now, or no? Feeling constricted, he merely said, "Okay, I'll see you then."

As Laura waved and walked off on her separate spoke of sidewalk, Justin's smile changed from one of happy disbelief to one of panic. Was he an idiot? How could he go through all of this again? Why in the world did Laura want to? Yet, another part of him was pleased: an ember he had thought extinguished for all time was flaring up again. Whether he got burned by it, ultimately, or watched it go out completely, either way he'd know for certain now whether it was ever going to catch fire.

All week, he thought about their date, anticipating, fearing, speculating. He scarcely said a word to Kyle or Craig -- not certain what to say -- and, when he stood outside Laura's door again that night, it was as though he'd been caught in a time warp. Everything was still the same: the thinking he had done this week had brought back all the nervousness and fear he'd felt before, and for a second, Justin thought of flying down the hall and flinging himself off balcony, like the girl who'd tried to cast love out: that desperate attempt to get outside the body and away from its desires -- to literally fly free of them. But then the door was opening and Laura stood before him once again, and Justin walked into the hyper-feminine boudoir: an actor walking through the scene again, to try to get it right. He leaned down to kiss her on the cheek, and Laura looked surprised.

"Oh, thanks." She stood there, flustered for a moment, then said. "I'm still getting ready. Sorry. Would you like some wine? I'll only be a minute."

"Thanks," said Justin as she headed back into her bathroom. Looking round, he found two glasses on her dresser, and a bottle on her coffee table. He looked inside her little brown refrigerator for an open bottle, but there wasn't one. Still, he wasn't certain whether he should open up a brand new bottle: he feared it might commit them into staying there a while. He picked the corkscrew up and fiddled with it, then decided he would go ahead. He'd only used a cork-screw once or twice before, and he felt suddenly tremendously unworldly. He'd heard Kyle talk about his summer waiting tables -- how he'd had to open up the wine for people as they watched. The thought made Justin cringe, feel terribly inferior: he couldn't even pee with someone standing next to him, yet Kyle could pop champagne as people watched, and had no trouble having sex. *Calm down*, he told himself. Then, in a minute, to his immense satisfaction Justin had the bottle opened up, and poured two glasses, which he set down on the steamer trunk. He noticed Thornton's yearbook on the top and started looking at it idly. *Thornton College 1978* was silver grey, and smaller than his high school yearbook: there were, after all, only 500 students in the whole school. There were pictures of the seniors, candids in the Student Union, pictures of the underclassmen and the clubs, among them Thespians and Madrigals. Then, Justin turned a page and there, bare from the waist up, was a photograph of Kyle, his black-haired torso glistening with sweat. It was a picture from a dorm event -- some relay race which Kyle had apparently participated in. Until now, he'd never thought about the fact that Laura's years and Kyle's on campus coincided. Now though, Justin started hunting through the book to try to locate other photographs of Kyle, then turned back to the beefcake photo, staring at it hard.

"I see you've found the yearbooks," Laura said.

Justin felt like she had caught him masturbating. Sheepishly, he set the book down, wondering if she had seen what he was looking at.

Then, Laura sat beside him innocently, saying, "Sorry I took so long."

"Oh, not a problem." Nervous and self-conscious, Justin handed her a glass, avoiding the offending yearbook.

"Thank you," Laura said, and smiled. "You want to see some really awful pictures of me?"

"Sure," he said, feeling guilty still, and noticing her thighs pressed up against his own as Laura grabbed the book. His felt his penis stiffening, and as she pointed at the random photos of herself, he tried to focus on her words. He took a larger swig of wine than he had ever done before, then watched her hunt about to find herself. She pointed out a photo of herself in choir, in dormitory group shots, and he grew aware that he was growing even harder, like a fire that manufactures its own wind. The wine was burning in his stomach, and his groin was growing hungry as a mouth.

She touched his knee and said, "Oh, God, you can't see this one: it's too horrible!"

Her fingers lingered on the inside of his knee, and Justin felt a jolt run through him from her hand straight to his crotch.

"Here, let me see," he said, his hand now brushing hers. He felt too shy to look her in the face, and yet, her eyes were there beside him, warm and green, her lips warm, red, and full. He kissed her, leaning over so the book slid to the floor, then somehow was on top of her, his hips pressed hard into her lap, a wave of lust consuming him. He closed his eyes, to glory in the feel of it, then opened them and glanced down at the floor to see if there was any chance the book had fallen open to Kyle's photograph. It hadn't, and he cursed himself for even thinking of it. He was totally aroused now, feeling Laura underneath him, feeling what a man should feel.

"Wait," said Laura breathlessly. "I thought we weren't going to do this?"

"It's okay," he said, surprised to feel so strong, so masculine. It was as though, somehow, the photograph of Kyle had given him a model. As he moved now, he was conscious of the Kyle that opened up wine bottles unselfconsciously in front of other people -- became him -- then was conscious of the thought of being in Kyle's body, moving with Kyle's muscles, and this thought suffused him now with wondrous new excitement and arousal.

"You're sure?" said Laura.

"I am," said Justin. As he stood up now and carried her into the bedroom (something he would never dream he could have done before), he felt like he was Kyle, and in his arms was Maureen. They were on their honeymoon, Kyle's torso poised above hers, entering her masculinely. As he pulled off clothes and climbed beneath the covers in the moonlight, he began to rub against her body bluntly, gracelessly, until she reached down patiently to guide him into her.

"Wait, don't I need to put a condom on?" he said, the warning voice of Kyle's responsibility instructing him.

"Well, aren't you sweet? Don't worry, though, I'm on the pill."

"Oh," said Justin, remembering the agony of traipsing to the drug store earlier that week and asking for the anguished "prophylactics," all for nought. He felt himself slip in her then, his penis gliding till it felt as though he'd hit a bone. He was surprised at that: he'd always thought the feeling would be one of being swallowed, of complete envelopment; and yet, as he continued pushing in and out, he felt like he was only half inside, as though he couldn't thrust as deep and hard as he would like. To counter that, he flashed again on how Kyle's body must have looked and felt as Kyle had entered Maureen, Justin summoning an image of Kyle's penis, thick and hard; and, in a few, short minutes, lost within his reverie, he felt his own eruption bursting from him. Laura gasped when Justin came, hips arching as she grabbed his hair and pulled, the two of them collapsing afterward and drifting into sleep.

Now, as he lay there in the night beside her, pallid winter moonlight falling on their naked bodies from the window, Justin felt a curious and blank elation. He had done it! He could scarcely believe it, but he had! He'd been the man Kyle would have been, and he had nothing now to fear or envy. Looking at her there beside him in the windowpane-striped silver light, an ochre nipple poking out above the sheet, he said it to himself time and again: *I'm normal. I've had sex now with a woman. I'm a man.* Why did it still seem just a little unconvincing?

CHAPTER 9

NEXT MORNING, HEADING HOME THOUGH, Justin felt an almost out-of-bounds elation as he walked across the early morning campus, thinking how he'd share this news with Kyle and Craig; imagining the looks upon their faces as he told them what had happened -- how he'd proved himself with Laura. All his fears and worries seemed so groundless in this light! The shadows on the quad were shortening, contracting, every object snapping into place as light arrived. He saw each rock, each indentation on the red-bricked buildings, every pane of glass up in the stone-carved, Gothic windows of the chapel, in a new and different way. It was as though his soul were freed, as though he saw things only now quite clearly, plainly: as if all the shadows and the clouds had suddenly dispersed, and he could see each color and each thing in fresh-washed light. In this mood, he imagined telling Kyle, at some point far into the future, of his (obviously naïve) fears about his sexuality -- about the fact that he had even feared once that he was in love with Kyle himself. He thought how they might laugh at that: two adult friends recalling youthful foibles, thinking suddenly with melancholy of how innocent those days and years had seemed -- how trifling those concerns.

He reached his dorm and entered in the early morning stillness, shaking off the chill of campus. Since their finals week officially began today, some students were about: those students who had pulled all-nighters were wandering the halls, while others, who had 8:00 exams, were headed to the dining hall to get some breakfast. He felt suddenly outside of all of this -- outside of school right now. He had a test tomorrow, but he didn't care a bit. The world seemed different to him, changed: he'd passed the biggest test of all, and nothing else seemed capable of touching him.

He opened up his door a little timidly -- with Jacob, he could never tell what he might find -- but Jacob must have had a final, or stayed overnight somewhere. Stale beer in plastic cups and empty potato chip bags littered the room: Jacob must have scored last night. Well, he had, too. Justin slipped his clothes off, grabbed his gear, and headed toward the showers, anxious to be done with cleaning up, so he could head to Craig's to break the news. He showered quickly, almost sad now as the evidence of Laura slipped away from him and down the drain. Then, when he'd dressed, he headed out to Craig's room, not sure whether Craig would be awake, but almost bursting with the need to share his news.

Craig's dorm was quiet, too. As he climbed the stairs up to the third floor and reached his wing, he found Craig's door was open. Craig was up already, sprawled across his bed with tea cup in his hands, books spread around him on the bed.

"Hey," said Justin.

"Hi, how you doing?"

"Fantastic," said Justin coming in. He felt bold and masculine, returning from the room of his most recent conquest with the winter air upon his clothes. As he sat beside Craig on the bed, he was conscious of the difference in him: they were just two friends now, no uncertainty at all about his sexuality.

Craig looked up at him. "You look happy."

"I am. I slept with Laura last night."

Craig looked at him, speechless. "You did what? You mean .... "

"Um hmm. I think you're right," said Justin, beaming. " I think it *was* just nervousness."

"Wow," said Craig, seemingly taken aback. "You really think that's all it was?"

"I think so, yeah," said Justin, hesitating. "Why, don't you?"

"Well, no. I mean, I don't know. That's great," he said uncertainly. "That's great. So, tell me everything."

He was on the verge of speaking when they heard a knock and Kyle walked in.

"Hey, guys," said Kyle, all bushy beard and smiles. "What's up?"

Craig smirked at Justin. "Well, this guy was, I guess -- all night, it seems."

Kyle closed the door and sat beside them on the bed. A steely smell of morning came in on his clothes, as if they'd just been freshly ironed, and Justin felt the bed bounce from his absolute solidity. Kyle's torso towered next to him, a muscular exuberance emanating from him even from beneath his winter coat, and Justin felt himself begin to slide a little way into the deep declivity Kyle's body made.

"What's this?" said Kyle.

"I spent the night with Laura last night." He felt a bit ashamed at saying this, considering what Kyle had said before about not rushing into sex, and yet his pride won out.

Kyle slapped himself upon the forehead comically and laughed. "Oh, boy. So much for going slow, huh?"

"Yeah," said Justin.

"What a lady killer this guy is!" Kyle turned to Craig now. "You and I could take some lessons from this little devil."

Kyle reached out and chucked him on the chin, and Justin felt both pleased and somehow saddened. Suddenly now, he realized there wasn't any turning back; when he told them that he'd slept with Laura, he had crossed a barrier of some kind, and on the other side stood Kyle. Kyle slapped him on the back, and Justin tried to tell himself that he was being silly: everything was different now, and it was better. Still, as close as Kyle was right now, Justin felt as though a little glass wall separated them: a wall preventing him from touching Kyle.

———◆———

In the dining hall at lunch that afternoon, the three of them were laughing, talking over Christmas plans, and he felt flushed with love for both of them. It was the same love Justin always felt, yet somehow magnified today, increased by his success with Laura.

"Hey," said Craig. "Here comes your squeeze."

He looked across the room, saw Laura walking with her tray, and only then did he connect the phrase, "your squeeze" to her.

"Oh, yes," he said, for lack of something else to say. He felt a strange indifference, and a certain helplessness. It was as though he'd never thought beyond last night, had never thought how he and Laura would relate from here on out. Were they now "a couple" then, and did he treat her that way? Somehow, he had never thought of that. Now, as he thought about the consequences -- of the expectations Kyle and Craig and Laura had -- he felt absolutely unprepared.

"Will Laura come and sit with us, is what I want to know," said Craig a little impishly. "How public is this 'thing' you guys have?"

"I don't see why not," said Justin, conscious of their eyes upon him, of the way he knew he should behave.

As Laura neared, however, she looked lost, preoccupied, and didn't seem to see them.

For a second, Justin thought she was headed somewhere else; he almost hoped she was. But, as she neared, he flagged her down.

"Laura, would you like to sit with us?"

"Oh," she said, as if awaking from a daze. "Thanks." She sat down next to Justin and glanced at him a little shyly.

"Do you guys know each other?" Justin said. "This is Kyle Rhodes and Craig Anderson. And this is Laura Dickinson."

"Hi," said Kyle. "I know you, but I don't *know* you."

"Right," said Laura. "I've seen you before, but never knew the name."

"Exactly," said Kyle.

"I think I've had a class with you," said Craig.

"Oh?"

"Yeah, Psych 100, I think" said Craig.

"Oh, God, yes," said Laura. "One of those 8 a.m. classes. How could I forget? I drank so much coffee that semester trying to stay awake."

"You and me both," said Craig. "I think I probably slept through most of it."

"Me, too."

"Well," said Craig. "I guess we *must* know each other, then, seeing that the two of us have slept together .... "

Justin felt himself begin to blush, the color rising in his cheeks, but Laura laughed, the same loud, earthy laugh she'd laughed when Justin told his joke the other day. "I guess so," she said.

Craig flashed a brief, *What was I thinking?* look at Justin, then sheepishly went back to eating.

"What's your major?" said Kyle to Laura, rescuing them from the awkwardness.

"Marketing."

"Ah," said Kyle. "I have a Business minor. Psych's my major."

"So you can psych the competition out?" said Laura.

"Hopefully."

"Psych and Business," said Laura, gravitating disconcertingly to Kyle. "That's interesting. Are you thinking of going into corporate psychology or something like that?"

"I'm not sure, really. I'd actually like to be a therapist, but I haven't quite decided yet about going on for a Ph.D."

"We should talk sometime," said Laura. "I'd be interested in hearing what you decide."

"Sure," said Kyle. "Well, I hate to race off, but I have a Child Psych final in an hour. Nice meeting you."

"You, too," said Laura, smiling at him as he stood.

Justin felt a little throb of jealousy at the way she looked at Kyle -- the quick but shy, approving glance: it was the way so many people seemed to look at Kyle.

"I have to run off, too," said Craig. "I have a Painting final in half an hour, and I still don't know my primary colors yet."

"Oh, well," laughed Laura. "Good luck."

Kyle and Craig picked up their trays and left, and Justin felt the weight of expectation settling upon him. He looked at Laura shyly now, not certain what to say.

"So, how are you?" said Laura.

"Just fine. I want to thank you for last night."

"I had a good time, too." She paused, then said, "So what's the plan?"

"I beg your pardon?"

"What does your finals schedule look like?"

"Oh," said Justin. He had thought she meant, *What is the plan for you and me?*

"I have a test tomorrow, but that's no problem," he said, regaining himself. "Then I have two Wednesday, and the last one on Thursday."

"Would you like to stop by my apartment after dinner?"

"Sure," said Justin, feeling trapped and panicked suddenly, and not sure why. Hadn't he been successful last night? On the other hand, would Laura want him dropping by to see her every night now? When would he see Kyle and Craig, if that were the case? Justin pushed the thought out of his mind and said, "What time?"

"How about at seven?"

"That's fine," said Justin, feeling still a bit conflicted.

"Good," said Laura, smiling happily.

They took their trays to the conveyor belt, and as they walked out, Justin felt tremendously self-conscious. He wasn't certain where to put his hands, and felt like everyone was watching them: the brand new item on the campus. He reached out shyly, taking Laura's hand, and for a moment, they were boyfriend/girlfriend exiting the cafeteria.

"Aren't you sweet," said Laura, looking up at him, surprised.

They moved out to the frigid quad and stopped, and Justin felt the cold air hitting him. The campus seemed in limbo: breathless, motionless, as Justin pecked her on the cheek.

"See you tonight at seven, then," he said, and smiled weakly.

"I'll be waiting," said Laura, looking pleased, and moving off obliquely toward her dorm.

As Justin turned and walked across the stiff grass toward his own room, he felt confused. The two of them had slept together now, but he was troubled by the fact that all of it felt so mechanical to him, so like it wasn't from the heart. And if it wasn't from the heart, what did that mean? He really didn't think he was supposed to be in love with Laura yet, or was he? They'd had sex, and yet he hardly knew her -- certainly, he didn't feel for her a tenth of what he felt for

Kyle or Craig. But might that change? Somehow, it all felt very much a sham to him right now, and he was not sure what to do. How could they take it slower now -- now that they'd slept together, and he'd started treating her as though she were his girlfriend? Kyle was right: they *had* gone way too fast. But what else could he do? There was no going back.

———◆———

As Justin stood outside her room that night, he still felt awkward, pressured. Justin knocked, and Laura opened up the door, dressed modestly in jeans and sweatshirt, hair pulled back. Before he even could say "Hi," she'd pecked him on the cheek and stood there smiling.

"Hi, how are you?"

"Fine. Come on in."

"How'd your test go?"

"Oh, all right." She motioned to the couch, and after taking off his jacket, he sat down. She settled next to him familiarly, long legs folded underneath her.

"When are your other tests?"

"That was my only one. My other classes all had projects or a paper. So, I'm done."

"Oh," Justin said. "When are you leaving, then?"

"I haven't made my mind up yet." She looked at Justin, as if this decision rested partially on him. "I could have left tonight if I'd really wanted to. Instead, I'll probably leave tomorrow afternoon. When's your last final?"

"I'll be here 'til the bitter end, on Thursday."

"Ouch," said Laura.

"Yeah. So, are you going to your parents for the holiday?"

"I'll be with my mom on Christmas day. For most of it, though, I'll be staying with some friends down by St. Louis. My parents are divorced, and I've been gone from home a while, so going back home isn't really a big deal for me."

"Oh," said Justin, not sure what to say. A look came into Laura's face now, something he had seen before: a look which touched him, but which also made him feel a certain helplessness. Her face looked simultaneously wounded and defiant, self-sufficient and yet full of need. Justin wished he could move like a lover through the space between them and erase that need somehow. He reached to touch her cheek, and Laura started.

"Sorry."

"No, I'm sorry," Laura said. "You just keep surprising me."

"What do you mean?"

"I keep on getting different vibes from you. I wasn't sure I'd ever see you again after that first night. Then, there you were. And then, after we'd slept together, I thought: Well, that's it. But there you were again. And now, here you are again."

"You thought I'd just drop you after having sex?" said Justin, trying to deflect the rightness of her words.

"I wasn't sure. As I said, I think you're really sweet and all, but I keep picking up contradictory messages. Like today, in the cafeteria, when you took my hand, just like we were a couple or something. That really surprised me."

"And aren't we a couple?"

"I'm not sure. Is that what you want?"

"I think so. Yes," said Justin, wondering if it sounded as hollow to her as it did to him. "Why wouldn't I?"

"I don't know. I just wasn't sure if that's what *you* wanted."

"I think a lot of it is just my inexperience," said Justin, feeling scared, defensive, and a little startled by her frankness. He was not sure what to do, but thought a kiss would somehow ease the awkwardness. He leaned to kiss her, and she watched him coming toward her. He was hoping to persuade her -- hoping to persuade himself -- of his sincerity. Still, as they kissed more fervently, as Justin felt himself take on the role of Kyle -- moved in the guise of being in Kyle's body, and felt himself grow stimulated by that once again -- he also felt dishonest, watching Laura be won over by someone who wasn't him. Before, he told himself, he hadn't known for certain where his own arousal came from. He had seen Kyle's picture, and had been aware he was aroused. But Laura's legs were touching his the whole time, and there hadn't really been a clear-cut line. This time, though, he felt quite certain his arousal didn't have a thing to do with Laura. It was only as he thought of Kyle that his erection grew, and Justin felt it fan the flames -- felt his desire mount. Then, in a short time, lust consuming him as he imagined being in Kyle's skin, it was as though he, Justin, weren't there anymore at all.

It was the same when, later, after making love and drifting off to sleep exhaustedly beside each other, he awoke and felt her body next to his: one stranger sleeping vacantly beside an even greater stranger. Carefully, he peeled the comforter aside and moved across the room to be away from her a moment. Everything inside the frigid, dust-still room was silent as he crossed and pulled the curtains back to look out at the inky quad, its street lamps not illuminating anything, just doing more to call attention to the utter dark.

He went into her bathroom, flipped the light on, and was surprised to see the way the room was decorated. Laura's bedroom had peach colored walls, and was full of pastel pinks and blues. This room, though -- possibly a remnant of the decorations of the previous resident -- was silver and black, with huge, stylized yellow sunflowers on the foil wallpaper. The mirror was a 1950s Deco vanity with beveled glass, and it was markedly in contrast to the early 1970s update. Looking at himself here in the midst of all this incongruity, he felt a shock to see the same old visage looking back at him. What was he doing here? What had he done? What kind of man was he, to treat a person this way, when he knew he didn't really feel a thing for her? Looking at himself now on the inconsistent wall, he wasn't sure how he could crawl back in the bed again, assume the role of someone he was growing more and more aware that he was not; yet, he was also not sure how he couldn't.

He left the disconcerting room at last and, walking out, could see the pale light glowing on Laura's dreaming body. He was trying to decide if he should leave, put on his clothes and go. But in the next moment, conflicted, he crossed the room and sat atop the comforter despite the chill. He watched her guileless, trusting face, and leaned down to kiss her softly on her shoulder, warm breath playing on her skin, the coolness of the peach-toned satin she was wrapped in warming to him. Lying down beside this sexless package, feeling only warmth and bulk, he felt now, for the first and only time that night, relief. As Justin lay beside her then, he hoped that Laura would not waken in this dim, intransigent half-light, or seek to kiss him passionately, touching him in order to rekindle roles of sexes that opposed each other in the dark. Deep in his heart beside her on the bed, he wished that he had not been born a man, nor she a woman.

Just then, though, Laura stirred beneath the covers, turned, and reached to touch him. Justin lifted up her hand from where it fumbled at his hips and kissed it, as if hoping somehow to deny its implications.

Next morning, he and Laura said goodbye a little awkwardly.

"You think you'll leave today, then?" Justin said.

"Yes, I think I will," she said uncertainly.

"Will I see you at lunch?

"Maybe we should say goodbye now," said Laura, looking at him for some sign. "I'm not sure when I'll take off."

Justin steeled himself to ignore her need, bad as he felt about it. "Okay," he said, leaning in to kiss her.

"Well, take care," said Laura.

"You, too."

As Justin closed her door and left, he was both disgusted with himself, yet incredibly relieved. Despite himself, he realized, with sudden joy, this left him free to spend these last few days with Kyle and Craig. Somehow, right now, that was all that mattered to him.

The last night of the term, he, Kyle, and Craig were sitting once again at dinner. The campus would officially close tomorrow, and the halls all had that empty, vacant, wintry feeling. Many of the students had departed, and the ones that still remained seem tired, their minds now focused on the holidays.

"Are you guys coming to the party in my dorm tonight?" said Kyle. "Sounds like it should be pretty wild."

"*I* am," said Justin, primed for being with the two of them.

"I think I'll take a pass," said Craig. "Estelle and I are going to try to fit in one last date. Plus, I have to get out of here at the crack of dawn tomorrow, so I probably should say goodbye to you guys now." Estelle was the girl he'd taken to the movie recently, and Craig had been spending more and more time with her lately.

"Things are getting pretty serious between you two, huh?" said Kyle.

"They're developing nicely, thank you," said Craig comically. "Of course, nothing like this guy here." He nudged Justin, and for a second Justin had to think what he was talking about. Then, when he realized, he clutched.

"Estelle and I still haven't *slept* together, like some people I know," continued Craig.

"Oh, but that's okay," said Justin, "since, as you say, you and Laura seem to have slept together already. Besides," said Justin after a moment, conscious of falling into the role of the young stud: "there's always that 'last night' thing you could take advantage of."

"Yeah, right," said Craig. "Estelle is *very* Catholic, let me tell you. Who knows when -- if ever -- that will happen. Most likely, not until she's married."

"Wow," said Kyle. "You sure know how to pick 'em."

"Yeah, but I think she's worth it," said Craig. "Sometimes love is worth the wait."

"Good for you," said Kyle, clearly impressed. "I was just being a dick. Sorry." He smiled, one of those smiles that made the world seem right, then turned to Justin. "So, when is Laura leaving?"

"Laura's gone," said Justin with barely concealed satisfaction.

"Ah," said Kyle. "Are you two going to talk to each other over break?"

"Yeah, I guess so," said Justin noncommittally, annoyed again at being snapped back into the reality of his situation, reminded of the consequences.

"He guesses so," said Kyle. "My boy, my boy. Let me offer you some advice: a woman likes to be *appreciated* a little bit. Not calling her up over break when you've just started sleeping with her, for instance, might be something of a bad move, if you catch my drift. Then again, who am *I* to be offering *this* guy advice?"

"Yeah, yeah," said Justin, cringing at his dishonesty, and feeling bad again about acting in this charade.

After they had said goodbye to Craig, Kyle turned towards Justin. "So, looks like it's just you and me tonight, huh buddy?"

"That's right," said Justin, beaming suddenly as Kyle began to rub his shoulders, swaying them in opposite directions like the flimsy corners of a large sheet of plywood: "You and me."

———

That evening at the party, though, Justin felt a wave of sadness overtaking him. The party was a loud affair, the students sparse yet boisterous, but there was something sad and desperate and thinly concealed beneath the surface of it. He was thinking of how awful everything with Laura was, how complicated it had all become, as well as about Kyle and Craig, and how -- soon -- the two of them would graduate and leave him here alone at school. He felt the beer beginning to affect his head, and thought of leaving; but the thought of bidding Kyle goodbye prevented him. He wished there were some way he could have talked to Kyle, but he was scared of doing that, and anyway, wasn't it possible -- just barely possible, still -- that even after all this, he was still wrong? Possible that Laura simply wasn't someone he could love, but that there was still a woman out there waiting for him somewhere? He didn't really think so anymore, but he was also confused and drunk and desperately lonely at the thought of walking back to his empty dorm room alone. He wished again that he and Kyle could be alone to talk this over, that maybe he could even stay at Kyle's tonight; and yet, he also felt afraid to ask that.

A short time later, though, he found himself begin to waiver: what was wrong with asking Kyle if he could stay over in his room with him? They were as close as friends could be. Still, it was a while before he worked his courage up to say, "Kyle, could I crash here on your couch tonight? I'm really drunk."

Kyle slapped him on the back enthusiastically. "No problem, bud. Just let me finish this beer. Mi casa es su casa."

Kyle's voice was hoarse, inebriate, and Justin vacillated over whether he should back out now. Was he so drunk he couldn't stumble back across the cold quad to his room?

But then, Kyle was tapping him upon the shoulder and they were stumbling down the stark, reverberating hall to Kyle's room, flicking on the light and shutting out the noise behind them. They stood for a moment, Justin feeling suddenly self-conscious and dishonest in the harsh fluorescent light. Then Kyle was grasping him in an inebriated hug, and Justin found himself responding with a burgeoning intensity. Kyle smelled of stale beer, sweat, and in Kyle's arms, he felt his groin swell; felt the tears beginning -- tears he sniffled back immediately.

"I'm gonna miss you, bud," said Kyle.

"Me, too," said Justin, feeling everything inside him fall into place within Kyle's arms. It was as if his body rose, then settled, like a boiling pan that, with the flame removed, calms down to stillness once again.

Then Kyle was struggling to pull his shirt and pants off, toppling heavily onto the mattress on the floor, and Justin looked at Kyle's body clad in only underwear: this body he had spent so many moments agonizing over, and which he'd told himself he didn't love, but which he found it hard to say now that he didn't. Kyle was lying on the floor, out cold, his chest hair matted and disheveled in his drunkenness. Justin thought again that he should leave -- he wasn't all that drunk -- then started shyly taking off his shirt and pants, and sat down gingerly upon the sofa. Kyle was breathing hard already, and as Justin leaned back on his elbows, he could feel the room begin to spin. He looked at Kyle, took in his deep-set eyes, the heavy shoulders and the graceful collarbone, and felt his penis aching stiffly and implacably. He wished now he could lay his cheek against Kyle's beard, or lose himself against that chest. He flashed on Laura laying there beside him in the moonlight: how different he had felt then in comparison to this! The things he'd done, the promises he'd made since then -- all that had been a sham! Kyle's underpants were bunched around his muscled legs, the leg holes open slightly at the crotch, the whiteness barely covering Kyle's dark, soft genitals, and Justin felt the tears appearing in his eyes. He was ashamed that he had looked, that he had had these thoughts -- had transgressed in this friendship so. He watched Kyle's hairy stomach heaving in and blowing out, felt suddenly the too-long squelched desire begin to mount and knew he had to leave. He pulled his pants back on, slipped on his shoes and coat and said, "I think I'll head back after all, Kyle. You have a safe trip." Kyle didn't stir, and Justin leaned down, speaking too loud, trying to make him understand.

"Kyle."

"What?" said Kyle groggily.

"I'm heading back. You have a great vacation."

"Okay. You too."

Outside, the dull blast of the hallway hit him with its noise and light, the party still in full swing down the hall. He tumbled down the stairs and raced across the frozen campus in the dark calm, stumbling in the snow and lying there face down for a moment. Even in the pack of ice, the yearning in his penis was unquenchable, a voraciousness that couldn't be appeased. He wished the snow would freeze his penis off, so that, at last, he might walk sexless though the world, without desire. He wished they'd find his frozen corpse here in the drift tomorrow, all his struggles over. Desperately, he pressed his hips into the snowbank, breathing hard into the snow. At last, ashamed, outcast, he picked himself up slowly, listlessly, then headed back across the frozen campus to his empty dorm.

Inside his room, ensuring first that Jacob had, indeed, left, Justin threw his coat down on the floor, whipped off his belt and opened up his pants, his penis rigid as a dandelion stalk: try as he might to yank desire for men out of his soul, the root had stayed there, sprouting back as irrepressibly as dandelions in a lawn. He massaged the shaft, the head, felt how the penis strained to meet his touch. He thought of Kyle again, then squeezed the angry shaft as if to force the blood back in his body. Suddenly, he felt as though he might explode. He worked his hands along the shaft, his penis so engorged there was no loose skin to massage it with: the length of it was filled with Kyle. He grasped it, doubling over at the feel, and felt a thunder welling up inside -- a force, acropetal -- which he felt powerless to stop. He thought again of Kyle: the hairy bellows of his stomach; pumped tearfully and desperately, his hips unleashing handful after handful of his sperm, seed spraying in the air the way the seeds had flown that day out in the dandelion field: caught lightly in the wind or plopping heavily as spit upon the ugly, blue-green carpeting.

There, jismed in the winter light of the abandoned dorm, he realized now, unmistakably, he was in love.

BOOK II

———

Before I was in love I, too, knew what love was.

ANTON CHEKHOV

CHAPTER 1

———•———

At home that Christmas, Justin felt more isolated than he ever had before. All through the long drive home, through bleak and frozen cornfields, past soulless urban malls and houses outlined to the hilt in garish, flashing bulbs, he felt like all of it was false. Or was it that *he* was the false note in this cheerful Christmas landscape? As Justin's mother prattled on about plans for the holidays, he couldn't concentrate. He kept replaying in his mind the little plops of jism on the floor, the awful certitude of what he'd done. This, then, was who he was, the evidence of what he felt for Kyle spilled out across his hands, across the cruddy carpet of his room, its floor stained with the stains of countless other unknown, wasted things. He was in love with Kyle. He was a gay man: gay, gay, gay, and there was nothing he could do, apparently, to change that.

In the car, his mother -- surprising him this holiday by picking him up instead of his father -- spoke as if he were the same child she had always known, and he was trying not to scream. She had no notion who he was now, who he'd ever been. What would she say if she knew the truth? She had never even met Kyle, never knew his trials with Laura. He was totally and completely alien to her -- to both his parents. And he felt even more a stranger to himself.

As they'd turned off the highway onto I-55 at the start of their long drive north, he'd gotten yet another jolt. Driving along the highway, which paralleled the small town of the college, now visible through the denuded winter trees, he'd suddenly seen the campus in the distance going by: cafeteria, main hall, and then his dorm. But the order of it wasn't right.

"Wait," said Justin. "You want to be going north."

"Oh, did I take a wrong turn?" said his mother. She looked at the dashboard, then said, "Well, the compass says we're going north."

"That can't be right."

As Justin looked up at the dashboard, though, he saw that it was true -- saw suddenly the whole town laid out in reverse of how he'd thought it had been set up that whole semester in his mind: the cafeteria due south instead of north, his dorm due south -- all of it just the opposite of what he'd thought. "But how?" said Justin, struggling for the next few minutes to resolve the orientation in his mind, thinking through the lefts and rights that got them to the place they were now, trying to make it right, but failing. How had he gotten so confused? He still could not quite figure it out. After they'd continued resolutely in the same direction for a long while, he said simply, "I got turned around somehow, I guess."

All through the holidays, he felt a similar confusion, discombobulation, and restlessness. He thought repeatedly of calling Kyle -- confessing everything -- then thought about him, busy with Maureen, and quashed the idea. He thought of calling Craig, but that, too, seemed too complicated. There was so much to explain, so much that was embarrassing, and so much he was still unsure of. All he knew was that he felt alone, ashamed, and sordid. And the truth of what and who he was seemed inescapable at last.

One day, in January, the start of school still more than a week away, the Christmas season having come and gone rather mechanically, Justin borrowed his mother's brand-new, divorce-consolation car and headed out to Readmore Bookworld in the next town over, Rock Island. It was well known as the only bookstore in the area that sold erotic magazines, and as he drove there, he felt determined to take some kind of next step. But, he also felt nervous and ashamed.

Justin drove clandestinely out past his grade school, his heart beating as nervously as if he were skipping school, then kept on driving through a part of town he didn't travel often. Moline was an old town, perched atop the bluffs that overlook the Mississippi river. On the other shore was Davenport, in Iowa; Rock Island lay across the hills that formed the older section of Moline. He passed huge, old, Queen Anne and Second Empire mansions: three-story houses gazing blankly at the river moving lazily below. He turned and headed toward the oneway now: an ugly, semi-interstate that headed straight past Augustana College, past the railroad tracks and factories, and toward the land of the forbidden content.

As Justin pulled into the bookstore parking lot, filled with a few stray cars, he felt his heart begin to race with fear. He stopped the car and looked up at the ugly, beige, brick wall in front of him, only vaguely aware of what lay inside. It was a Thursday morning, 10:00 a.m., and he had told his mother he was going shopping. He sat there for a moment longer, trying to decide whether he should actually go in. What would he say if anybody saw him? Was he old enough to enter? What if someone should approach him inside? Justin took a breath and opened up his frosty car door. As he locked it, he checked two or three times to make certain he had the car keys in his hand: to lock himself out here and have to have someone come rescue him would be disastrous. He walked around the side and opened up the bookstore's black door, trying not to look back toward the street.

Inside, the store smelled hugely of newsprint, but was nicer than he'd thought, with racks of paperbacks and wood plank shelving holding hardbacks. Fully half the store, though, was comprised of periodicals -- two long brown rows of shelving holding them -- and in a corner of this section were a group of men all looking at the porno magazines. He made his way tentatively among the hardbacks, moving, as if absently, from aisle to aisle, then headed down the dirty, white-tiled aisle at last, where *MotorTrend* and *Car and Driver* melded into *Muscular Development* and *Strength and Health*. He stopped a while in front of these, the stunning male physiques displayed so prominently on their covers, then walked still further back to join the group of men perusing *Playboy*, *Hustler*, and the like. Next to these, there was a smaller rack that held *Playguy*, *Mandate*, and *Honcho*, but it took a while before he worked his nerve up to the point where he could actually lift one of these magazines down from the shelf. He wasn't sure if he should look at it right there, or buy the thing and leave, and just then someone shoved him from behind. He moved out of the way to let the man walk past, not sure if he was being merely rude, or if the shove was due to what he chose to look at, but it made him suddenly resolve to stand his ground and take a peek.

The magazine was filled with mostly trashy shots of men with hard-ons: men dressed up in leather harnesses and chaps, or unattractive, slender youths with pimply skin who stuck their asses out pathetically toward the camera. Next to this, there was a *Playgirl*, though, and Justin flipped through page on page of gorgeous men, his penis grown so hard he felt like he might faint. He'd been there now about five minutes, and as someone else squeezed past him, Justin looked up to discover that it was his eighth grade English teacher, Mr. Phipps. Justin was too scared to move, and stood there, shocked, but Mr. Phipps pushed past, not looking back at him.

Justin moved off quickly, but continued watching from behind the stacks. Mr. Phipps glanced at the group of men, then picked a *Honcho* off the shelf -- the magazine that featured men in leather on the cover -- and began to flip through it. Mr. Phipps was in his 50s, thin and angular, with pompadoured blond hair. As Justin watched him, he perused a half a dozen magazines, then picked one up and walked up to the counter, paid, and walked out. Justin stood there, too unnerved to move, then made his way back down the aisle, grabbed a *Playgirl* and a *Mandate* from the shelf, then wasted time inside the store until he thought that Mr. Phipps was probably long gone.

Up at the register, the old man didn't even look at him as he checked out, a pair of black half-glasses riding on his nose. He guessed the man had seen it all, and left the store as quickly as he could.

Outside, he looked around for Mr. Phipps, but luckily didn't see him. He walked quickly to the car and glanced around, but saw no one, and sat there in the cold car glancing through the magazines. He was afraid someone would see him, but he was far too curious to leave before he looked at them. He'd been so overcome with lust before, he'd wished that he could masturbate right there. But Mr. Phipps had scared him -- made him feel both lurid and depressed: this man who'd taught him English, buying porno.

As Justin looked at *Mandate*, which he hadn't liked as much as *Playgirl*, but which he'd bought specifically because he thought that he should buy an out-and-out gay magazine, he couldn't help thinking how strange the gay men looked to him -- how alien and unattractive. None of them looked anything like normal men -- like Kyle -- or like the men in *Playgirl*. Instead, the magazine was filled with photographs of men in crew cuts wearing leather jackets, rings through nipples, and the like. These were the things that Mr. Phipps was looking at now, he reflected. As Justin sat there in the freezing car, the covert magazines spread out upon his lap, he felt adrift, alone. Was this, then, who he was, and what he was supposed to like? Was Mr. Phipps' fate -- buying porno magazines alone when he was 50 -- his fate as well? Was that to be his life? As Justin sat there in the fogged-up car outside the sleazy shop, he'd never felt so far away from Kyle.

CHAPTER 2

———◆———

C OMING BACK TO THORNTON WHEN the holidays were over, Justin wondered what, exactly, it was he was returning to. Was he ready to confront the truth about himself at last? It seemed he was. But was he also ready to have other people know it? That he felt a lot less certain of.

As Justin and his mother drove across the January landscape, snowflakes blowing up across the road, Thornton seemed a nest of traps and nettles waiting for him, Kyle there at the center of it all, the way he'd been out in the dandelion field that fall day months ago. Justin had been pondering all week long what he was going to do about his feelings for Kyle; he almost thought he was going to have to break things off with him, despite the fact he was not sure how he'd ever do that. Yet, he loved Kyle so much that, to keep on feeling all the things he felt -- to sully and transgress the boundaries of their friendship so -- was growing just too hard to bear. The feelings he was having, the clandestine nature of his physical attraction -- all of this -- was clearly wrong, and if that meant he had to break with Kyle, he guessed that he was going to have to do it. How, or if he truly could, he had no clue.

Now, as they drove along, Justin suddenly became aware that his mother, who was driving him back to school this time, hadn't spoken for some time.

"You're very quiet," said Justin.

"Am I? I guess I am. You are, too. Is everything all right?"

"Not really," said Justin, not having anticipated confiding his troubles to his mother, but wondering suddenly whether he should. His mother had seemed so brittle lately, however, that he couldn't imagine discussing this with her until he had things a bit more figured out himself, and she did, too.

"What is it, girlfriend troubles?"

Justin paused, realizing that, in a way, he *did* have a girlfriend problem at the moment, though not in the way his mother meant. One of the things he'd decided over break was that he had to break thing off cleanly and quickly with Laura, though there was no way he wanted to give his mother even a hint that he was seeing anyone. He decided to shift the conversation totally away from himself.

Justin paused, surprised to find himself saying what he was about to say, and feeling suddenly naked and vulnerable as he did so: "Last semester, there was this kid from Thornton who tried to commit suicide, and everybody tried to ignore it until it happened. Sometimes things can be right under your nose, and you don't see them. But you've got to pay attention to them, mom. You have to." Justin found himself getting suddenly very emotional. "You've got to open up your eyes and look at things the way they really are."

"Oh, my dear, " said Justin's mother, looking at him as much as possible while still trying to keep her eyes on the road. "I had no idea! Here I am worrying about myself, and there you are, poor boy, going through all this by yourself! This boy," she continued after a moment. "What was he depressed about?"

Justin debated whether he should mention anything about Steve's being gay, but again decided to steer clear of it. "He was in love with somebody -- somebody who couldn't love him back," he said finally.

"Oh, how awful."

"Yes, it *is.*" said Justin.

"Did you know him well?"

"Fairly well," he said, feeling his defenses begin to kick in.

"Why didn't you ever say anything about it, for heaven's sake? A boy you know tries to commit suicide -- how could you never even mention that?"

"I don't know, mom," he said, guilty and defensive in the ensuing silence. "I guess maybe I feel like I should have done something. That's why I'm feeling guilty." Thinking of all the things he'd left unsaid -- and of all the things he was on the verge of saying -- his heart begin to race.

His mother sighed. "Well, that's horrible news, but I'm glad you told me, and you can't blame yourself. Do you really think you could have done anything to prevent it?"

"I don't know. Probably not," he added, after a moment.

"I think probably not, too." His mother sighed. "Love makes people do some crazy things."

Justin hesitated, uncertain what else to say, but then his mother continued,

"If you want to know why *I'm* quiet, it's because your father and I slept together again. I guess I might as well talk to you about these things: you're an adult now."

"What do you mean, you slept together? I thought you were really mad at him."

"Well, I am, or *was*. But feelings don't just stop, Justin. You can't just shut them off. Your father was over getting some things after you were home for Thanksgiving, and even though he's with Peg now, for some reason -- maybe for old time's sake, I don't know -- we made love. Which would be fine, except it's got me all confused again. I thought I was more or less over your father. I told myself I'd have to go my separate way, then in he walks and upends my life again. The problem is, your father and I have always been in each other's lives, and I'm not sure how to live without that. The love part -- the sexual attraction -- hasn't really been there for a long time. We're like two people who *used* to have feelings like that for each other, but now it's like a distant memory. And yet, we still care about each other, we're friends. So how do I separate the friendship from that love, and vice versa? That's why I'm taking this vacation after I drop you off, to try to sort things out."

"How do you do that?" said Justin.

"I don't know," said his mother.

"No," said Justin after a moment. "I mean, how do you separate out the love part from the friendship?"

"Well, I'm not sure you can," laughed his mother. "You know, I thought I'd die when your father abandoned me. I couldn't believe he could just run off and leave you and me like that. I hated him and Peg, and spent all my time being angry and hurt about the situation. Now, though, I feel like your father didn't so much leave me as go off to try to find himself. Which is what I think I have to do. Somehow, I have to get a bearing on who I am and what I feel."

"I guess that's what we all have to figure out a way to do," said Justin quietly.

After he and his mother had eaten lunch in town (Justin noting, at last, as they turned off the interstate, the one turn he hadn't accounted for before, and understanding now -- finally -- how it was, exactly, that he'd gotten his north and south mixed up all last semester), she'd dropped him back on campus, then continued on her trip.

As Justin walked the empty dorm hallways restlessly, a small fear gnawed at his bowels. The weak light fell in rhomboids on the scuffed-up white tile of the hallway, dust motes rising in the emptiness, and Justin was reminded how the sun had fallen just like this in the hallways his first week last semester, when Sam had helped him move in all his things, and he'd eventually met Kyle and Craig: the two men who had changed his life. A new life seemed in order now, a new life where he faced the truth of who he was. But how hard that was going to be! How hard, considering the love he bore for Kyle and Craig, and the uncertainty of everything that lay ahead. Why couldn't he meet someone who would help him with his feelings? Someone who was not a leather man in harness, or a faded teacher living out his lonely life, or a flamboyant fellow student driven to attempt suicide? Why couldn't he meet somebody like Kyle?

Justin walked into his room filled with the cold, dead weight of things he'd carried in, and wondered whether Kyle or Craig were back yet; Jacob didn't seem to be. He grabbed his coat and boots and headed out across the quad, the Sunday-vacant silence of the snowy campus making him feel ostracized and lonely.

He reached Kyle's dorm and wandered in, stomping off the new, clean snow upon the sodden carpet, a solitary stereo behind a closed door playing Meatloaf's "Two Out of Three Ain't Bad" somewhere. Kyle was not in yet, apparently, so Justin wandered back into the cold across the quad to Craig's room, climbed the stairs in silence, just to find that Craig was not there, either.

Walking back outside into the crunchy snow, he trudged across the campus, wondering what to do. The thought occurred to him to go see Laura -- end that sorry episode at last -- but Justin didn't feel prepared to face that yet. Then, in the middle of the campus, Justin stopped and stood there for a moment, conscious of the silence, of himself clad in his red down jacket and his black boots, standing in the snow. So this was him, just him: this person desperate to find a berth, like some lost ship out on the ocean looking for a port. For a second, all he heard was his own breathing and the sound of blood inside his veins. He watched the frozen campus, ravens flapping noiseless and pathetic in the chestnut's wet black limbs. Poised halfway in between his own dorm, Craig's, and Kyle's, he suddenly felt pathetic and alone. Who was he? What, now, was he seeking? Friendship? Love? What did he hope to find if Kyle or Craig were in? What would he say to them? He watched his breath before him like a cloud, his gonads small and hard as cherry stones here in the cold. He stood a moment more, his glasses fogging up, then felt himself blind-sided by a body hurling at him from his right.

"Woah, woah!" said Justin, cheered as he realized it must be Kyle or Craig. He picked himself up, brushing off the snow, and saw that it was Kyle.

"You *knuckle*head," said Kyle, and Justin felt his spirits start expanding like a sponge. Kyle stood up, brushed the snow off of the two of them, and said,

"How are you?"

"I was fine until you bowled me over." Justin clutched a moment, having heard his *double entendre*.

"How was your vacation?" said Kyle, laughing.

"Fine." He ventured timidly: "I missed you guys."

"I missed you, too. Come here, you stranger."

Kyle hugged him though his plaid wool winter coat, and Justin felt the world begin to slow and center. It was as if the hole he'd had all Christmas in his chest was being covered, calmed and stilled like waters in a lake at sunset. Kyle embraced him hugely for a moment, then released, but Justin hung on for a moment, head still curled to fit Kyle's chest, as though by holding the position of the hug, he might somehow preserve the warmth and feel of it. Kyle smiled, his white teeth perfect, close, and Justin felt himself impelled again toward him, the way a tree leans out across a river when its roots are washed away. He thought another hug was probably excessive, so he merely touched Kyle's arm and stood there rooted and immobile, looking at the light upon Kyle's face. He felt a throb inside him, felt the joy, the ache, the yearning. Yet he also felt a twinge of something else, some vague new fear or dread. His smile faded as he thought, *Yes, here I am, here's Kyle again, and everything is still the same.*

Then, Justin felt himself assaulted from the other side, a blue blur crashing into him, Craig suddenly on top of him and laughing, heavy snow caked whitely in his blond beard.

"Oh, my god, there he is! All right, you savage," Kyle said. "This means war!" Leaping up, Kyle cupped a snowball in his hands and pelted Craig full in the face. An all-out war began as Craig retaliated. Soon, the three of them were running tree to tree, attacking gleefully. Craig hid behind a chestnut tree, and Kyle said, "Come here, you chicken."

"Chicken fight," said Justin, running up and hopping up on Craig's back. For a moment, he and Craig walked toward Kyle threateningly, a kangaroo-like man with curiously foreshortened arms, until Kyle sent them toppling. Craig leaped up and splatted both of them with snowballs.

"Oh, you traitor, you," said Justin. Hopping up and turning now, his back toward Kyle, he said, "Hop on."

"No, no," said Kyle: "I'd break you."

Justin stood a moment, stupidly bent over. "No, you wouldn't," he persisted. "Come on."

"No, that's all right," said Kyle

"All right," said Justin, straightening up, attempting nonchalance but feeling mortified.

All through the evening, though, he felt the sting of that remark, the casual, unconscious cruelty of Kyle considering him a weakling. *As if there were no possibility that I could lift him,* Justin thought resentfully, incessantly. *As if I hadn't borne his monkey on my back this whole year long.*

He still could feel the smart a little later on when Craig went off to find Estelle, and Kyle decided that he'd give a quick call to Maureen. Abandoned suddenly like this, he thought he might as well seek Laura out. If he knew one thing at the moment, it was that he had to break things off with her.

Still, as he sat across from Laura, Justin felt his resolution wavering. He'd knocked reluctantly -- indeed, had walked across the campus to her dorm like someone walking toward his father with the whipping branch that would, eventually, be used on him. She'd opened up the door, face lighting up to see him.

"Hi," she said. "How are you! I'm so glad you stopped by."

"Well, I wanted to come see you," he said guiltily.

They sat down on the white duck sofa, Laura crushing two mauve satin accent pillows as she sat, a pool of warm light from a curved brass reading lamp cascading upon her. Some nerve-wracking, free-form jazz played just a bit too loudly in the background.

"I was hoping I would hear from you over break," said Laura, with some effort at remaining noncommittal.

"I know," said Justin, clutching. "I'm sorry."

"So, how was it?"

"Just fine. And yours?"

"Fine."

"Could I get you some wine?" said Laura after a moment.

"No, thanks" said Justin. The longer he waited, the more his heart pounded. Finally, he knew he simply had to launch into it. "Listen, Laura, I need to talk to you about what's going on with us."

"Okay," said Laura, sounding suddenly on guard.

Even after thinking of this all break long, he still had no idea what he was going to say to her. All Justin knew was that it seemed unfair to her to string her along, when he knew in his heart he didn't feel for her the things he should.

"I feel like things have moved a bit too fast," he said at last.

"Fast how?"

"Well, I think we may have moved too fast in having sex, for one thing."

"Okay," said Laura. "Why was that a problem?"

"I feel like I'm not sure how to relate to you now," said Justin, uncomfortable -- "like a boyfriend or a lover. We didn't really get a chance to get to know each other all that well, and here we are suddenly being very intimate."

"We can take it slower if you want to."

Justin felt surprised, and realized he was botching this. The truth was, he was not sure he saw Laura as a friend; that thought had never really crossed his mind. But since they'd slept together, how could they go back, now that they'd gone as far as they had gone?

"But don't you see? How can we do that? How can we try to get to know each other now, when we've already shared the most intimate thing of all?"

Laura looked at him in that needy and defiant way -- that look that so hopelessly confounded him.

"I'm confused. I really don't think I'm asking you for very much at all. I'm not asking you to be in love with me, just to be my friend -- friends who maybe occasionally also sleep together. Why can't we leave it at that?"

"Because I think that would be too confusing for me."

Laura looked at him trenchantly, like someone who -- despite all the movements of the huckster's cups -- can still point to the pea. "You know, if you were just going to use me for sex and then dump me, I wish you'd have had the balls to tell me in the first place."

"Laura, I'm sorry. It isn't like that."

"No, what's it like then?"

Justin struggled with an answer, but the whole scenario and its complications overwhelmed him.

Laura paused, and looked reflective suddenly. "You know, I see you with these wonderful friends of yours, and I have to say, I feel a little jealous. I sometimes feel like I don't fit in anywhere at all. I know we've gone a bit too far, but on the other hand, I don't understand why someone wouldn't want to keep a friend."

Justin's first thought was to say, *But we weren't friends first,* though he didn't really want to say that. For a second, he almost thought of saying, *Well, maybe we could take it slower* -- thought maybe he could find a way, despite the confusion he still felt. But somehow, even so, he felt the sex thing would always be there, coloring everything -- that since they'd crossed that line, there was no going back.

"I'm not sure I can do that," he said guiltily, uncertain how to go on.

"Fine," said Laura petulantly. "Just go, please."

"Laura, I'm sorry," said Justin.

"Go sleep with those wonderful friends of yours if you're so in love with them," she hurled at him, fighting tears.

Justin froze, afraid that she had guessed the truth. He rose and skulked out like a scolded dog.

Drawing the door behind him quietly, he stood for a moment, shaken and ashamed. His hand was still upon the knob, as if unwilling to let go. Yet, as he stood, uncertain, in the winter-warm, indifferent hall, he also felt amazingly relieved. He hesitated for a moment more, released the knob at last, then groped his way across the night-dark quad in a direction that he hoped was right.

CHAPTER 3

———◆———

I N THE DAYS AND WEEKS that followed, Justin felt as rootless as a dandelion
 seed. He downplayed his and Laura's breakup to Kyle and Craig, citing the
time that had passed during the break, saying merely that things hadn't worked
out. But, in his heart, he knew he had to talk to Craig again -- come clean about
the things he felt: the certainty that he was gay; but, more than that, the fact
that -- as he saw him once more on a daily basis -- he was sure, at last, that he
loved Kyle. He kept on looking for an opportunity to talk to Craig, but couldn't
seem to find one. Then, one evening after they'd been back a few weeks, Justin
told himself the time was now. He'd been curled up all day in the library in a
corner on an avocado nylon sofa underneath a white cloth globe lamp, immersed
in *Moby Dick*, watching as the winter darkness settled on the campus and -- suddenly unable to concentrate -- grabbed his coat and book bag and headed out
across the blue-black, February quad to have a talk with Craig.

As he walked across the campus looking at the ice upon the sidewalks, frozen into hard, black, glassy patches -- ice that once was water, laying in its still
little pools -- Justin found himself beginning to wonder. The ice here was the
water he'd seen earlier that week, pooled up on an unseasonably warm day; yet
now it was changed. Was this, then, what had happened with him in his feelings
toward Kyle? If so, where exactly had that happened? When had his feelings
coalesced into this glossy, slippery thing called love? And if that's what had happened, did that mean that love was just a matter of degrees? That, at a certain
temperature, his feelings were mere friendship, while at another, they were love?
His father's feelings toward his mother never made the change, at least according

to his father. But, had they felt like love at one point, only later melting back to friendship? Now that his feelings for Kyle seemingly had shaded over into this firmer substance -- into love -- what did that mean? That they would always stay that way, crystallized forever into this hard thing? Or would they, too, change like the seasons? Did love do that?

Still unresolved about this, Justin reached Craig's door and knocked.

"Hey, how you doing?" said Craig as he opened up the door.

Craig's room was warm and still, the only light coming from his reading lamp. A cup of Constant Comment tea, with an orange flag still dangling from it, sat on the register beside his bed.

"Fine," said Justin, setting down his books and taking off his red down jacket, which crackled with static. "Are you busy?"

"No," said Craig. "Have a seat."

Justin sat beside the bed, looking at the creases on Craig's yellow woolen blanket where he'd lain. It looked so warm and cozy that he wanted to crawl into it. He smelled, as well, the cinnamon in Craig's tea, calling to him like a memory of Christmas mornings past.

"You've been studying?" said Craig.

"Yeah, *Moby Dick* over at the library."

"Oh, God."

"No, actually, it's really good. Listen to this: 'Yes, these eyes are windows, and this body of mine is the house. What a pity they didn't stop up the chinks and crannies though, and thrust in a little lint here and there.' I think that's incredible writing. And that part was actually cut from the original edition. Can you imagine?"

"I guess I'm not understanding," said Craig, perplexed.

"Oh," said Justin, taken aback. "The metaphor, or what?"

"No, I got that. But why do you like it?"

"Well, I guess because he's comparing himself to a house, but saying the structure isn't very sound -- there are gaps in it. He's feeling very drafty, like his soul is exposed somehow -- I don't know. It just struck me and I liked it."

"I see." There was light and warmth in every part of Craig's blond beard: the delicate hairs framed his dark maroon lips, swirled around his neck and ran down into his shirt. Looking at this, Justin felt a rush of love: a love that seemed composed purely of warmth and belonging, though as he dwelled on it, he grew aware of something physical stirring inside him as well, and admitted to himself that Kyle was hardly the only man he'd ever felt attracted to.

"Don't Ishmael and Queequeg sleep together?" said Craig.

Startled -- afraid, even -- that perhaps Craig had somehow read his thoughts, Justin said cautiously, "They share a bunk together, if that's what you mean."

"But aren't they naked and all? I seem to remember something about that."

"I don't know," said Justin, recalling the episode vividly in all its titillating ambiguity, but still nervous and unwilling to characterize it as being actually sexual.

"Or, no," said Craig: "I remember. There's a scene where they're squeezing the oil in the barrels, and Ishmael is squeezing everybody's hand. Anyhow, it's all a little giddy as I recall. And then there's the fact that it's *sperm* whale oil, right?"

"Right," said Justin a bit defensively.

""Was Melville gay?"

"Well, there's a theory that Melville was attracted to Hawthorne, who happened, I guess, to have been extraordinarily handsome. And Melville *did* dedicate Moby Dick to him."

"Um," said Craig. "And, of course, there's nothing Freudian at all about Melville creating a character who chases this huge phallic symbol across the globe as he dedicates his book to the gorgeous Hawthorne..."

"Right," said Justin, now somewhat flustered. At last, though, he summoned his earlier resolve and plunged ahead: "Craig, I want to talk to you about something," said Justin.

"Okay," said Craig.

Justin struggled for a moment, trying to find his way in, then said tentatively, "When we had our discussion before, last semester, and I told you I thought I was mistaken about my being gay .... I guess I wasn't being entirely honest with you. Actually, I guess I wasn't being entirely honest with myself."

"Well, I have to say, the whole episode with Laura was confusing to me," said Craig after a moment.

"What do you mean?"

"I just wasn't sure what was going on, is all. So, how are you feeling about it all?"

Justin hesitated for a moment, then said, "I think I have to admit there doesn't really seem to be any doubt about it anymore: I'm pretty sure I'm gay." He sat there for a moment, feeling as vile and naked as Ishmael, cold wind whistling through his chinks.

"You're sure, despite the fact that you had sex with Laura?"

"Yes," said Justin.

"But what makes you so sure?"

"What do you mean?"

"Why are you so sure now, when you weren't before?"

"Well," said Justin, squirming on the bed, "I think it's just undeniable, you know? I mean, I can't deny it anymore."

"But you succeeded with Laura. So, what makes you think now that you're gay?"

Justin sat for a moment, trapped, defeated, then said suddenly, "I didn't succeed with Laura -- not really. I mean, I did, but I know now that was a fluke: it isn't who and what I am."

"But what's making you think that?"

Justin squirmed again. So here it was at last: the moment all his doubts and fears were summed up in one simple utterance, one simple declaration. Justin took a breath and said at last: "Because I'm in love with Kyle."

"What?" said Craig. His face was vaguely fearful.

"I think I've known it all along; I've just been afraid to admit it to myself."

"I see," said Craig after a moment, his face inscrutable. "I guess that makes some things clearer, and others not. So, what are you going to do?"

"I don't know."

"Are you planning on telling Kyle?"

"I know I have to, but so far I just haven't had the nerve."

"Justin," said Craig gently. "I'm sure you must be feeling scared right now, but you can't keep hiding a thing like this. It isn't fair to Kyle *or* you. At the same time, you can't deny who you are."

"I know, I know," he said. He felt his upper lip begin to quiver, felt the hot salt of the start of tears. "So, do you think I'm awful?"

"Awful? Of course not, Justin. But to be honest, I guess maybe I *do* need a little time to let this sink in."

"I understand," said Justin, feeling hurt despite his words.

There was a pause when neither one of them knew what to say.

Then, Craig said: "I think I've always realized you're closer to Kyle than to me. In a way, I've been kind of hurt by that. Now, it sort of makes sense to me."

"You think I'm closer to Kyle than *you?*" said Justin, startled.

"Yeah. I mean, given what you've just told me, that's kind of obvious, isn't it?" There was a look of mild defiance on Craig's face, but also, a kind of plea to Justin to tell him it wasn't true.

"No, I don't think it's obvious. I mean, I may be telling you I'm attracted to Kyle, but look who I'm telling: *you.* I've always felt as though you and I were on more of the same wave-length than him. If anything, I feel like *you're* the confidant -- not Kyle."

"Well, thanks for that," said Craig, softening. "I guess in a way it just hurts a little that what you're telling me is that you're attracted to Kyle and not to me. Isn't that weird? I guess I've always been kind of jealous that he seems to be the object of everybody's affections. I shouldn't say that, I guess. I mean, I love Kyle, too, though not in any physical way. I *do* feel a really strong bond with both you and him and, yeah, we're all pretty huggy with one another -- pretty touchy-feely -- but there's nothing sexual going on for me. At least, I've never felt there was. And you're sure there is with you?"

"Well, I don't know," said Justin, feeling enormously grateful for being given this out, yet hating himself for taking it. "I've been over and over it a thousand times, trying to figure it out. Like what you say about us hugging each other so much."

"Yeah, we *do* do that a lot. I think we all kind of took our cue from Kyle in that."

"Do you and your family hug each other a lot?"

"Yeah, quite a bit. My family's from the south, so there's a lot of open affection going on."

"See, not for me. That's why it's been so amazing for me to be friends with you and Kyle. I mean, I really feel like you guys taught me what love is, showed me what affection could mean. I don't ever remember my parents even touching me, and we *never* hugged each other. The first time Kyle hugged me, I was shocked -- I absolutely couldn't believe it. And that's just how Kyle is. But, it's confusing to me, too. I mean, I love you guys to death, and would never want to do anything to jeopardize that. But what is love? How can you really love someone without feeling some physical attraction?" Justin sensed that he was straying from the point, not making any sense, and yet, wasn't there some truth in what he said?

"Well, I think love is both physical *and* emotional," said Craig carefully. "And what you're saying is, you feel something physical toward Kyle?"

"Yes," said Justin. He was feeling both relieved and unsure of himself at the same time in saying this.

"Enough so to say you think you're in love with him?"

"Yes," said Justin after a moment. Craig had a look on his face that was so naked and vulnerable, so scared yet level-headed, that for a moment Justin almost wanted to say, "I love *both* you and Kyle; it's not just Kyle."

"I'm not sure what to say," said Craig. "You're going to have to figure out exactly how you feel, and what you want to do, obviously. I won't say a thing, but honestly, I think you're going to have to talk to Kyle."

———

Washing up late that evening, thinking over everything he'd discussed with Craig, Justin placed his brown leather kit upon the aluminum shelf above the sink in the bathroom of his dorm. Despite the fact that the aluminum shelf was shiny, it was impossible to see himself reflected in it: its surface was as nicked and dull as an old table knife. Beginning to brush his teeth, he noticed an unfamiliar face walk in behind him and place his gear upon the shelf as gingerly as if he weren't quite sure it was allowed.

"Hi," said the boy shyly, not looking up at Justin.

"Hi," said Justin.

They continued brushing their teeth for a moment in silence, Justin taking in the new boy surreptitiously: he was tall, dark-haired, and somewhat athletic, yet there was also something gentle-seeming about him. In a flash, Justin wondered whether he might be gay, and yet concluded that he probably wasn't: he was too cute, too boy next-doorish.

"Are you a new student?" said Justin.

"Transfer," said the boy with difficulty through the toothpaste.

"Oh," said Justin, rinsing. "From where?"

A pause. A rinse. "State."

"Well, nice to meet you. I'm Justin."

"Tom," said Tom, banging the water off his toothbrush and shaking hands wetly.

"What made you transfer out of State?"

Tom shrugged, putting his toothbrush back in his kit, then said, "It was so big, and anyway, this school is closer to home, to my girlfriend." He added this last almost guiltily, looking at Justin almost as if he expected to be accused of that not being a good enough reason to change schools.

"Oh," said Justin, trying to prevent his face from falling.

"What room are you in?" said Tom.

"One twenty-seven."

"I'm in 116. Drop by some time."

"I will," said Justin, thinking to himself, however, that he almost certainly would not.

Walking back into his empty room, it hit him sadly now that Jacob hadn't come back this semester. Days had turned to weeks with still no word, until at last he'd heard Jacob had some visa problems and would not be back this year. He'd braced for the arrival of another roommate, but none had come, and so it seemed he had a single now. Before, he'd often felt annoyed and pressured by the constancy of Jacob's womanizing; now, without him, though, the room felt curiously cold and lonely. Looking at it this evening, it seemed almost Scandinavian modern, with its white brick walls and black wrought iron window frame. It was somehow like a room in January, when the Christmas tree and all the decorations have just been removed, and in a way it was. In his mind's eye, he saw Jacob standing naked in the center of it, as he'd done often in the past, and Justin missed the cozy male familiarity, like Ishmael suddenly bereft of Queequeg. He moved then to the stereo and put on the Dan Fogelberg album he and Craig had listened to earlier in the semester. The gentle opening chords of "To the Morning" filled the room, and Justin listened, emotion building in him as he heard the words: "And maybe there are seasons,/ and maybe they change;/ and maybe to love is not so strange." He sat thinking about Kyle again, staring into space.

Then, suddenly, conjuring up images of all the men he'd ever felt attracted to and couldn't have -- the disappointment and frustrations of that pent-up love becoming uncontrollable -- he felt his groin begin to swell; and in the emptiness -- love shading over into lust -- at last he lay there grinding his hips into the darkness, as if trying to push a little closer to the one he loved, to Kyle. As he came, the image of Kyle nearly naked on his mattress last semester flitted through his brain, and Justin knew that Craig was right: he had to tell Kyle everything.

———◆———

A few nights later, Justin sat across the room from Kyle, heart hammering with fear. The February night was pressing on the window panes outside, and Justin saw himself reflected miniaturely in the glass. He looked away, then tried to stare back through his silvered image to the quad outside, but couldn't do it. It was like the night he'd gone to look for Kyle and Craig inside the gallery where Craig had studio space, the lights inside turned off, save for a small bulb way in back. He'd cupped his hands to try to peer in, but could not see past his own reflection -- through his own breath -- fogging up the glass. Now, Justin looked at Kyle -- Kyle's brown eyes warm, attentive, unsuspecting -- trying to summon up the nerve to broach this subject. The wheat stalk in the poster on the wall above his desk said "Bend," and Justin stared at it a moment, flashing back again on Steve's naively optimistic rainbow poster last semester. Was he headed for the same fate now as Steve? Was this the moment his life changed as well? At last, he said, "Kyle, can we talk about something a minute?"

"Sure," said Kyle, as blithely as if he'd just asked him to pass the salt.

Justin had been struggling with how to broach this, without much in the way of resolution. Did he just plunge into it, or come up on it slowly? Looking at Kyle, feeling the yearning start once more inside, he said, "There's something I need to talk to you about, but I'm not really certain how to do it."

Kyle sobered up a bit at this, and Justin looked away. Justin would have given anything to spare Kyle this -- not be the one who dumped this extra pressure on him, especially given the ordeal with Steve last semester; yet he felt as though there wasn't any other course. How could he remain Kyle's friend and not confess this? Wasn't it deceitful not to come clean?

"It's funny you should say that, Justin, because there's something I've been wanting to talk to you about, something that's been bothering me -- something I feel I need to tell someone."

"Okay," said Justin, surprised by this turn. "What is it?"

Kyle hesitated. "I don't know how to say this any other way than just to say it: I slept with Karen Taylor."

"What?" said Justin, stunned, remembering the Peer Group Counselor who'd joined them at the bar last semester. "When did this happen?"

"Right after the whole thing happened with Steve."

"But what about Maureen?"

"I know," said Kyle, looking as though he'd just been punched in the stomach. "That's why I've been feeling so guilty. Here I've got this great woman -- this woman I love and want to marry -- and then I go and fuck it all up."

"Did it only happen once?"

"Yeah, just the once, thank God."

"And what is Karen looking for from you now?" said Justin, remembering the discomforts of his own breakup with Laura.

"Nothing, really. When I brought her up to the bar that first night back after Thanksgiving, we'd already talked about it and decided that was it -- that we were just friends, and it had really meant nothing: it just happened."

"What do you mean, it meant nothing," said Justin, his mind reeling not only from the news, but also from Kyle's casual assessment of it. Once more, it seemed to him, the lines were being blurred between things. If Kyle could sleep with a friend and say that it had meant nothing, what did that mean? He flashed back on his mother sleeping with his father after they'd broken up, and felt even more confused. Still struggling to understand, he said, "If it didn't mean anything, then why'd you do it?"

"Well, I guess I shouldn't say it didn't mean anything, because it did at the time. I think I was just feeling so vulnerable and needy about Steve and all, I just wanted some affection. Karen, being a good friend, noticed I was looking pretty wrecked and, well, one thing led to another .... "

"I see," said Justin, hurt to hear that, when Kyle had felt he needed some affection from a friend, he hadn't turned to him.

"And now I'm torn," continued Kyle. "Do I tell Maureen what I did, and risk losing her? It's just tearing me apart, not telling her. Well, that and other things."

"What other things?"

"I'm sorry, Justin," said Kyle. "You were telling me you wanted to talk about something, and here I am trampling all over it."

"No, no," said Justin. "That's all right. What is it?"

"I've been thinking over things with Steve, and I'm not proud about the way I handled that. I think I held on way too long -- got in over my head. There must have been some part of me that was flattered by Steve's being in love with me, I guess, hard as it is to admit that. It must have been hard for him."

"Well, you did what you could," said Justin uncertainly.

"The truth is, I worry that maybe I was more culpable in the whole thing than I admitted to myself before."

"What do you mean?"

"I'm afraid maybe I was even giving him mixed signals, leading him to think I might be responding, even though it didn't seem to me like I was." Kyle hesitated a moment, then said: "Have I ever told you about my friend from high school? The one who committed suicide?"

"No, I don't think so," said Justin, feeling curiously off balance.

"He lived down the street from me. We were never best friends, but we went all through school together. Anyway, he committed suicide when we were sophomores."

"Are you saying he was attracted to you, too?" said Justin.

"No, no," said Kyle, looking pained. "Nothing like that." Despite having said this, he paused a moment as if re-examining it. "Anyway, you can imagine how it resonated with me when Steve slit his wrists. I've thought about that ever since last semester. Was I trying to make up for Eric killing himself by trying to save Steve? I've been very upset and confused about the whole mess. That's one of the reasons I wound up in bed with Karen. Maureen thinks I'm upset about Steve; she doesn't know about the incident with Karen, but I think she can tell something is wrong. Things are actually a little strained between Maureen and me right now."

"Dealing with Steve -- with that whole mess -- was a hard thing for everyone," offered Justin tentatively. "Especially if you went through it with another friend."

"Yeah, I know, but ... I guess there are some things I need to sort out in terms of how I acted. Was I just trying to play the older brother with Steve, or was I more at fault than that?"

"What are you saying?" said Justin, feeling strangely upset. "You're only a student, for god's sake. You did what you could. You don't have that much training in counseling."

"I know," said Kyle, swallowing hard, and looking heart-breakingly vulnerable. "What I'm wondering, I guess, is -- like you said about Eric -- am I guilty of leading Steve on at all, maybe even Eric, though I'd never even thought of that?"

"Why would you do that?" said Justin, hardly able to believe his ears.

"I don't know," said Kyle. "I guess I need to take a hard look at myself, at my emotional involvement with both of them -- even at my own sexuality -- to see if there's anything going on there. Is it possible I may have been ... responding -- even wanting -- more than I thought?"

Justin couldn't move. He tried to think what he should say, but couldn't: everything was too confused. Kyle looked at him, and Justin couldn't meet his eyes.

"Maybe it would help me if you told me what you're feeling," said Kyle earnestly.

"That's just it," said Justin, seizing on this opportunity, this unexpected door. "I think I'm feeling exactly the way you are. This thing with Steve has got me so confused. I mean, I know I love you and Craig, but I don't quite know what to make of that."

"I've thought about that, too," said Kyle. "I feel so close to you guys -- such a strong bond. Is it possible it's more than that? I can't think I've been aware of any sexual feelings toward either you or Craig -- not consciously anyway, and certainly not the way Steve was. I don't think it was there with Eric, either. Still, we all hug each other a lot -- don't think I haven't thought about *that*. And I *do* feel something from that: a kind of release, I guess. So what does that mean?"

All Justin wanted at the moment was to tumble into Kyle's arms. The thought that Kyle might be admitting he was gay -- or even that he was confused -- was far beyond his wildest dreams. Perhaps he wasn't as alone in this as he'd thought! Perhaps Kyle shared the same confusions and frustrations after all!

"So, you're feeling something similar?" said Kyle, jolting Justin back.

"Yeah," said Justin, suddenly astonished at the turn all this had taken. "I was very confused by the whole episode with Laura. I think maybe we *did* jump into having sex too fast, just like you said. And I was always bothered that I didn't feel for her what I feel for you guys." Even uttering this, he felt nervous and afraid; still, Kyle didn't seem to flinch at all.

"It seems like it really bothered you that you two had sex when you knew you really didn't love her," said Kyle agreeably.

"It did. I mean, there's no question the bond I feel for you guys is strong -- really, really strong. So what do I make of that? Then this whole thing with Steve was so upsetting .... "

"I know," said Kyle.

They sat there for a moment, then Justin stood impulsively and took a step toward Kyle, embracing him. Kyle hugged him back in reflex, the way a person, startled, manages to catch a tossed ball.

"Thanks, guy," said Kyle. Then, as if filling space while Justin kept on holding him, he said, "It must feel good to you to talk about it, too."

"It does," said Justin, beaming at these words. He wasn't certain what the truth about himself was anymore, but obviously, he and Kyle were feeling similar confusions. What he'd feared would drive a wedge into their friendship seemed, ironically, to have forged an even stronger bond. How strange life was sometimes! Squeezing a last, summary little hug from the embrace, Justin looked up toward the window, black with night. He couldn't see himself at all. All he could see, reflected in the pane, was Kyle.

CHAPTER 4

A FEW NIGHTS LATER, CRAIG AND Justin sat in Craig's room, a fiery late-February sunset pressing on the long, tall window panes. A pine tree poked the crowning finger of its exclamation point -- the sum of all that it had grown to be -- into the bottom of Craig's third-floor window, altering the view forever afterwards. Justin looked down at the slushy roads of campus winding past the Gothic chapel and down the hill, the gentle luminosity of snow at sunset spreading out across the campus to the other dormitories, which were ringed around the outer edges of the campus like huge, 19th-century mansions. Craig lay on the bed, his shirt untucked, unbuttoned, blond hair flowing gently down his chest and belly like an exhaled breath. Picking up his beechwood guitar, inlaid with walnut around the hole, Craig started strumming softly, then sang:

> Lover, there will be another one
> Who'll hover over you beneath the sun
> Tomorrow, see the things that never come today.
> When you see me fly away without you,
> Shadow on the things you know
> Feathers fall around you, and show you the way to go:
> It's over.

"Wow, said Justin. "That's beautiful. What is it?'
"*Birds*. It's a Neil Young song."
"It's really beautiful. Beautiful and sad."

"Yeah, it's a great song."

Craig started strumming softly again, and Justin felt as though his heart were going to burst. Craig looked so beautiful sitting there, his shirt open masculinely, revealing his soft, unblemished skin, the furry hair matting thickly around the belly button. Justin felt so close to him right now -- so emotionally intimate and happy -- that he rose and crossed the room, kneeling in front of the bed and embracing him.

"Woah," said Craig, his guitar bouncing between them as if he'd dropped and kicked it accidentally.

"What's wrong," said Justin, feeling stung. He raised up now and perched, a bit humiliated, on the bed beside Craig.

"You just surprised me, is all. I'm sitting here half naked. Jeez! Give me a little warning, will ya?" Craig gathered his shirt tails together and glanced up toward his open door, but saw no one.

"Sorry," said Justin. He sat there for a moment, feeling hurt, embarrassed and aggrieved, then moved across the aisle back to the chair.

"No, it's okay." An awkward moment passed, then Craig said, "I'm sorry. So, how did your talk with Kyle go?"

"Actually, it went great."

"Really?" said Craig, setting the guitar back on his bed behind them, in the space where one would lay.

"Yeah, why wouldn't it?" said Justin, still feeling a bit defensive.

"I don't know. I'm just surprised, I guess. You told him?"

"Yeah," said Justin, realizing he was being a bit vague.

"And how did Kyle take it?"

"Okay."

"Okay. What do you mean, 'okay?'" said Craig. "What did he say?"

"Well, I don't know," said Justin, suddenly embarrassed, and not sure how much of Kyle's indecision he should divulge to Craig. He and Craig had always told each other everything, and yet now, in the full bore of Craig's apparently unsympathetic scrutiny, he felt curiously reluctant to discuss it, as though it were a secret he and Kyle shared. Once, at a party, he had reached his arm out along the back of a sofa and discovered Kyle's arm was already there. Kyle had winked at him handsomely, good naturedly, squeezing his hand and then, amazingly, did not let go, just held on, as if to say, *We have this secret little link together, you and I.* This secret felt like that clandestine, momentary little bond.

"You didn't tell him, did you?" said Craig.

"I *did* -- we talked about it," insisted Justin.

Craig got up from the bed, closed the door, and then sat back down on the bed. "You told him you're in love with him?" said Craig skeptically.

"No, not exactly," said Justin. "But we did talk about things."

"Things. What things?"

"About being attracted, about being confused. We talked about how upset the thing with Steve Norberg made us." Justin stopped suddenly, unwilling to tell Craig any more about Kyle's fears: apparently, the same fears he had had about himself, and which he now felt he must protect -- must shelter from undue analysis or revelation.

"And Kyle understood, you're questioning your sexuality?"

"Yes, I think so. We talked about love and friendship. Frankly, I'm still confused about the difference between them."

"Well, Justin, there *is* a difference. Love's a *part* of friendship, just the same way friendship's a part of love. But one thing isn't necessarily the other. Just like now, for instance. I have to say: it really seems to me your hug went past the bounds of friendship -- that it wasn't friendship so much as sex."

"I see," said Justin tersely. "I'm sorry if I made you feel uncomfortable."

"Justin, don't get angry. I'm just trying to help."

"What happened to not labeling myself?" said Justin. "Didn't you tell me Freud says we're all bisexual.'"

Craig gave an exasperated sigh. "I think that's true, to some extent, but I also think there comes a time, given all you've told me, when you have to say, okay, most of society would probably categorize me as ... having feelings outside the norm."

"I see. And what is normal?"

"Justin, you know what I'm saying. I'm not trying to attack you .... "

"Well, maybe I'm still not ready to categorize myself, to slap some label on myself."

He was on the verge of saying, "Maybe Kyle's not either," when they heard a knock upon the door.

"Who is it?" said Craig.

"It's me, Kyle."

Craig hopped up from the bed and swung the door out to his arm length.

"Hi," said Craig.

"Hi," said Kyle, glancing at the two of them. "I'm not interrupting anything, am I?"

"No," said Justin, not quite looking up at Kyle. He felt a breath of fresh air coming in with Kyle, a smell like health, as if he'd just arrived from skiing in the Alps. "We were just yakking." He stole a glance at Craig, who dropped his arm as Kyle came in. Craig didn't quite meet his eyes either.

"You guys want to go shoot some hoops? said Kyle.

"No, thanks," said Justin after a moment. "Basketball isn't really my forte."

"That doesn't matter," said Kyle. "I just wanted to do something with you guys, is all." He looked at Craig, who looked listless and indecisive. "Oh, come on," said Kyle.

"I'd be fine with that, I guess," said Craig.

"Why don't you guys go ahead," said Justin. "I'll watch."

"Come on, you silly person," said Kyle.

"I'm really bad. I'm really, *really* bad. And I'm not just being modest."

"I'm not asking you to be Wilt Chamberlain, for crying out loud," said Kyle. "Just put on some shorts and come with us."

"All right," said Justin. Given the look of warmth and friendship in Kyle's face, how could anyone resist?

Later, in the steamy incandescence of the gym, the warm air smelling of old rubber mats and sweat, and filled with the sharp, high squeak of rubber shoes on varnished wooden floors, Kyle passed the ball to him and Craig, and once or twice, he tried to lay it up without success. Kyle passed the ball to him again, but this time Justin said, "That's all right, I'm useless."

"Fine," said Kyle. "But we're not leaving here until you make a basket."

"Oh, Kyle," said Justin: "You have no idea what you're getting yourself into."

"Yes, I do. Just try." He passed the ball to Justin, who looked at Craig standing gangly and oversized in his short blue shorts with thin white piping. Craig's arms were folded, and he was watching them curiously. Padding around in his high top black tennis shoes, his blond hair and too-short shorts, Craig looked like an oversized German shepherd puppy crammed into a too-small sweater.

"Kyle, really, I don't want to do this."

"Because you're afraid."

"I'm not afraid. I just don't want to do it."

"You're afraid you'll look stupid."

"I *will* look stupid."

"Okay, so you'll look stupid. Do it anyway."

Justin stood there, exasperated, raised the ball, flung it like a girl throwing a softball, and missed the basket completely.

"See? I'm hopeless."

"You're *not* hopeless," said Kyle. "And personally, I think it's stupider not to try to do something because you're afraid you'll fail rather than to actually *do* it and fail. So what if you're bad? You expect to be perfect your first time out?"

"I guess you're right."

"Hasn't anybody ever showed you how to shoot?"

"No," said Justin, Kyle having hit upon a sore spot. His father, for all his masculine bravado, was just as miserable at sports as Justin was, and thus had never made any attempt at tossing a ball to Justin.

"Here," said Kyle. "You take the ball like this." Kyle came up behind him, putting his arms around him, guiding his hands. "You don't toss the ball so much as pop it up, let it roll off your fingertips and into the basket." He took the ball from Justin and executed a perfect free throw, the ball swishing through the basket hitting nothing except the net. "See? Like threading a needle from across the room."

As Kyle touched Justin's hands, he felt a current running through his body -- felt the eyes of everybody in the gym upon him. Justin tried a few free throws that missed; then, finally, he sunk a basket.

"See?" said Kyle. "It's not that hard. Somebody simply has to show you."

As Justin looked at Kyle, he felt such a flush of love and gratitude, such a bond of tenderness with Kyle, he was afraid he might cry. He looked at Craig, who looked at him inscrutably, though for the moment anyway, it looked as though he wanted peace between them. Justin thought how rare these friends were. In particular, how rare was Kyle: this man who made him feel so loved, who kept encouraging him to take these shots.

CHAPTER 5

——◆——

ONE EVENING, WITH SPRING BREAK approaching, Kyle tossed out the idea of
the three of them spending their break together:

"Why don't the two of you come up to Stevens Point and spend the week
with me? We'd have a blast, and anyway, I'm sure there's much less ice and snow
up there than down in Tennessee." Kyle winked at Craig.

"Wow, that'd be great," said Justin, leaping at the thought. Not only was
the idea of spending more time with Kyle and Craig great in itself, but this plan
would also take care of the painful thought of having to spend time with his
father and the new love of his life. Justin's mother was still off somewhere on
her adventure, and Justin wasn't even sure his father knew he had a spring break
coming. At any rate, he wasn't going to let the opportunity to see Kyle's home
slip by.

"You think you could, too?" said Kyle to Craig.

Craig looked at Justin for a moment strangely, then said, "I guess so.
Honestly, I wasn't real keen on driving all the way back to Tennessee anyway."

Now, in the car and on the road, the hazy twilight afternoon before them
and the clouds an eerie white against the blue, Justin felt elated -- freed -- as they
drove open-windowed down the interstate, the March wind whipping up their
hair into a greasy-feeling frenzy. Justin hung his arm out of the window of Kyle's
black-and-yellow 1968 Le Mans, touching the gritty dust upon the warm side of
the car gingerly. He let his hand ride up and down the air planes, flat-palmed,
wondering at how the motion of a finger here or there could make it soar or
crash within an instant. He was humming to himself another Neil Young song

which Craig had introduced him to: "Now you stood on the edge of your feather, expecting to fly;" repeating to himself that line; unable to remember what came next, except the last line ending on that unexpected Major chord, the same one it had started on. He felt elated looking at Kyle sitting across from him, the hair wispy across his temples and his deep, brown-shadowed eyes. Kyle's slightly thin, brown arms sat squarely on the steering wheel, guiding them all assuredly. Kyle glanced at him and said above the car's roar, "Are you singing 'Many a tear has to fall?'"

"No, Neil Young. The tunes are pretty close, though, now that you mention it." They rode in silence for a while more, then Justin glanced behind him and discovered Craig was dozing, after having spent the last half-hour pouring idly over maps.

"Looks like our navigator's out," said Kyle.

"Yeah," said Justin, feeling even more delighted at the coziness of this -- of having Kyle all to himself.

When they reached Stevens Point at last -- a town not greatly different from Moline, Justin saw to his amazement -- then turned the corner into Kyle's late 1950s subdivision, Justin felt momentarily disappointed. When he'd conjured up in his mind the city and the street Kyle lived on, he'd imagined it to be an old resort town filled with huge Victorian homes and tree-lined streets. Yet, as they pulled up, all he saw were 20-year-old ranch style homes painted white, with two or three shrubs plunked around the cinder-block foundations, driveways ticked off with amazing regularity, and at the end of all of them, a gaping mouth that waited to accept the family car. It was a neighborhood much like his own, and as he thought of this, his disappointment eased somewhat. Didn't this mean, ultimately, that he and Kyle were from more similar backgrounds than he'd thought? Didn't it make sense, then, that they'd struck a bond so easily -- that they had far more in common than he'd imagined?

Craig was awake now, and they sat in the driveway for a moment, belting out the chorus of The Police's "Every Little Thing She Does Is Magic." Justin reveled in this sudden bond -- indeed, it seemed that everything they did together *was* magic -- before they grabbed their things and walked up to the black aluminum door of the ranch-style house, a curved sidewalk lined with white stones leading up to it and dotted here and there with mauve and yellow crocuses appearing in the freakishly warm weather. Justin kept on trying to imagine Kyle down through the years as he had walked into this doorway: coming home from grade school, junior high and high school, stumbling in the house in sweaty clothes from playing basketball or hockey in the street. He wished he could have been there all those years to see Kyle in the various gradations of his youth. There still was so much about Kyle's life he didn't know, so much of it he wished he could have been there for! The fact that they were here, now, was a start, but so much was elusive still: behind the bland exterior of this house was an entire life he now stood on the threshold of, and as they neared it, Justin had to hold himself a step or two behind to keep from trampling Kyle, excited as he was to be here, seeing finally where Kyle had spent his childhood.

"Well, this is it, guys," said Kyle, stepping across the threshold, setting down his bags and gesturing with a handsome, black-haired forearm.

Justin -- sunblind -- immediately felt a sharp, insistent poke in his crotch, and nearly doubled over in surprise. As his eyes adjusted to the darkness, he saw a tawny Labrador attempting to decide whether he should jump up on him. Instead, he jumped up in the air in front of them repeatedly, and barked. He tore over to Craig and nosed him similarly in the groin.

"Woah!" said Craig. "He's really friendly, isn't he."

"Yeah," said Kyle laughing. "He always manages to poke people right in their privates like that." Kneeling down, he grabbed the dog and startled wrestling with it. "How are you, you great big beast?" The dog, whose head was now at the level of Kyle's, reared its head and barked again, at which all of them laughed.

"Mom. Dad. I'm home," said Kyle, walking down some stairs into the living room. Justin watched Kyle's squarish rear-end padding off and thought again how immature he felt, how adult Kyle seemed in comparison. He wondered whether he would ever feel that grown up in his life.

Kyle's house was split into a kind of level-and-a-half: the living area and kitchen were downstairs; the bedrooms up a half a flight. The walls were paneled in dark walnut, and the carpeting was avocado green. Rust-colored macrame plant hangers hung upon the landings and the living room. As Craig and Justin followed Kyle, they rounded the corner and came upon a short, stocky, elderly couple sitting and smoking at a brown Formica table with copper-colored metal legs.

"Hi Mom, hi Dad," said Kyle, walking up and giving both of them a hug.

"Well, we didn't expect you until tomorrow," said his mother, not rising from her seat, and looking up at him as if he'd merely come across town. Justin was shocked: if Kyle had been his son, he would have known exactly when he was expected to arrive, and would have welcomed him home like a returning prince.

"What?" said Kyle. "I told you when I talked to you last week we'd be here on Saturday."

"Were you expecting *us*?" said Justin shyly.

"Yes," said Kyle's mother, smiling. "Kyle told us he was bringing friends. Now, which one is Craig, and which is Steve?"

"Steve?" said Kyle, momentarily flustered. "No, no -- that was ... somebody completely different. This is Craig, and this is Justin."

"Nice to meet you both," said Kyle's mother. "I'm Mona, and this is Bud." At this, Kyle's father nodded silently, and flicked his cigarette into a scalloped, black Bakelite ashtray.

"How long are you boys up for?"

"Just a few days," said Kyle.

"Is Maureen on break, too?" said his father.

"Yeah, she'll be home tomorrow."

"Well, I'm sure you'll both be glad for that," said his father, winking.

Justin, who'd felt off-balance ever since Kyle's mom thought he was Steve, now felt a second sting upon hearing how happy Kyle would be to see Maureen. Wasn't Kyle happy to be there with them?

"Yeah," said Kyle. "It'll be nice. It's nice these guys could come up, too." Kyle smiled at both him and Craig, and Justin felt immediately assuaged.

"You boys make yourselves at home while you're here," said Kyle's mother.

"Thank you," said Craig and Justin.

The parental obligations having been dispensed with, Kyle said, "It's beautiful weather outside. How'd you guys like to play some tennis or something?"

"Tennis?" said Craig skeptically. "Oh, God. I don't know."

"Oh, come on," said Justin, feeling suddenly energized and happy. "It'll be fun." Tennis was one of the few sports Justin actually played, having been a member of the second-string tennis team in high school. Perhaps, he thought, this was something, sports-wise, he could actually hold his own in against Kyle.

"I don't really know how to play," said Craig.

"Look," said Justin. "You guys made *me* play basketball .... "

"Peer pressure, peer pressure," said Kyle.

"All right, all right," said Craig. "But I'll be terrible."

"That's what *I* said," said Justin. "You see how far that got me."

After Kyle found some rackets in the basement (*what an athletic house*, thought Justin, *that they'd simply have spare racquets sitting around!*), Kyle said, "You guys go ahead and change in there, pointing to a room that Justin guessed had been Kyle's old bedroom. As he walked into the early afternoon dimness, he could make out pennants and trophies lining walnut-paneled walls, the crush of album covers, and a mildewed, healthy boy-smell. Outside, he could just make out the green street sign reading "Hampshire Lane," and instantly he felt connected to Kyle's history, waking up on all those sultry, early summer mornings to this sign outside the window. *Lucky signpost*, he thought, *that had witnessed Kyle growing up through all the years!*

Kyle switched the room light on, and suddenly, Justin felt self-conscious at the thought of changing here beside Kyle and Craig.

"Are you guys set with shorts and T-shirts and stuff?"

"Yeah," said Craig. "I didn't bring a jock, though."

"You want to borrow one?" said Kyle.

"You have an extra?"

"Yeah, I think so," said Kyle, rummaging through a drawer, then tossing one to Craig. "Look, here's even another. You want one, Justin?"

"Sure, if you've got it," said Justin, startled again. What an amazing man this was, his masculinity so limitless he didn't even pause at loaning pieces of it out for friends to wrap themselves in!

Kyle shot the jock strap to him like a rubber band, and as Justin stepped out of his pants and into it, he felt something envelop him: a magic intimacy and a sense of courage such as ancient warriors must have felt when girding themselves ahead of battle. Now, as they changed, their eyes were downcast in the universal manner of the locker room.

"All set?" said Kyle once they had changed.

"As ready as I'll ever be, I guess" said Craig.

Out on the court, the ground around the playing area was soggy from the recently melted snows. The Southwest-mesa red of the outer border looked faded and dusty around the forest green of the court as they discovered, much to their dismay, that the nets had not yet been hung up yet for the season.

"Shit," said Kyle.

"Can't we just bat the ball around? I don't know how to play anyway" said Craig.

"I'd as soon write unrhymed poetry," said Justin.

"What the hell is this guy talking abut?" said Kyle, good-naturedly.

"I think he's being intellectual," said Craig.

"'I'd as soon play tennis without a net as write poetry that doesn't rhyme.' Robert Frost," said Justin.

"Right. Whatever," said Kyle, bonking Justin on the head with a tennis ball. "Or I guess we could just spend time 'Mending Wall.'"

"Very good," said Justin, impressed.

"What do you guys think? I guess we could still give it a go. It's going to seem a little pointless, though." He turned to Craig. "What do you say? Are you game for batting the ball around a while?"

"Like I said," said Craig, "I really don't know how to play anyway, so whatever you want to do is fine with me."

"Great," said Kyle. "I tell you one thing, though. It's way too beautiful to keep this shirt on." With that, he braced the racquet in between his legs, shucked off his shirt cross-armed above his head, and stood there, black-haired, white skinned, the twin mounds of his pectorals each culminating in a lip-red nipple. As always, Justin looked at him in awe: the two matched tablets of his chest hair meeting in the center like some ancient script which Justin wished he could decode, dark hairline running down the center of his belly deep into his shorts. He felt inspired to join him, and removed his own shirt. Standing awkwardly, he pulled the whole thing like a tube sock overhead, then stood there pale, unshirted, in the weak March sun. The chill cool rubbed up like a cat against his skin, the goose bumps breaking out across his back like sweat, then disappearing once again.

"I'm gonna leave mine on," said Craig.

"Oh, come one, you baby," Kyle said. "Get some sun."

"No, I'm fine," said Craig, and Justin knew it was because he was self conscious of his body in comparison to Kyle's. But for the first time ever, Justin felt a strange, contagious masculinity, perhaps inspired by their girding-up together in the jockstraps earlier. He felt like they were fellow warriors -- young and strong and vigorous -- and he was ready to join in.

"All right," said Kyle, "But it's a beautiful day."

"Oh, all right," said Craig, and dragged his shirt off hastily at last. In the sun, the yellow-blond hair on his chest looked weak and colorless, like grass beneath an upturned rock.

"Why don't you take the other side," said Kyle to Justin. "Craig and I will take you on, since you know how to play."

Justin felt a stab of hurt to be put on the side against Kyle, yet had to concede the plan made sense: Craig didn't know how to play, and Kyle was looking out for him. Now, as he crossed the courts all by himself, however, he felt a little ostracized: the odd man out.

"Why don't we try to play it like a game, and just see how it goes?" said Kyle.

As Justin watched Kyle step and stroke, he was astonished at the speed and power of Kyle's serve. It hit his racket with a dull thud, knocking it out of his hand. The ball lobbed off obliquely to the diamond chain link fence as Justin stood, sore wristed, shocked at the force with which it had come across. "God, take it easy," said Justin, embarrassed that he'd dropped his racquet.

"That was a fault," said Kyle.

"Oh," said Justin stupidly, not even thinking that the ball might have been out of bounds. "What does it matter, I guess?"

"Well, I'm just thinking we should try to use *some* guide," said Kyle. "Frost aside." He winked at Justin.

"All right," said Justin. He stood there readying again, intimidated by Kyle's strength, yet thinking that Kyle's second serve would come across much softer. Instead, Kyle burned in his second serve as hotly as the first, the ball bouncing from the racquet up into his face and, in the process, hitting one particularly prominent front tooth. Blood rushed to his upper lip as Justin wiped the tennis fuzz from his mouth. From then on, with each next service, Justin tried, but couldn't master what, essentially, was fear of how strong Kyle was serving.

"Maybe we should just do some volleying," said Kyle when they had played a game or two.

"No, that's all right," said Justin, struggling to be valiant.

"I'm just thinking this isn't too much fun for Craig," said Kyle, and it was true: Craig had merely stood like a sentry each time Kyle had served. Since Justin couldn't get Kyle's service back, essentially there was no play.

"Maybe you're right," said Justin.

They started batting the ball back and forth nonchalantly, Craig hitting awkwardly from time to time, but Justin fishing it out of the nonexistent "net" and knocking it back over. Pretty soon, they had a rhythm going; still, it was apparent from the skill with which Kyle placed and hit the ball, he would have killed the two of them in any competition.

As they stood later toweling off, the weak sun having drilled their shadows home, then lengthened them behind them, Kyle said, "Good volleying." As usual, he said it in his friendly, totally inaccurate way, looking past all Justin's obvious shortcomings, and Justin felt a rush of love for him again. He couldn't fathom yet that they were here in Kyle's home town. The whole thing seemed surreal, but wonderful. He couldn't keep his eyes off Kyle: his chest hair drenched, the weak sun on his graceful limbs. Kyle raised his arms and swept the shirt into the pockets underneath, and even this unconscious gesture seemed magnificent and beautiful. Standing beside him with the towel around his neck -- more draped to hide his shirtlessness than dry him off -- he felt so overcome with love and happiness to be in the presence of this kind, attractive man, he rushed across the court -- that faded, netless space -- and wrestled him into a bearhug gleefully, his whole soul thrilling as their bodies' slick sweat met.

"Oh, God," said Kyle, stiffening uncomfortably. "Knock it off, will you? I'm gross."

———◆———

That evening, late, they sat, sunburned and listless, in Kyle's living room, watching TV and drinking beer. They were tired from the afternoon of playing tennis; and, after they had showered, and had a huge meal of pot roast, string beans, spinach, mashed potatoes and gravy, and apple cobbler, they sunk into the faded golden velvet sofa for some television.

Now, Kyle's parents having gone to bed, the TV flickers moved across the dog curled at their feet, the floral curtains drawn across the glassed-in patio doors, and the pictures of the children on the walls, their faces dark beside a great, black mirror on the far wall. Justin looked at Kyle and thought about the day, still overjoyed that he was here. Today was like that day out in the dandelion field again: the weather strange, unseasonable, the light surreal. The whole thing was so like a dream (but one he never wanted to awaken from!) Justin scarcely could contain himself. Kyle sat beside him on the sofa squarely, hugely, shadows playing in the corners of his beard, some soft, black chest hairs poking out below the throat. It seemed to him he'd never loved Kyle more -- had never wanted more to be a part of him.

"You guys up for some more tennis tomorrow?" said Justin brightly, feeling ready to conquer the world with Kyle beside him.

"You're assuming this weather's going to last," said Kyle.

"Why wouldn't it?"

"It's pretty unusual for this time of year, especially in these parts. We'll see. What do you say, partner?" said Kyle to Craig. Craig had been quiet all day, and Justin wasn't certain why.

"Whatever," said Craig. "We can play it by ear."

"Sure thing. Well, guys," said Kyle, looking at Justin again, then at Craig: "What do you say we hit the hay?"

"Yeah," said Craig. "I'm pretty beat."

Kyle stood, and Justin merely moved up to the sofa's edge. The question Justin had been pondering all day was, who would sleep where? Since he'd had his talk with Kyle, was there a chance that they might even bunk together? He had seen the sofa bed here in the living room, and there was Kyle's bed. So, who would sleep with whom, and where?

"This flips out into a double bed," said Kyle.

"Great, so do I," said Justin. Kyle and Craig both laughed.

"I thought you guys could sleep in here, okay?"

Justin cursed himself. As soon as he had made his comment, he wished he hadn't. If he had just stayed quiet, was there any chance he might have slept with Kyle? Perhaps he'd ruined it by hugging him out on the courts -- presumed too much? Or was Kyle perhaps being shy with Craig around? But this was proper on the surface, Justin guessed: the guests should sleep out here, Kyle in his own room.

Watching now as Kyle moved off and brought them blankets, pillows, sheets, then indicated where the bathroom was, he wondered, too, if Craig felt odd at all about the situation: they had never dealt with anything like this before. Given what Craig knew, what things would change from now on? Would the issue of his sexuality be in the air between them always? Yet, all three of them had changed together side-by-side earlier today, with no apparent problem.

When they'd finished washing up, Craig -- clad in his shorts and T-shirt -- climbed underneath the blankets next to Justin and turned his back toward him.

"Night," said Craig into the emptiness of the living room beside him.

"Good night," said Justin automatically, wondering, however, if Craig had turned his back because he felt uncomfortable. After a moment had passed, he said, "Craig?"

"Hmm?"

"Is this all right with you?"

"What do you mean?"

"Us sharing the bed together. Is that all right?"

"It's fine, Justin."

"Is everything all right? Are you glad we came?"

"Yeah, I guess I'm glad."

"I just wondered. You seemed a little quiet today."

"I'm fine, Justin. Go to sleep."

As he lay for a while hearing Craig's breath growing regular, he would have given anything if it were Kyle beside him. Not that he did not love Craig. Yet from the evidence, it seemed that it was he and Kyle who were confused, not Craig. In a way, it would have made *more* sense for him and Kyle to share the bed, and leave Craig out of it. All evening long, he contemplated that scenario; all evening long, he lay there in Kyle's living room, so near and yet so far.

CHAPTER 6

———◆———

A S HE WOKE NEXT MORNING, he was not sure where he was: the avocado carpet lay beneath him unfamiliarly, the sofa bed's bar pressed into his back, and Justin snapped upright so violently he was afraid he'd made a noise. Beside him on the bed lay Craig, still laid out cold despite the violence of Justin's waking. Justin watched the dust motes rising in the beams of light that poked around the floral curtains in the living room, then lay back down and let the circumstances of his being in this room at Kyle's house settle on him once again. He had a hard-on like a rock -- he would have given anything to be alone -- though at the base of it, he knew, was pee. What to do? If he continued lying there and Craig awoke, he'd have no way to hide it; if he got up now and went into the bathroom, he risked running into Kyle or someone from his family. Justin rolled onto his side and felt the erection slap his thigh. He lay a moment more, not feeling it slacken at all, then actually reached down to grasp the shaft a moment. Concluding that it wasn't going to die, and that he really had to pee, he eased himself out of the bed as noiselessly as possible, and crouched beside the drowsy bed, the house as still as a sheeted winter room. He slipped his jeans on from the day before, but left his shirt off, feeling sexy suddenly -- one of Kyle's strapping college pals -- and eased his way across the cold room to the bathroom, which was just across the hall from Kyle's room.

After he had peed successfully, by fits and starts, then flushed as quietly as possible (still, however, deafening in the silence), he emerged from the bathroom and noticed Kyle's door was half-open: a hazy, early morning light illuminating things inside. He took a soundless step or two across the hall and paused, wondering whether it was too early to wake Kyle. He knocked softly on the frame, and in a second heard Kyle saying groggily, "Come in."

Inside the room, Kyle lay flat on his back, the covers swathed about his middle, the long, brown dog laying sphinx-like atop Kyle's feet, looking up at Justin curiously. Kyle was laying there not so much *in* bed as resting on a thing he had used, as though the blankets and the sheets were clothing he had worn and then cast off. One arm was propped behind Kyle's head, and Justin could see the black hair of his underarms -- hair that ran disheveled down his chest and belly and continued underneath the blankets. Morning light was glinting from the trophies on the paneled walls, the figurines of baseball players, and monolithic basketballs and footballs shiny gold as Christmas ornaments. Justin stood there looking at them all: the plaques and pennants, albums lined up heavily beneath the stereo, the window with its green street sign outside in early morning fogginess proclaiming Hamphire Lane -- he saw all these and died a little death again that he was such a stranger to Kyle's past.

"Good morning," said Kyle, his voice so hoarse he laughed.

"Hi. I wasn't sure you were awake yet."

"I'm not either," said Kyle, laughing once again.

Emboldened, Justin walked into the room and perched beside Kyle gingerly upon the bed, the dog now sloping to him at an angle as he did so. Kyle moved a bit in order to accommodate Justin, but otherwise, did not seem self-conscious in his undress.

"I'm really glad you asked us up."

"Me, too," said Kyle.

Justin would have like to broach with Kyle the subject of the conversation they had had before, to find out more about what Kyle felt, but suddenly they heard the water flush across the hall, and saw Craig enter sleepily, clad in some rumpled shorts and faded T-shirt. Immediately, Justin felt embarrassed to be sitting on the bed beside the half-dressed Kyle.

"Good morning. Sleep well?" said Kyle.

"Yeah, okay," said Craig.

"I know what you mean," said Kyle, extracting his legs from underneath the dog with exaggerated emphasis. "Lucky, on the other hand, slept great."

Craig and Justin laughed.

"He's gotten pretty spoiled lately, haven't you, old boy," said Kyle, tousling the dog's head. "I never used to let him sleep in here, but now my brother does."

"What do you mean?" said Justin after a moment. "You mean while you're away?"

"What?" said Kyle. "Oh, this isn't my room anymore. Since I went away to college, it's Frank's."

"So all this stuff in here's not yours?" said Justin, startled.

"Nope. Frank took over when I moved out."

"What about these trophies?"

"They're Frank's. All of it is his."

Justin looked around the room, amazed and a little disappointed about the scenario he'd conjured up since arriving. "I just assumed it was yours. So, yesterday we just borrowed his stuff, his...jocks?"

"A jockstrap's a jockstrap," said Kyle. "I really don't think Frank would mind our borrowing the stuff."

"So, where's Frank now?" said Craig.

"Actually, he's hardly ever here now, either," said Kyle. "He's got a job and a place in town he just moved into. I guess he just hasn't been back to pick up all his stuff yet."

"He's not leaving these behind, is he?" said Craig, pulling out some vintage Beatles albums.

"Actually, those are kind of everybody's. I'm not sure whose they really are."

"They're probably worth some money these days," said Craig.

"I was born a little too late for the Beatles," said Justin idly. "They were just a bit before my time."

"God, I was *weaned* on the Beatles," said Kyle with such an air of expansiveness, finality, and pride, that Justin felt stung. It was as if Kyle had suddenly pronounced a gap between their lives -- a little, seemingly unbridgeable chasm -- and Justin struggled for a way back in.

"I don't remember Kennedy or Vietnam, either," said Justin dejectedly, "except when we pulled out. In fact, I really don't remember anything about the Sixties but the moonwalk, and the reason I remember that's because my dad made all of us come in and watch it."

"Yeah, I remember that pretty well, too." said Craig. "You know, Neil Armstrong screwed up what he was supposed to say."

"What do you mean?" said Justin.

"He was *supposed* to say, "One small step for *a* man. One giant leap for mankind.' When you think about it, what he really said makes no sense: 'One small step for man. One giant leap for mankind.' There's no real difference between the two."

Justin weighed this for a moment, oddly sad. He thought back to the piece of stitchery his mom had done for him that had those words on it, a sampler that had hung in his childhood room through all those years -- a source of inspiration and aspiration which, he'd now found out, was actually a mistake. He stared absently at Kyle's chest, still reflecting on the difference between "a man" and "man" -- about the things he'd missed by just a little -- when Kyle said:

"So, I'm hoping tonight you guys can finally get a chance to meet Maureen. Sound good?"

———◆———

When they finally met Maureen that evening, Justin was again initially a little disappointed. He'd imagined all this time, and from the way Kyle talked about her, that she'd be tall and model-like, exuding elegance and beauty. Instead, Maureen was short and robust in a kind of gymnast's way, and just a little plain. She was also, in an inexplicably startling way, brunette (somehow, he'd imagined she would be a blond) -- the kind of girl who looked like she'd be just as happy in the kitchen whipping up some pies or in the garden weeding out the vegetables. Her wholesome, all-American look fit Kyle; still, Justin was a bit surprised she wasn't gorgeous. As they stepped into Maureen's front room, the floor done up in candy-striped shag, with country pine beams running along the ceilings and cabinets, Justin felt as though he'd just stepped into a picture from the cover of a *Family Circle*. Everything was done in such a manner you could sense the impetus behind it: "Fifty Decorating Tips for Under Fifty Bucks" or "Beautify Your Home with Evergreen."

"Now, which one of you is Craig and which one is Justin?" asked Maureen as they entered and removed their jackets.

"This is Craig, and this is Justin," said Kyle, pointing them out to her.

"Well, it's nice to meet you," said Maureen, hugging both of them exuberantly. "I've heard so much about you."

"Wow," said Craig, laughing. "If you hug strangers like that, how do you greet your friends?"

"Oh, you guys aren't strangers," said Maureen. Immediately after having said this, however, an awkward pause ensued.

"It's nice to finally meet you," said Justin shyly. "We've heard a lot about you."

"And I've heard a lot about you."

"What about me?" said Kyle. "Don't I get a hug?"

"What, you?" said Maureen. "I've got these two new good-looking guys here, why would I want to hug you?"

Kyle pouted, looking heartbreakingly handsome. Justin would have given anything to be the one to wipe the sad look from his face.

"*You*, mister, get a kiss." At this, Maureen stood up on her tiptoes and Kyle embraced her hugely, easily, as though he were passing a ballerina in a *pas de deux*.

"Aw," said Craig. As they continued, he and Justin looked at one another. Then, after another moment, Justin -- attempting humor -- said, "Alright, you two, break it up."

"Woah," said Kyle. "I guess *that's* how she greets people she knows."

"Not just people I know, you dope," said Maureen. "People I *love.*"

"Well, I guess she put me in *my* place," said Kyle, smiling.

"And it doesn't seem like a bad place to be, either," said Craig.

"No, indeed," beamed Kyle.

Later that evening, after they had headed out to dinner, then gone bowling -- Justin watching enviously all night long as Kyle and "Mo" mooned at each other, held hands during the entire meal, and clowned for each other in the strangely empty bowling lanes -- Craig and Justin waited in the car as Kyle and Maureen said reluctant lover's goodbyes, spotted in the headlights in the doorway like two late-night opossums.

Watching them caught in the beam surrounded by the 1 a.m. darkness, Justin was confused. Hadn't Kyle admitted that he wasn't sure where he and Maureen stood right now, especially after the business with sleeping with Karen back at school? And yet, it seemed like things were fine between them. However, was it possible Kyle was going through what he'd just gone through with Laura -- liking somebody enough, but in the end, not loving her? Remembering the indecision he had felt with Laura, he wondered what agonies Kyle must be going through right now. Justin had been looking for the signs of hesitation on Kyle's part all evening long, but so far hadn't seen them. He assumed Kyle was being very discreet, which was exactly what he would expect from him: Kyle was the soul of courtesy. But was he, perhaps -- even at this very moment -- looking for a way to break up with her?

After a moment more, watching them in the headlights, Justin said testingly to Craig, "So, what did you think of Maureen?"

"She seems fine. Why, don't you like her?"

"No, she's fine. I guess she's just not what I expected."

"What did you expect?"

"I don't know, someone pretty and tall and sophisticated -- someone like a model. Maureen seems very nice, and very down to earth, but not what I would have expected Kyle to pick."

"Yeah, she's a bit perky for my taste. I hate perky. But I'm not sure I could see Kyle with a model. He seems like somebody who'd want the all-American type."

"I guess," said Justin uncertainly. "I'm just not sure she seems special enough for him. I guess I never think the girlfriends of my friends are good enough for them."

"I see. And is that how you feel about Estelle?" said Craig a little icily.

"No, I didn't mean that," said Justin, though in truth, when he had met Estelle -- a very well-scrubbed, dark-haired woman with an erudite, but slightly stiff quality about her -- he had immediately recalled Kyle's disparaging "vegetarian virgin" assessment of another girlfriend from earlier in the year.

"You just meant that you don't feel anyone's good enough for Kyle?"

"No," said Justin, feeling suddenly constricted. "I guess I don't know what I meant."

"I think I know exactly what you meant," said Craig.

Justin was surprised by Craig's tone, and was on the verge of saying something, when he saw Maureen wave at them gaily and go in. Then, Kyle was heading back toward the car, and Justin let the comment die.

———•———

Next morning, they met Maureen for breakfast, then took a drive, the day more typical of March than the previous day had been. They needed winter jackets once again, and as they drove around, the earth looked bleak in the way that only the end of winter can: all the fields were muddy and flattened by the weight of snow, the grass a frosty yellow, and no buds had yet appeared on any of the tired-looking winter boughs. They might have been in Sweden for the starkness of the unplowed farmland all around them, and in truth, Justin felt almost as displaced. He and Craig were here in Kyle's hometown, but now Maureen was there with them, and everything seemed different and awkward, the dynamics changed. Driving around in the car, it almost seemed as though the four of them weren't certain where to go or what to do, and again, Justin wondered what Kyle was feeling about it all. Did he feel the same awkwardness in the situation as he had with Laura, and was his and Craig's presence there a help or a hindrance? Nice as Maureen was, Justin felt impatient for the three of them to be alone again, and wondered whether Maureen would be with them now for the duration.

———•———

That afternoon, the four of them decided to play cards in Maureen's parent's rec room. Walking down into the basement, which was like the renovated basement seemingly every person in the Midwest had: white walls; grey indoor/outdoor carpeting; a ping pong table; huge TV set designed, no doubt, for watching Sunday afternoon football games; a black leather sofa and a small bar -- Justin speculated on this world that almost everybody else seemed perfectly comfortable in, save him. What were the aspirations of the people who lived in rooms like these? To have a house, a family, a room in which one kicked back, had a beer and watched the ball games on the weekends? Was this the life Kyle wanted, too? Justin couldn't quite believe he did, and yet, he seemed perfectly content and at home here as Maureen set up the square card table, flipping out its four legs in their opposite directions, overturning it, then placing it squarely on the floor. He could imagine Kyle here in this world, with kids, but wondered whether Kyle still wanted it. What was he feeling now: Ambivalence? Guilt? Regret?

Maureen put in a tape, and soft folk music filled the room.

"Who's this?" said Craig as they staked out their little territories on the four opposing faces of the table.

"Chris Williamson. She's all the rage at ISU right now."

"Oh, yeah?" said Craig. "I've never heard of her."

"Big fave with all the lesbians." She looked at Justin as she said this, then at Kyle. Or was he dreaming that she'd looked at him with any meaning?

"Oh?" said Kyle.

"Don't worry," said Maureen: "I'm not a lesbian."

"Well, that's good to know," said Kyle, laughing a bit uncomfortably, thought Justin.

Maureen began to shuffle cards, and Kyle said, "Hey, can we have the game on as we play?"

"Sure," said Maureen, flipping on the oversize TV. The roar of cheering fans filled up the room.

Justin wasn't even sure what sport "the game" would be, and watched the ease with which the other three: Maureen, Kyle -- even Craig -- accepted this as background noise, this sport that, from all evidence, the vast majority of people cared about, save him. In truth, Justin's heart sank, for there was nothing more soulless and empty to him than flipping on a game and realizing that what he was doing was so out of sync with what the rest of the world was doing on that particular day.

Maureen got up and brought in chips and salsa. Again, for Justin, it was like a glimpse into another world: one he had read about or seen on TV, but which he'd never seen first hand -- a ritual as alien and far away to him as, say, a Jewish Seder. His swift initiation into this made Justin feel both curious and agitated. He would rather have been alone with Kyle or Craig, or seeing Stevens Point, and yet, he was intrigued to be included in a ritual like this he'd never really experienced. His family had never watched TV together like this, and certainly not sports. He guessed Kyle's family must have done this often, judging from how comfortable Kyle looked.

"Which game is this?" said Craig.

"Georgetown and Indiana. Looks like Indiana's up."

"Shit," said Craig. "I don't want Indiana to win: I hate Bobby Knight."

"He's a good coach, though."

"Yeah, but he's such an unbelievable asshole."

Justin was astonished by this interlude, surprised that Craig -- like seemingly all other males -- could come up with a comment like this on his own. To Justin, it was like the lingo of Wall Street people: as they started talks of stocks and bonds, not only did he fail to understand it, but he also had no interest in it, either. As they watched a while -- Craig groaning every time his team was thwarted, Kyle and Maureen joining with him -- Justin tried to like their team as well, but truthfully, his interest in this was as distant and *un*interested as if they'd been watching passing clouds.

After a while, Kyle said, "I guess Justin's not too thrilled by this, huh?"

"Oh, that's all right," said Justin, flattered and assuaged by Kyle's concern.

At last, the game winding down, they dealt the cards to play a game of hearts, and Justin felt relieved. Even if the three of them were not alone, the truth was, he was here in Stevens Point with Kyle and Craig, and he would make the best of it. Just then, Kyle laid the queen of spades on Justin, and his momentary happiness dissolved. How could Kyle do that? Justin asked himself as he endured their groans of sympathy as stiff-lipped as he could. Flustered, he let the next two hands go by before adopting his resolve. Emboldened then, he took the next trick full of hearts.

"What are you doing?" said Kyle.

Justin merely smiled at him.

"Is he trying to shoot the moon?"

There was a momentary silence, in which Craig said, "I don't think you're going to be able to do that, because a heart's already been played, hasn't it?"

"Oh, God," said Maureen, like an overeager cheerleader. "Is anybody sure?"

"I don't know," said Kyle. "I was pretty sure. The question now is, can anybody stop him?"

Through all this, Justin merely smiled to himself, uncertain whether he could pull off the trick or not, but going for the gamble. With each successive hand, he pulled in all the points, but in the end, his bid to shoot the moon, indeed, fell one heart short.

———◆———

That evening, sitting in Kyle's darkened living room, Kyle curled up in Maureen's lap, and Craig and Justin sitting in their chairs, apart, Justin watched Maureen caress Kyle's hair. Kyle was sprawled bare-stockinged, face flushed, shirttail loose, enthralled, and maybe even tumid in her lap, and Justin wondered what it must feel like to hold Kyle in one's arms like that. Kyle looked up into her eyes, then raised up from her lap to kiss her in that self-consciously demonstrative way young lovers had. Justin watched and wondered: did Kyle feel anything more for Maureen in these moments than he had toward Laura, or was he just being mechanical, too?

"These guys must be having loads of fun right now," said Maureen, self-conscious of their eyes, but also proud about her prize in Kyle.

"We're fine," said Craig.

"Well, I guess I should probably get going anyway," she said tentatively.

"Yeah," said Kyle, rising. Turning to Craig and Justin, he said, "If you guys just want to hang out here, I'll run Maureen home."

"Oh, no," said Craig. "We thought we'd come with you and say goodbye, too."

"Yeah, think again," said Kyle.

For a second, Justin thought Craig was serious about them going: he, too, had just assumed they would, and had been looking forward to the last few hours of the night alone with Kyle. Now, as Maureen and Kyle took off, Justin understood at last that he and Craig were giving the two of them some time alone. He felt a little hurt at being left; still, he thought it might be for the best. Was this, perhaps, the time when Kyle was finally going to have his talk with Maureen, maybe even break up with her? Maybe that's the reason he wanted to be alone.

As Craig and Justin climbed the strangely quiet stairs now, Kyle's folks asleep long ago downstairs, Justin was hoping Kyle would not be gone long -- that he'd have a chance to talk to Kyle when he returned, in order to keep exploring the confusion they had talked about. Of course, if Kyle broke up with Maureen now, he might come back upset. But that might mean even a better talk, since he would be on hand to comfort Kyle, to share his indecision and confusion.

"I wonder how long Kyle will be," said Justin idly.

"I don't know," said Craig, stepping in their room and closing the door behind them. "Maybe he'll just stay at Maureen's and fuck her all night long. After all, they're in love."

"What's your problem?" said Justin, shocked by Craig's antagonistic tone.

"I don't know. What's yours? I mean, what are we even doing here?"

"What do you mean, 'What are we doing here?' We're seeing Kyle."

"Um hmm," said Craig. "And our being here wouldn't have anything to do with the fact that you're in love with Kyle, now, would it?"

"Sure, I love Kyle," said Justin, taken aback and lowering his voice. "But I love you, too."

"Oh, don't give me that crap, Justin! You told me you were in love with him, remember? Or did you forget?"

"Okay," said Justin, gathering himself. "I love Kyle. So what?"

"I'm just saying, if Kyle weren't gorgeous, didn't have this hot little bod you're running around lusting after, would we even be here? I don't know. I don't see you running around lusting after *me* like that."

"Is that what this is about? That I'm more attracted to Kyle than I am to you?"

"Of course not! All I'm trying to say is, you don't just love Kyle, you're *in* love with him. And that makes a hell of a lot of difference."

"All right," said Justin, nearly paralyzed in the face of Craig's unexpected attack. "So, I'm in love with him. But Kyle and I talked about that. He even said he wondered about his own feelings."

"Oh, this famous conversation you guys had," said Craig, interrupting. "I don't know what the hell you two said to each other, but something tells me you read a lot more into it than Kyle ever intended. I mean, where is Kyle now? Do you see him here, Justin? No, and I'll tell you why: because he's in love with Maureen. Maureen, and not you."

"Okay, so maybe he can't love me the way I love him," said Justin, trembling. "Maybe he can -- I don't know. But I don't get why you're so angry."

"If I'm angry, it's because I feel like you're deluding yourself. I've been watching you this whole trip, Justin, watching how you moon around Kyle, hanging on his every word, his every action. I don't care if you're in love with him -- that part doesn't bother me at all. But Kyle is not in love with you -- he's not -- and you're not facing up to that. I'd be amazed, in fact, if he felt what you feel toward him. I guess I'm hurt a little, too, because right now I'm feeling like the only reason I'm along, the only reason we're here sleeping on this sofa bed, is that's as close as you can get to Kyle."

"Fuck you," said Justin, enraged and trembling, part of him feeling the validity of Craig's remarks, and yet the other half feeling totally betrayed and speechless.

"That's just it," said Craig, looking at him calculatedly. "I don't want to. And I don't think Kyle does, either."

Justin stood for a moment, stunned, then walked away in silence. He groped his way blind down the darkened, unfamiliar hallway, furious, guessing at rooms and switches, at a loss for what to do, then slowly began the process of washing up. He and Craig passed each other in the hallway wordlessly, maintaining their silence and their distance. Justin wondered whether Craig was right that Kyle would stay the night at Maureen's. He couldn't believe that Kyle would be that inconsiderate: they were guests staying at his house after all; yet, maybe Craig was right. But what if Kyle came back and said he'd broken things off with Maureen? Who would be right then? Craig would see -- he'd have to see, then -- that he'd been right all along, that he hadn't read things into this.

But, as the hours passed and Kyle did not return, he started gradually to understand how feeble that belief had been -- how foolish and naive. As time went on without Kyle coming back, he started to accept the truth, the way the parents of a missing child begin to know the worst when days and weeks have passed without the child's return: that love is gone. Half a dozen times that night, Justin thought he heard a car door slam, yet as they went to bed, Kyle still had not come home -- was out there somewhere still, locked in his passionate embraces with Maureen.

Next morning, they were awakened early by a newly-showered, ebullient Kyle, who greeted the two of them propped up wearily on their pillows like a return-ing conqueror. Justin had hardly gotten any sleep again last night -- had been up nearly all night tossing, turning, and thinking -- and, glad as he was to see Kyle, it was a happiness strained by weariness and worry. He could hear Kyle's parents stirring below, busily preparing breakfast, and wondered how in the world he was ever going to be able to discuss this. But, as Craig headed into the bathroom to clean up, Justin rose and followed Kyle into his room, hoping to seize this opportunity to talk to him. Kyle, who looked -- as usual -- fresh and handsome, had a robin's-egg-blue polo shirt stretched taut against the broad expanse of his pectorals, the small V at the throat betraying a tuft of thick black hair that pro-truded like a patch of pubic hair. Try as he might to ignore this, Justin had to tear his eyes away when Kyle said, "Hey. How are you, bud?"

"Fine. What time did you get back last night?"

"That would be this morning, I'm afraid," said Kyle. "Maureen and I kind of got carried away. Sorry to leave you guys on your own like that."

They sat down on alternate sides of the bed, and Justin listened, nervous and distracted, feeling Kyle's words wash over him like water moving over stones. How easily he could have sunk beneath that onrush. He felt then like a stone one finds along the water's edge and thinks a treasure, thrilling at its pretty, agate-like transparency, only to find a short time later, when the stone has dried to powdery opacity, that what initially seemed amber-hued and jewel-like now seems luster-less and repellent. Justin felt this way about himself -- about this truth Craig had made him face again: this truth he had to hoist up from the stream bed and con-front Kyle with; to set between them so that Kyle could see it as it truly was. And yet, how easily he could have let Kyle just continue coloring his own essential col-orlessness; how easy just to sink, heart-flutteringly, to the bottom of Kyle's words!

He looked at Kyle now, thinking how unfair this was to him -- how sordid and grotesque and pitiful was his desire: this covert, foolish love of his that he had so long sought to hide, quite conscious he was playing Russian roulette with his heart, one of whose chambers Kyle had filled, but not sure whether it was the full or empty chambers he was most afraid of.

At last he said, "Kyle, can I talk to you about something?"

"Sure, Just. Is everything okay with you and Craig? Things seem a little tense between you. Did you guys have a fight or something last night?"

"Kind of. That's what I want to talk to you about."

"What's up?"

"Craig thinks I need to be more honest with you -- no, actually, Craig thinks I need to be more honest with myself. That's what we were arguing about."

"I see," said Kyle, sobering.

"Do you remember what we talked about a while ago, how you said you might be questioning your sexuality?" Justin felt his heart begin to pound as he uttered this.

"I do," said "Kyle, "and I've been meaning to talk to you about that."

"You were? Oh, good. So, what did you mean, exactly?"

"Well, that's what I mean. I think maybe I misspoke, or maybe I gave you the wrong impression when I said that."

"I see," said Justin, swallowing hard.

"I think maybe for a while I got confused about where the dividing line was between love and friendship," said Kyle. "I realized I had a lot of really strong feelings for you and Craig, and I realized you were wrestling with your own feelings -- maybe even your own sexuality. I thought, well, if I feel something, too, is there a chance that *I'm* gay? Especially given all the stress surrounding the incident with Steve, and then, doing what I did by sleeping with Karen. I was very confused. I still haven't told Maureen about it yet, but I'm going to. I know it's going to be really, really difficult for her to forgive me, if that's even possible. I feel bad I didn't do it last night, but it'll come in time. I know I'll have a long, hard road getting her to trust me ever again, but that's what I'm going to have to do.

"Anyway, to get back to what you were saying, maybe I shouldn't have said anything to you when we had our talk, because I'm afraid I confused you. That may, ultimately, have been the problem with Steve, too, I'm sorry to say -- maybe even with Eric. You really gave me a jolt when you said what you said about him being attracted to me; I'd never really thought about that before. Anyway, I've been thinking about it ever since we talked, and while I *do* feel a very great affection for you and Craig, it's not love -- not *that* kind of love. I think it's important for me to say that to you, because sometimes I get the feeling you've been looking to me for clues about yourself. Like yesterday, when you hugged me on the tennis court. It was pretty obvious to me you were feeling something I wasn't, looking for me to be something I'm not. I'm not gay, Justin -- I know that without a doubt. I don't know where *you* stand, but I *am* sure about myself, and I don't want to do anything to mislead you."

"I think it's really important for me to hear that," said Justin, hardly hearing his own words -- speaking them, rather, because he knew he had to, though the sense of them was almost lost behind the roar of blood inside his ears. "I want to be honest with you, Kyle, and I haven't always been -- I haven't always been honest with myself." He sat there now, lower lip trembling, the hot salt pressing from behind his eyes, then said, "This isn't easy for me."

"I'm sure it's not."

"It's a pretty hard thing to admit about myself, I guess," said Justin, stopping as the tears began to well. "The truth is, I think I *am* gay. What's more, I think I've known it for a long time. I was just too afraid to admit it."

"I'm sure it's really scary," said Kyle.

"I was really afraid I'd lose you as friends if I told you," continued Justin.

"Justin, do you really think that would have made us stop liking you?"

"I didn't know. And you guys are *so* important to me. You have no idea."

"I just wonder what all this means for our friendship, I guess," ventured Justin cautiously. "I couldn't deal with the thought of losing you and Craig as friends -- that's been my fear all along; but at the same time, I can't continue denying myself, denying the fact that I'm probably gay."

"It's going to be a difficult road, I'm sure, but I know you'll pull through all right," said Kyle.

"I guess," said Justin.

"You will," said Kyle.

Summoning up his last reserves of courage, Justin said, "There's something else, too."

"Okay," said Kyle a little warily. He leaned back casually on one magnificently splayed bicep.

Justin looked at it abstractly for a moment, then said, "It's great that we're talking about all this, but I think I need to be really clear about something else." Justin took a deep breath, wondering how in the world he was ever going to utter these fateful words. Then, gearing himself up one final time, he said, "I've told you now about my sexuality, and I'm glad you're aware of it; Craig is, too. But are you also aware that…that I'm in love with *you*?"

"Yes," said Kyle after a moment. "I guess I am."

He felt again the wave of sadness, guilt, and love that seemed to be so much a part of his relationship with Kyle, paused for a second to look searchingly at him, and thought -- not for the first time -- that by loving Kyle, he'd botched the only real love he had ever known.

"You say you understand I'm in love with you," said Justin, faltering, "But do you also understand how hard that is for me? I mean, how can we continue to be friends?"

"I don't know, Justin," said Kyle, looking heartbreakingly scared.

Justin felt a strange emotion creeping in -- an outrage at the way Kyle lay there so complacently, accepting all the things he was saying. He almost wished Kyle *would* get mad, throw iron barriers around himself -- at least, express the obvious discomfort and impossibility about the situation. "I keep on thinking about that night when Steve attempted suicide," said Justin. "We went back to your room and I was holding you, and you *kissed* me. What was *that* about?"

Kyle looked pained, defensively suddenly. "I'm sorry, Justin. I see I *have* been confusing you, and I have to take the blame for that. But that kiss -- that kiss was genuine." Kyle paused, the hint of a tear beginning to form in the corner of his eye. "I *do* love you. It's not a sexual thing with me, but I feel so close to both you guys, and that night, that kiss was what I felt. I can't explain it, but I meant it. My dad has never shown me a whole lot of affection, either, and in many ways, even my desire to be a counselor and go into psychology, has been a conscious working against that old-school belief that men shouldn't show emotion. Actually, I've been really consciously trying to get myself to the point where I *can* show affection to someone regardless of their sex, wherever and whenever I feel it."

"But can you see how confusing that kiss was to me?"

"I do."

"So what do we do, then?" said Justin, almost accusatorily, overloud and hopeless. "How do we stay friends at all?"

Kyle shifted and said, "Let me ask you something, Justin -- and I *have* been thinking about this. Do you feel *only* physical attraction for me?"

Justin felt bewildered. "I don't know," he said uncertainly.

"Think about it. Is what you feel for me exclusively sexual, or is there more to it than that?"

"No, I don't think it's just sex," said Justin, suddenly uncertain where all this was going. "I guess it's like you said: sex is a part of love, but love is more than just sex."

"That's what I mean," said Kyle. "I'm beginning to think that maybe love is not an either/ or -- not purely this or that. I'm not even sure I think sexual attraction overshadows all other aspects *overwhelmingly* when you love someone. It's certainly extremely important; but I think love's a spiritual, emotional, and intellectual attachment, too. I feel those bonds with *both* you and Craig; and though I'm confident it's not a sexual attraction, I also know I feel a certain sense of something when we hug: a warmth, a bond, a certain sense of connected-ness and release. Those were some of the things I was struggling with before, all worried they might mean that something sexual was going on. But I don't think that now. I know I love Maureen. But, as I said, I'm even attempting to embrace those other feelings somewhat. It seems to me there has to be a place for us -- for people, in general -- to meet. There has to be a place for you, Justin, and for me -- a place where men and women can be friends platonically; a place where gay and straight men can meet."

"All right," said Justin. "I guess what you're saying is, you still want to try to be friends with me, which I want, too. But how do we do that?"

"I feel a little sad in saying this," said Kyle," but truthfully, I think it *is* going to have to be more up to you than me in terms of figuring out what the limits are. I think you also have to be the one to weigh the benefits against the cost. It hurts that I can't help you with that part, but I guess that's how it has to be."

"I guess it's one of those things we're going to have to take step by step," said Justin after a moment.

"One more thing," said Kyle.

"All right," said Justin, bracing himself.

"I want you to know how much I care about you, whatever you decide. If we can't continue to be friends, I'll understand. I'll be sorry, but I'll understand. If I had another life to give you, bud, I would. I just want you to be happy."

Justin felt as though his heart were going to burst. For the first time since they had begun talking, he felt as though maybe things weren't quite as bleak as they seemed. He'd been certain that, as soon as he professed his love, he and Kyle would not be friends anymore.

"Thank you," he said, although he wasn't certain that was what he meant -- not certain that was what he meant at all.

"Let me give you a hug," said Kyle uncertainly.

As they rose to hug each other, Justin felt Kyle's arms around him, and felt the old familiar yearning deep inside. Then, in a surge of unassimilable grief, he thought, *I've wasted so much time.*

Later, as they were preparing for the return trip to school, Kyle decided to run out to perform a quick errand, and to say a private goodbye to Maureen. In the unexpected interval as they waited for his return, Justin said tentatively: "Craig, I'd like to fill you in on my conversation with Kyle this morning."

"Good," said Craig tersely.

"We had a really good talk, and I just want to let you know where things stand."

"Okay."

After Justin filled Craig in on all the details of the conversation, recounting as honestly and exactly as possible everything that was said, he said, "So, do you think there's any chance Kyle and I can actually still stay friends?"

"I don't know," said Craig. "I think it gets real complicated whenever sex is involved. I'm not really sure it can work out, but I hope you know I want the two of *us* to stay friends, regardless of what happens between you and Kyle. Mostly, I just don't want to see you get hurt, and honestly, I think you're going to have to watch really hard to make sure that doesn't happen."

"I know," said Justin, not certain of anything anymore at all. "I want the two of us to stay friends as well." He wanted so much to say, "I love you," but again, wasn't certain that he should.

"Come here," said Craig, inviting him into his arms.

As Craig embraced him -- as he felt Craig's care envelop him -- Justin thought, *here it is; here is the difference:* with Craig's arms wrapped around him, there was only peace, contentment; whereas with Kyle, he felt quite certain there would never be any of that at all.

CHAPTER 7

———◆———

STANDING IN THE DIM LIGHT of the bathroom in his dormitory after they'd been back from Stevens Point almost a week, Justin felt the toothpaste swirl and foam inside his mouth. It ran and dripped along the brush, his hand, and still, he felt listless, thinking vacantly about the trip and where the situation stood with Kyle. He was wondering how in the world they were going to hold onto a friendship now that he'd confessed to Kyle he was in love with him. A fat, blue blob plopped on the white porcelain of the sink, and Justin looked at it idly. He'd been brushing and brushing, staring off into space for who knew how long, until finally he started thinking, *Sooner or later, you have to spit things out. Sooner or later, you just have to get rid of them.* He felt himself begin to gag on the toothpaste, and -- spitting it into the basin -- began to clean up the sink, his hand, the brush.

Suddenly, beside him once again was the new boy, the transfer student he'd run into sometime before. *Tim. No, Tom,* thought Justin: *Like 'every Tom, Dick and Harry.'*

"Hi. How was your break?" said Tom.

Turning now, Justin saw the look of eagerness and hopefulness in Tom's eyes. It was a look he found intimidating and a little off-putting. Certainly, Tom was cute: dark-haired, boyish, and a little vulnerable. There was something about him, too, that reminded him a little bit of Craig, though he couldn't place his finger on precisely what. Tom had Craig's air of disheveled lovability, he guessed. He seemed like someone you'd see walking in a rainstorm without an umbrella -- someone you would want to offer yours. "All right," shrugged Justin. "How was yours?"

"Okay," said Tom, placing his brown kit bag on the occluded aluminum mirror of the shelf.

They stood for a second awkwardly, then Justin said, "How's that girlfriend of yours?"

"What?" said Tom, looking startled.

"Your girlfriend. Didn't you move here because of her?"

"Oh, we broke up," said Tom, looking a bit uncomfortable, and still not commencing his tooth-brushing operations.

"That blows, huh?" said Justin.

"Yeah," said Tom, standing there jumpily.

What's this guy's problem? thought Justin. He gathered his gear, preparing to leave, but not wanting to seem rude. Tom still had not begun to brush his teeth, which would have made leaving easier. Instead, he stood there with his arms akimbo.

"Hey, I heard your roommate didn't come back," said Tom.

"No," said Justin. "I'm not sure what happened. He was from Nigeria. I think things got too complicated with his Visa somehow, and he couldn't come back." Justin picked his gear up from the shelf, preparing to leave.

"Oh. Do you miss him?"

"Yeah, I do," said Justin, stopping in his tracks. He felt so surprised by this question that all he could think to say was, "Why?"

"Oh, I don't know," said Tom. "You just seem really lonely to me, and I thought that might be why."

Justin stood there, frozen, Tom a step or two away, blocking his way out. It seemed to Justin that Tom had fingered something deep inside him even he was not aware of. He'd been wandering the campus dazed and lost these past few days, as if he couldn't quite remember how to get home. Tom's words echoed like a dream voice, resonating as if he'd just snapped awake, and Justin blinked, trying to register the sense of it.

"Because if you are, I wish you'd stop by sometime," continued Tom. "I'm lonely, too."

Justin looked at him, and absurdly felt himself begin to tear up. "Thanks," he said, "I'm fine." He wasn't certain what was happening to him: he felt as though he might explode.

"I'm not sure you are," said Tom. "In fact, I'm pretty sure you're not." Then, Tom leaned in and hugged him, trapping Justin's arms.

He stood there for a moment, shocked, then felt himself begin to cry. Immediately -- petrified -- he choked the tears back. Yet, looking in the mirror, Justin was transfixed by what he saw: two men embracing in the half-light of the room. One of the men was him; he couldn't quite assimilate the sight. He kept on staring at his face -- his own face -- looking at himself. Finally, he managed to say tearfully, almost inaudibly, "Thanks. I'm not sure what's the matter with me."

"It's all right," said Tom. "I think we're both a lot alike. I've been watching you."

"Watching me?"

"Yeah. Ever since you got back, you've been out of sorts."

"Thank you for noticing," said Justin, feeling oddly scared.

"I'll tell you something else," said Tom.

"What's that?" said Justin, feeling almost like he knew what Tom was going to say.

"I think you're really cute. In fact, I've wanted to get to know you since the moment I first saw you."

"But, I thought you had a girlfriend," Justin stammered.

"I don't have a girlfriend, Justin, any more than you do. I was scared before, and so I said that. But I'm gay. And if I'm not mistaken, I think you are, too."

Tom leaned in as if to kiss him, but Justin pulled back fearfully, eyes glancing toward the door.

"I'm sorry," said Justin, reeling. He pushed past Tom and headed to the door.

Justin walked the strangely detached hallway to his room, upset, upended, sitting on the bed and feeling like the room was spinning, turning on its axis like the globe he'd seen Kyle take out of its huge wood cradle in the library one night. Justin had been shocked that Kyle could lift the globe at all; then that he did: the huge, *papier-mache* ball moving slowly through the stacks; Justin watching in amazement as the oceans and the continents rolled gently down the aisle, propelled by Kyle's soft touch; the world now spinning strangely -- north to south -- as if reverse-poled, which was the way he felt right now: reverse-poled Justin.

Then, Tom was standing in his door.

In a second more, he felt his world begin to spin again as Tom walked in and closed the door behind him, taking Justin in his arms and kissing him. Tom's mouth pressed breathlessly against his mouth, their bodies meshed together. He felt starved and paralyzed, tried to resist, and yet the sheer force of Tom's ardor held him in his place. He felt as though he might faint. They swayed for what seemed like eternity -- eternity inside a single moment.

Then, Tom was leading him back to the bed and laying down on top of him, Tom's weight pressed down upon him, centering and enveloping him. Justin lay there feeling petrified, Tom's fingers fumbling at his shirt, his mouth on Justin's nipples and a jolt -- electric -- running straight to Justin's groin. He tried to make the room stop -- tried to focus on Tom's body, on the calmness in *his* body as he felt Tom growing frantic. *Hold me,* he was thinking -- tried to say, but nothing came out. Tom was tearing off his own shirt, fumbling with his belt, and Justin felt like someone caught in nearly hard cement -- like someone trying to run away from something in a dream, but finding that his limbs would not cooperate. He felt his brain protesting, wondered, *What would Kyle think?* -- felt Tom pulling off his pants and underwear, then felt a strange, uncanny dehiscence as Tom took him in his arms. A force within was burgeoning -- a yearning so intense and hungry that his penis might have been a womb: a place that needed to be filled. Yet, at the same time, he was having difficulty in not turning Tom flat on his back and thrusting deep into his soft-haired thighs. He pressed his face against Tom's chest, and it was like being lost within a bay, like water moving out into a larger body of water. Tom continued kissing him; it was as though he'd found the center of his body somehow, and was filling it with only him. They moved and swayed together for an endless time, both undulating, cradling, striving with each movement to climb further into one another. He could feel a pressure building deep inside him, flowing upwards, then gone past as they collapsed upon the bed.

"Oh, my God!" said Tom, still panting afterwards. "That was incredible!"

Justin lay there feeling spent, exhausted, but a little strange. Now that the act was over, he felt agitated, and unaccountably afraid. "What did we just do?"

"We did what you've been wanting to your whole life: you made love to another man."

"But I don't even know you."

"Justin, listen, it's okay: relax."

Justin felt so strange. Part of him felt calm; the other part was taxed beyond belief: spent; winded; caducous.

"I'm sorry, Tom. All of this is happening so fast. I'm not sure what to think or feel. I hate to be rude, but I think I need a little while to take all this in."

"Alright," said Tom reflectively, "as long as you promise me you won't start feeling guilty."

"I promise," said Justin, lying.

Tom got up reluctantly and started gathering his clothes, then stood for a moment, naked, in the incandescent light. The light backlit Tom's scrotal hair to make a fiery sun of it, his testicles pulled tight against the chill inside the room. Even after Tom had dressed, he kept on seeing that: Tom's scrotum like a dandelion puff exploding in the light.

———————

When Tom had gone -- an awkward hug, a brief, though stirring kiss -- Justin still lay curled up on the bed, confused and fearful. He was curled the way a leaf curls just before the fire consumes it, feeling guilty and ashamed.

What did this mean? What should he do now? He'd had sex with someone -- with a man! Or was it even truly sex? He lay there feeling oddly clinical, wondering what the technical definition of sex was, then got out his dictionary and read, "the penetration of a woman's vagina by the male genitalia; b. the contact of the genitalia." He guessed they qualified on "b," but thought there wasn't even really a precise term for what they'd done. What would Kyle say if he knew what had happened? Then again, why should he care? In a very real way, Tom was the answer to his prayers. Yet, Justin still could not help thinking how much differently he would have felt if it were Kyle who had seduced him, rather than Tom. Somehow, guilt would not have been an issue if he'd just made love with Kyle, precisely since he *did* love Kyle, and therefore, wouldn't have felt an ounce of guilt about whatever they had done. What was he saying, then: that love between two people -- even two men -- was all right, as long as it was love? What he'd just done with Tom was not that different from what he'd done with Laura. Yet, how much different it had felt! One felt uncomfortable and wrong, the other, so natural and electrifying, there wasn't any comparison. And yet, he didn't love Tom any more than he loved Laura. What was startling to him now as he thought about it, however, was the sense that he could finally envision making love with someone in the future -- some man -- that he'd feel alright in loving, if the thing he truly felt was love. He'd never felt that way before, and it amazed him. Was it possible, someday, that he could love Tom? He wasn't sure; but for the first time ever, Justin felt that maybe love -- whatever that was -- might be out there somewhere, waiting to be found.

───❖───

Next morning, though, the guilt was back, and -- walking out into the weak warmth of the April day -- he still felt just a bit off. He kept examining his clothes to make sure he was fully dressed, and yet, as many times as he assured himself, he kept on reaching down to make sure his belt and shoes were there, or that he had his shirt on. Walking past the dorm Head Resident's apartment on his way to Craig's room, Justin found himself thinking idly that, in England, the position would have been called the Head Master. *The Master of Head.* He flashed again on Tom's body on top of his -- felt his penis burgeoning -- and told himself to stop it.

He continued walking in the spring air, seeing students walking in their clusters underneath the Gothic arches of the chapel windows; saw the grass returning to its greenery, the red and yellow tulips bursting with their sexual organs thrust shamelessly into the air: black pistils crowded yearningly around the yellow stamen. *Sex, sex, sex,* he thought. *The world is all just sex.*

Suddenly, Justin panicked as he thought about the very real possibility of running into Tom this morning. What would he say to him if he did? As he thought about it, Justin's first impulse was to run and hide, to avoid him entirely. But why should he avoid seeing Tom, when the experience he'd had with him had been so amazing and fulfilling? What was wrong with him?

Now, as he came to Craig's room, Justin felt as dislodged as a roulette ball: encircling the banked green of the quad, waiting for the wheel to slow to find a temporary home -- to lodge into a safe slot. Justin reached Craig's dorm and stood for a moment, steadying, as though the point of contact had gone past, and he was waiting for the wheel to make its circuit one more time, and things to kick, at last, back into place.

He climbed the stairs and wondered how on earth he was going to tell Craig. He recalled the day he'd raced here after Steve had slit his wrists, Craig answering the door as groggy as a bear. Steve wanted Kyle to love him; Justin did as well. Now he'd made love with a man: he was a gay man knocking on Craig's door. He heard the heavy shift as Craig moved in his bed, and flashed again on Tom's bare torso lifting heavily from him in bed last night. Then, Craig was there, his warm face in the doorway and a scent like cinnamon and wax emitting from his bedroom.

"Hi," said Craig. "What's up?"

"Well, last night was an interesting evening." Justin walked past Craig and sat down on the bed, shucking his light, spring jacket like the outer, papery layer of an onion.

"Oh, yeah? How so?"

Justin took a breath and sat for a moment, like a platform diver collecting himself before he decides to bounce off the diving board at last. "You know that new kid in my dorm -- the transfer student, Tom?"

"Yeah, I think so."

"Well, I was washing up last night; he came in the bathroom and we started talking. One thing led to another, and before I knew it, he was hugging me in the bathroom."

"Oh yeah?"

"I was just as startled as you are. I thought he had a girlfriend, and that he'd transferred here because of her, in fact. Turns out, that wasn't true. He told me he was attracted to me, and that he'd wanted to get to know me from the moment he first saw me."

"And then he hugged you?"

"Yeah."

"So what'd *you* do?"

"Well," said Justin, feeling suddenly ashamed once more. "I was really confused and scared, and I just went back to my room. But he followed me down the hall, and the next thing I knew, we ... were having sex." As Justin said the word, he was extremely conscious of the hissing of the initial sibilant, a sound that seemed synonymous with "sin."

"And is that good?" said Craig after a moment. "That you had sex?"

"I don't know," said Justin, surprised. "I mean, it does seem kind of sordid, doesn't it?"

"You just a*maze* me sometimes, Justin," said Craig, exasperated. "How are you ever going to know the way you feel unless you test it out? Now that you've admitted to yourself you're gay, what, you're never going to act on that?"

"You're right, I guess. It's just ... I guess it's just a little difficult to stave off all that guilt, you know? I mean, even coming here today to tell you, thinking how you'd react to it -- what Kyle would think about it -- was really daunting."

"Oh, now I get it," said Craig, stiffening. "You're worried about what *Kyle* will think; I should have known. Justin, listen to me: you're going to have to let Kyle go. You can't keep hanging onto him, expecting things from him. He just can't love you in the way you want."

"Don't you think I know that?" said Justin, his upper lip beginning to tremble uncontrollably.

"No, I'm not sure you do. I mean, I think intellectually you understand it, and yet you act as though you don't. Honestly, Justin, I'm sorry to say it, but sometimes I think you're like one of those stupid little ducks, the ones that hatch out of their eggs and imprint on the first thing they see: a goose or swan or scientist -- some way-wrong thing they think is 'mother.' You've said a number of times you thought Kyle and I had showed you what love was, but I think Kyle's what's gotten in the *way* of love for you. You can't move on with him around, and yet you've *got* to. Just like now: you're here, ashamed of what Kyle or I will think of what you've done, all worried we can't stay friends, and yet you still don't get it. What *I* think, or what *Kyle* thinks of what you've done, is not important. Whether we stay friends or not is not important, though I hope we can. The only thing that counts is that you're all right with *yourself.*"

"I know," said Justin, though, in truth, he was a little startled: he had not arrived at this conclusion on his own. "I know," he said again, as if by repetition he could make it so.

———•———

As he walked back to his dorm room late that morning, the spring day warm and humid, with the scent of clover yielding to the hotter, drier smell of cut grass -- grass trimmed back perennially from the point of seeding to a state of constant, unachieved fruition -- he felt detached, a little agitated. Walking down his hall, the dorm felt dead, what with the campus winding toward graduation. As he walked into his room and set his bag down, he could not decide what he should do. Should he go talk to Kyle, despite what Craig had said, or should he go see Tom? He felt uncertain what he'd say to Tom. He felt attracted to him -- that much now seemed obvious. And yet, he also felt ambivalent about pursuing things with Tom, when he was still in love with Kyle. As Justin pondered this, he turned around and saw Tom standing in the doorway.

"Hi," said Tom a little bashfully.

"Hello," said Justin, just as shyly.

"How do you feel today?"

"I don't know."

"Yeah, I know, that's why I thought I'd stop by."

There was something beautiful about Tom's lashes, moist and black and boyish, that made Justin want to kiss them. Scared and mixed up as he was, he felt a yearning deep inside him for the feelings Tom had given him last evening when they lay there naked with each other. Suddenly, he saw himself draw Tom into the room and close the door. He felt their arms enfolding one another. Then, their lips met softly as a deer's mouth touching a lake at sunset. He felt their bodies moving as if underwater, but with fluidity and clarity, not with clumsiness. They cradled each other, rocking, fitting perfectly; and yet, despite himself, he still felt just a little sad Tom wasn't Kyle.

When they had finished making love again, they nestled quietly against each other, staring into space.

"How are you now: Okay?" said Tom.

"I think so," said Justin. Justin's body was at peace. His mind, however, felt regret: regret that he and Kyle would never make love as he had with Tom; regret that soon the year would end and his best friends would graduate; regret that here he was with Tom -- this beautiful, attractive guy -- and he was thinking still of Kyle. He thought about what Craig had said. Perhaps Kyle *was* still in the way of love for him. So, how did he remove that obstacle?

"You're far away," said Tom.

"I'm here."

"Okay, you're here *and* far away. What are you thinking of?"

"About how glad I am you cornered me last night."

"How come?"

"I feel like somebody needed to give me a place to put my foot down, you know? All this time I've just been floating along, talking about being gay and not knowing. But now this has happened, and I feel sort of like Archimedes: 'Give me a place to stand, and I shall lift the world.'"

"Oh, but I notice I've only given you a place to put *one* foot down, huh?"

"I'll get the other down eventually. Just give me time," said Justin, a bit embarrassed that Tom had noticed his ambivalence.

"I think you will," said Tom. "Come on. It's a beautiful day out. What do you say we take a walk?"

"Sounds great," said Justin, thinking he could use something to take his mind off of his worries.

As they dressed and wandered out onto the quad, he was reminded of the day he'd taken Laura's hand inside the cafeteria to signify they were a couple. Despite not actually doing that with Tom right now, he was aware how much more genuine the impulse felt this time -- strange, scary, and exciting, but vastly more spontaneous and real. They walked into the fields behind the dorms, now full of dandelions, and he remembered how the three of them -- he, Kyle, and Craig -- had stumbled on the dandelion field so early in their friendship. Thinking of it now, the memory was bittersweet. He wondered whether what he felt for Tom could ever equal that. They were attracted to each other, obviously, and they'd made love. But was it *love* yet? Was it even friendship? Looking at Tom -- at his beautiful, attentive face -- it seemed a quite real possibility. But were they merely two men who were mutually attracted to each other? Once again, he asked himself, how much of love was friendship? And how much of friendship was contained in love? Weren't they both, basically, root and flower of the same plant?

Tom bent down to pick a greenish-yellow bloom and held it under Justin's chin. "If I see yellow, it means you're in love," said Tom.

"Yeah, or the sun's reflecting off the flower," Justin said, and laughed.

"Such a romantic."

"Actually, I feel like I am," said Justin. "I just haven't had that much opportunity to put it into practice."

"Maybe now you'll get a chance," said Tom, holding out a yellow dandelion head to him: a mini sun.

"Maybe I will," said Justin bashfully. "I've always loved dandelions, even if they're weeds."

"Oh, don't call them weeds," said Tom. "A weed's just something people call a thing that's growing where they think it shouldn't. But they're wildflowers, just the same; it's all a matter of semantics. Besides, you've got to admire their will to survive. They're tenacious little things. And they *are* beautiful, no matter what people say."

Justin looked down at the incandescent yellow blossoms, as if seeing them for the first time. Thinking back to the day he'd frolicked in the field with Kyle and Craig, he said, "Does the yellow part become the grey puffball later on?"

"You've obviously never taken Botany 101," said Tom.

"No," said Justin, laughing, "I haven't. It's all a mystery to me: a great big cloud."

"Let's review our flowers, then, shall we?" said Tom, sitting on the apple-green turf underneath some fading forsythias. Pointing out a dandelion clump nearby, he said: "First comes the flower, all innocent and springy yellow, opening up its fresh new face to the world. Then, along comes some clumsy bumblebee, tracking its sticky little pollen on the dandelion's bright new head, like a man who forgets to wipe the mud off his shoes on the doormat. Now, the flower's been sullied: it's ashamed; it's dirty. Suddenly, it hides its head and sinks back in itself, afraid to show its face. For a while, the flower broods. Dark, inexplicable changes take place deep within. Then, finally, the flower -- newly energized and ready -- hoists its grey head proudly in the air. But still, it can't let go. It feels so *strange*. It doesn't realize that -- though it's changed -- the seeds of what it was are still there, waiting for a chance to grow again. It holds on for a while, tight as a fist until -- the time being right at last -- it simply lets go, lets the wind disseminate it, and the process all begins again."

Tom plucked a dandelion puff nearby and blew it into Justin's face, as startling as a spurt of semen.

"Make a wish," said Tom.

EPILOGUE

THEN GRADUATION WAS UPON THEM and Justin was racing across the rampant, mid-May quad, its thickly tufted grass tangled here and there with dandelion puffs, their dotted-Swiss coronas radiating like the last stage of some perfect, dying supernova. He watched his feet swish through them, leaving little white streaks on the asparagus-green turf as he advanced, thinking about the things Tom had said, about the fact that everything was now about to change. He headed down the hill and up the other side to Kyle's room, past the tennis courts and gym where he and Kyle and Craig had once played basketball. The parking lot beside the gym was crowded now with families in navy polyester suits and floral dresses emptying from Pintos, Plymouths, and Chevettes -- whole groups of men and women and their kids who had no notion of how sacred this ground was; who'd never know what he and Kyle and Craig had meant to one another; who had, perhaps, some distant memories of when they'd first encountered love, or found the one without whose presence all the rest of life seemed inconceivable. He wondered, though, how many of those lucky few had ever had to puzzle over whether what they felt was weed or flower? How many of them could have told him where love crossed the line of friendship, changing over, like the dandelion, from its sunny yellow innocence into the grey of sex?

He'd had a little fight with Tom the night before about today: he'd filled Tom in about his history regarding Kyle and Craig, and Tom said jealously: "You'd rather spend your last day with your old boyfriend than with me. You're still in love with him."

"Look, Tom," said Justin, feeling a certain sting of truth in this, but also a certain nascent resoluteness that it was not the whole truth anymore: "Kyle and Craig have been my best friends all year long, and yes, I *do* love them. I want to say goodbye. I *have* to say goodbye."

In truth, he did feel somewhat unresolved about his motives. Indeed, much as he'd begun to feel something for Tom, and wanted him there, a big part of him wanted these last moments alone with Kyle and Craig.

"Why don't you come with me if you're so concerned?"

"No, no, that's all right," said Tom. "You go. I'll be here when you're ready."

He'd been somewhat miffed and unsettled about the whole exchange, and yet, he wondered whether Tom was right. Was he still hoping, holding onto something that he'd never have, unwilling to let go?

Now, Justin stood with Kyle and Maureen in Kyle's boxed-up bedroom, the mattress lying guiltily upon the floor, the sheet pulled back, exposing to the light of day the light-grey, pinstriped mattress on which Kyle and Maureen had undoubtedly made love last night, just shortly after Kyle had met her at the train. Kyle had his black graduation robe on, the pale pink piping running along the outer edge of the stole to indicate his honor's status. He looked, for all the world, like some Prince just waiting to ascend the throne. Justin felt a tug of sorrow and regret, but tried to counter those feelings with thoughts of Tom.

Now, as they joined the other seniors on the quad, they found Kyle's parents, as well as Craig's and Estelle's. Craig's parents introduced themselves to Kyle's; Craig shyly introduced them to Estelle as well, who stood there looking nervous as a Catholic schoolgirl at her first communion. Looking at Kyle and Maureen, and Craig and Estelle, Justin suddenly felt as though he didn't fit in, and wished Tom *had* come. Then, in the next breath, he wondered what reaction that would have triggered? He knew that time would someday come, but not today: today was for celebrating what had been.

As they milled about, waiting for the ceremony to begin, Kyle's mother looked at Justin and said, "So, Justin's not graduating, is that right?"

"No," said Justin, feeling sad and awkward.

"Justin's a freshman." said Kyle, beaming at him.

"I figured he was either younger than you, or his parents stood him up," said Kyle's mother, at which they all laughed.

Kyle glanced over at Estelle, then said, "Justin and Estelle are the two youngsters."

"Now what class are you in, Estelle?" said Craig's mother.

"I'm a freshman, also," said Estelle, after which there was an awkward pause, and during which Estelle looked as though she wanted to die.

Justin had never met Craig's parents, and had only barely gotten to know Estelle, who seemed sweet enough. He felt another twinge of guilt about this: Kyle had so preoccupied him over this past year that everything else had been pushed aside. Craig's parents had stood there until now as silent and bewildered as the elderly residents in a nursing home, being showered suddenly with birthday party balloons. Craig's mother had a slight Southern accent, hair the color of brass, and large, gold-rimmed glasses, which gave her face a kind of Mother Goose quality. This was accentuated by a large, silk jabot that cascaded in motherly ruffles and frills all down her front, and made it look as though she might be carrying some kind of staff along with her.

"Where's *your* girl?" said Kyle's father to Justin suddenly.

"Oh, I don't have one," said Justin lamely, feeling stupid.

"You don't *have* one?" said Kyle's father, ribbing him good naturedly. "Well, why not, for goodness sake? I thought you college kids were supposed to be smart. That don't sound very smart to me, not having a girl."

"Dad," said Kyle.

"Well does it?" said Kyle's father, appealing to his wife.

"Now, Bud, behave," said Kyle's mother. "These kids didn't come here today for you to pick on them, did you?" She smiled at Justin with such warmth that Justin had to smile in return.

"Maureen," continued Kyle's mother, "How was your graduation?"

"Oh, it was wonderful!" said Maureen, who was wearing a peach-colored satin dress that set her bright blue eyes off wonderfully. "The only bad part was that this boo-boo wasn't there," she said, punching Kyle lightly on the arm.

"Ouch," said Kyle, shielding himself comically.

"Now, now, no fighting," said Kyle's mother.

"Yeah, save that until *after* you're married," said Kyle's father, laughing.

The ceremony was about to begin, and Justin sat on the sun-drenched quad with a thousand other parents on their wooden folding chairs, observing all the seniors marching through the corridor of black-gowned faculty. He watched the ceremony, saw both Kyle and Craig up on the platform, readying to exit from his life, and still was not sure how he felt.

Now, as the crowd stood, watching all the seniors file out, he watched the mortar boards sail up into the air -- watched Kyle and Craig conversing with their families -- and waited for his opportunity. He'd thought about this for a long time now -- about the way he wanted to say goodbye -- and only since he'd had his talk with Tom had he decided what he'd do. He waited for a break, then cornered Kyle and Craig.

"Hey, guys," he said, a bit self-conscious with Maureen around. "Come here a second, would you?" Bending down, he picked two huge grey dandelions from the lawn and handed then to Kyle and Craig.

"Alright," said Kyle, blowing on his and dispersing it immediately to the wind. "We're free."

Justin felt his insides clutch a moment, then release. *That's fine*, he told himself. *Perhaps that's how it should be, after all.*

Craig looked at Justin for a moment, then said, "Ah, I have a feeling you weren't supposed to do that."

"Oh," said Kyle. "I'm sorry."

"That's all right," said Justin. "I just wanted you both to know how much your friendship means to me. To me, this symbolizes a bond I think we'll always have."

"Because of that day out in the field?" said Craig, as always, understanding immediately.

"That's right," said Justin.

"Oh, that's really nice. That'll mean a lot to Kyle, won't it," said Maureen, inserting herself into the moment like an unctuous talk show host.

"Absolutely," said Kyle.

There was an awkward moment, a seeming acknowledgment of the inevitability of the change at hand. Then, Kyle hugged him suddenly.

As he felt Kyle's arms around him, Justin felt the same old, helpless, swamped-boat-in-the-stream-of-love sense he had always felt before; yet, for the first time, he felt something new in it as well: a certain self-awareness; a surprising knowledge that he didn't really need a rescue anymore. He loved Kyle dearly, yet he also realized, as Kyle continued holding him, that he was not so much receiving love right now as *giving* it. He clung to Kyle a second more, then dropped his arms, as if afraid to ask too much. But Kyle held on -- did not let go -- and somehow Justin knew that this was what he'd wanted; this was all that anybody ever truly wanted: one brief moment of complete connection; one brief feeling of reciprocation, understanding, recognition: one brief moment when he knew that he was loved. It was the moment he'd been looking for his whole life, and it felt as if a stone had rolled away. As Justin looked across the quad during the last few seconds of the hug, he felt a huge shift taking place inside.

Now, everyone was taking off, and Justin turned to Craig, whispering in his ear, "Thank you for understanding." Craig did not respond. Instead, he merely squeezed Justin for a moment, and then let go: it was enough as well.

Finally, Justin walked back to his dorm, and found the hallway door propped open, warm May sunlight pouring in. He heard some random voices calling to each other from across the quad, the way he'd called to Kyle and Craig that day out in the dandelion field. But here, inside, the hall was still and calm. He walked the cool, dark hallway until he stood outside Tom's door. His friends had graduated; he was just beginning. He had thought Kyle was the door, the way into his life, but he was wrong: Kyle was, at best, a window -- like some beautiful, but fleeting, glimpse that perfectly encapsulates desire. He wasn't absolutely sure Tom was the door either; but as he stood in the morning hallway, dandelions drifting through the warm, spring air outside, Justin listened to his heart at last, and knocked.

ACKNOWLEDGMENTS

———◆———

I WOULD LIKE TO THANK ALL the people over the years who have read the manuscript in its various stages, and who have made helpful comments. I would especially like to thank the following: Judy Handschuh, Bobbi Ischinger, Denise Leveron, Michael Moore, Curtis Smith, and Cornelius Wormely. Last, but certainly not least, I would like to thank Scot O'Hara for all his love and support, not only with this project, but also for a lifetime of happiness beyond my wildest dreams.

Dale Boyer was born in Moline, Illinois. He attended Blackburn College (B.A.), The University of Wisconsin-Madison (M.A.), and Vermont College (M.F.A.). His work has appeared in such publications as *The Writer's Chronicle*, *The Windy City Times*, *The Harvard Gay & Lesbian Review*, and many other publications. He is married to Scot O'Hara, and currently lives in Chicago.

Made in the USA
Middletown, DE
23 March 2016